Also available from Headline Liaison

Pleasure Points by Cheryl Mildenhall
Fortune's Tide by Cheryl Mildenhall
A Family Affair by Cheryl Mildenhall
Private Lessons by Cheryl Mildenhall
Second Chance by Cheryl Mildenhall
Intimate Strangers by Cheryl Mildenhall
Dance of Desire by Cheryl Mildenhall
Flights of Fancy by Cheryl Mildenhall
The Journal by James Allen
Love Letters by James Allen
Aphrodisia by Rebecca Ambrose
Out of Control by Rebecca Ambrose
A Private Affair by Carol Anderson
Voluptuous Voyage by Lacey Carlyle
Magnolia Moon by Lacey Carlyle
The Paradise Garden by Aurelia Clifford
The Golden Cage by Aurelia Clifford
Vermilion Gates by by Lucinda Chester
Sleepless Nights by Tom Crewe and Amber Wells
Hearts on Fire by Tom Crewe and Amber Wells
A Scent of Danger by Sarah Hope-Walker
Seven Days by J J Duke
Dangerous Desires by J J Duke

The Voyeurs

Cheryl Mildenhall

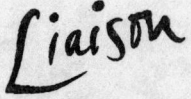

Copyright © 1998 Cheryl Mildenhall

The right of Cheryl Mildenhall to be identified as the Author of
the Work has been asserted by her in accordance with
the Copyright, Designs and Patents Act 1988.

First published in 1998 by
HEADLINE BOOK PUBLISHING

A HEADLINE LIAISON paperback

10 9 8 7 6 5 4 3 2 1

All rights reserved. No part of this publication may be reproduced,
stored in a retrieval system, or transmitted, in any form or by any
means without the prior written permission of the publisher, nor be
otherwise circulated in any form of binding or cover other than that
in which it is published and without a similar condition being
imposed on the subsequent purchaser.

All characters in this publication are fictitious and any resemblance
to real persons, living or dead, is purely coincidental.

ISBN 0 7472 5814 7

Typeset by Avon Dataset Ltd, Bidford-on-Avon, Warks

Printed and bound in Great Britain by
Mackays of Chatham plc, Chatham, Kent

HEADLINE BOOK PUBLISHING
A division of Hodder Headline PLC
338 Euston Road
London NW1 3BH

The Voyeurs

Chapter One

Anyone who knew Meredith Cooper well also knew that she was prone to the most bizarre and erotic daydreams. Time and place made little difference to her ability to fantasise. Consequently, bumping along the road on the front seat of a removal lorry, with the backs of her bare legs sticking damply to the warm vinyl, was no barrier to the uninhibited workings of her mind.

Without meaning to, she had cast the two removal men as the male leads in this particular fantasy. They were definitely not the type of men she would have normally chosen to fulfil her sexual needs. Certainly not in real life. The older one, Bradley, was coarse and brawny, with straggly hair that was thinning on top and dark patches of damp under the armpits of his blue overalls. The other, a lanky young lad called Steve, seemed to find it a challenge to put together a coherent sentence and scuttled out of her way every time she approached him. Yet both men had managed to undergo an incredible transformation in her current fantasy, thus assuming immense sexual desirability.

To concentrate on her fantasy Meredith kept her eyes tightly shut in the hope that Bradley and Steve would think she had fallen asleep. It wasn't far off the truth; the journey down the M1 motorway from her old flat in Nottingham to her new place in London had started to bore her before they hit junction twenty-two. As a result, she had decided to pass the time by indulging herself in her 'other world'.

More than anything Meredith wanted to orgasm. She craved it desperately but to do so she would have to touch herself. She hadn't yet achieved the level of sensuality where she could make herself come simply through fantasising. Even though she was carried away by her thoughts she was unable to ignore the reality of her situation. Almost weeping with frustration she bit down on her lower lip and forced herself to end the fantasy.

'Fancy a cup of tea and a bun, love?' A male voice jolted Meredith from her reverie. 'There's a services coming up.'

She opened her eyes and blinked hard several times. The sun was out now and it dazzled her as it bounced off the cars ahead. Rubbing a hand across her forehead, Meredith realised she felt tired and headachy. No doubt a shot of caffeine and sugar would be the best remedy.

She turned her head and smiled wanly at Bradley, the owner of the voice. For a moment the sight of his broad, strong hands gripping the steering wheel tempted her to pick up the threads of her fantasy again.

'Yes, please,' she said, banishing the thought and trying to sound enthusiastic at his suggestion, 'and I'm dying to go to the loo.'

Two miles later they stopped at the motorway service area. The lorry park was almost full. Meredith could see quite a few drivers who – as it was an emergency – took her immediate fancy. Briefly she thought about going up to one of them and propositioning him. It was possible that she could drag him into a secluded corner for a stand-up quickie.

In reality, she studiously ignored the many catcalls and wolfwhistles that accompanied her descent from the cab of the removal lorry. Clad only in the shortest of white shorts and a clinging tee-shirt with no bra underneath, it was hardly surprising that she commanded instant attention. Ducking her head and using her hair to camouflage her burning cheeks, she almost ran to the service area building.

The corridor to the lavatory was full of old-age pensioners all milling aimlessly about and chattering about the weather and their grandchildren. There were more in the lavatory – a clutch of old biddies clucking away and reeking of lavender – forcing her to wait for agonisingly long minutes for a cubicle. Her frustration was so great that, as soon as she was safely locked inside a vacant cubicle, she ripped down her shorts and knickers and rubbed furiously at her swollen clitoris. With the speed and intensity of a tornado, her orgasm ripped through her, leaving her feeling shaky, breathless and more than a little ashamed of herself.

Afterwards, legs trembling, she lowered herself, sat on the loo and rested the side of her head against the thin partition wall. With relief she simply let the floodgates of her bladder open. As the warm fluid left her body in a steady stream she felt the last residues of sexual tension flow out of her as well. It seemed to take ages until she felt totally drained. Then, ignoring the grumbles coming in stage whispers from the other side of the door, she sat and breathed slowly and deeply for a few moments until she felt capable of standing up again.

The rest of the journey was uneventful. Meredith sat next to Bradley this time while Steve took over the driving. A brief bout of small talk petered out quickly leaving Meredith to simply stare out of the window at the monotonous scenery. After a while the fields and bushes gradually gave way to a more urban landscape until they finally reached the end of the motorway. It took them another hour to crawl through the jam-packed centre of London until, finally, they were pulling up outside her new home.

Straight away Bradley and Steve began to complain.

'Where's the front door?' Bradley demanded.

'Just along the tow path,' Meredith said.

She glanced up at the converted warehouse where her new flat was situated. It seemed ages since she had last been there to view the flat and put down a deposit. Now it looked both familiar and yet exciting in its strangeness. The warehouse was built right next to a canal. On the other side of the glistening water, on which a pair of swans glided majestically, was another converted warehouse which was exactly the same.

'Do you mean to say we've got to lug this lot half a mile?'

'It's not half a mile,' Meredith interrupted him. 'Don't exaggerate.'

Feeling defiant, she jumped down from the cab and went around to the back of the lorry. Steve and Bradley hesitated then joined her. Looking thoroughly disgruntled Bradley made a great show of unlocking the roller door at the back and pushing it up.

'I'll take this box in,' Meredith said, grabbing the box with the kettle and all the tea things. 'Then I can make a pot of tea while you start bringing in the rest of my stuff.'

She decided a cup of tea was all they were going to get from her now. Sod helping them move her furniture and boxes, after all she was the one paying their wages. Grinning to herself she heaved the box into a more manageable position in her arms and puffed her way up the towpath away from them.

From a third-floor window of the warehouse on the opposite side of the canal Alex McGovern watched the little altercation down on the towpath with interest. He hadn't been living there very long and this was the first entertaining spectacle he had happened upon so far.

Since moving in, he had quickly discovered the joys of sitting and looking through the floor to ceiling French windows that opened out onto a small balcony. It helped to while away the long hours between auditions. But usually all he could see were flocks of ducks floating down the canal, or the odd person disappearing inside the building opposite.

He assumed the young woman heaving the Smiths Crisps box into her arms was a new tenant. Inside he felt a quiver of elation. He sincerely hoped so. From what he could make out she was lovely. Certainly a view worth watching.

At twenty-eight Alex had finally managed to tame his former wild, testosterone-induced behaviour into something close to sexual discernment. These days he didn't feel the adolescent urge to try and shag anything in a skirt. Instead he forced himself to use a measure of self control. Quality not quantity was his motto now – though it didn't always work. Sometimes, especially at post-performance parties when – high on the acclaim he received as a dancer – he would still go temporarily mad.

On such occasions he forgot all about his new image as someone of incredible sensuality and aloofness and behaved more like a kid let loose in a sweet shop. You'll hate yourself in the morning, he told himself at the time. But it didn't seem to matter. High on adrenaline, helped along by a bottle or two of champagne, he would find himself indulging in sexual encounters of orgiastic proportions.

Very good female friends – who he could just about count on the fingers of both hands and all fellow dancers as well as ex-lovers – told him that he was an incorrigible bastard but charming with it. They treated him indulgently, very much like older sisters. They told him off and massaged his ego all at the same time. With taloned fingers they would stroke him fondly and allow their fragile, bird-like faces to crease into thin-lipped but nevertheless genuine smiles. On these occasions he felt privileged. These women wouldn't risk laughter lines for just anybody.

He supposed it was true what they said about him and he was always vowing to try and curb his sexual appetites. Besides, he reasoned, it wasn't so much the sex that gave him the most pleasure but the build up. A born flirt, he loved the initial eye contact, the flattery, the charming sensual gestures, the thrill of the chase. What inevitably came afterwards was almost always a let down in comparison.

Turning his attention back to the window again, Alex felt a sharp stab of disappointment. The young woman had already disappeared inside. He cursed himself and the way he'd let his mind wander. Now he had missed the sight of that small, tight bottom straining against those small, tight shorts, and the sight of those slender tanned legs flashing like golden strobes across the dull backdrop of the warehouse as she walked.

Glancing up he felt his heart perform a surprise *jeté* behind his rib cage. Like a vision of indescribable loveliness she was standing at the window directly opposite him. Her hair fell over her face in a blonde curtain as she leaned forward and peered down at something below. He glanced down too and noticed that the two men in blue overalls were struggling with a battered red velvet chesterfield sofa.

Immediately his active mind conjured a vision of his new neighbour reclining across that sofa. She wasn't naked but dressed in a fluid gown of pistachio silk. He realised the image was similar to one he had seen in a painting hanging in a private gallery in Chelsea. The name of the painting escaped him but the vision of pale-haired beauty had not. The pose had been one of submissive wantoness – arms and legs sprawled carelessly, head flung back, silken strands of hair fanning the deeply buttoned red velvet backdrop. And the delicate fabric of the subject's dress had served to highlight the curves and contours of her sinuous body rather than conceal them.

Alex felt a pang of disappointment as the young woman straightened up and moved quickly away from the window. He could just make out her small, slender body disappearing into the obscure depths of the empty room behind. He waited for a while but she didn't return to the window.

When he realised she was probably busy unpacking the many boxes the men carried into the building and arranging her things, he moved reluctantly to the *barre* he had fixed to the wall at the far end of the sparsely furnished, bare boarded room. There he began to go through his standard routine of *pliés* and *battements* until his leg and buttock muscles were screaming and he had almost managed to banish all thoughts of his new neighbour from his mind.

Nightfall came as a surprise, the sudden blackout forcing Meredith into the realisation that the previous tenants had absconded with all the light bulbs.

'Bloody skinflints,' she muttered angrily as she searched blindly through still full boxes for candles and a box of matches. 'Now where are the damn things? Oh, thank goodness.' Pushing aside wads of crumpled newspaper her fingers curled around a long fat tube of wax. At the bottom of the same box she discovered the matches she knew she'd packed and quickly lit the candle. 'Let there be light,' she murmured with satisfaction as she watched it flicker into life.

The flame grew, illuminating the bare walls surrounding her and lending the spacious room a ghostly atmosphere. She shivered, feeling all alone for the first time that day. It was only now that it occurred to her how much she had left behind. All her friends. A way of life which, though not wholly satisfying, had become comfortable and familiar. Now, for the first time in eight years, she was truly on her own and the mistress of her destiny.

As she sat and stared into the darkened corners of the room Meredith felt a peacefulness wash over her. It replaced her earlier unease. Here in London she had a real chance for advancement. She could become anything. Be anyone. The thought was as exciting as it was scary.

For three years she had followed an art and design course at Nottingham University, specialising in fashion and textile design. Afterwards she had stayed in Nottingham, finding herself various jobs in the fashion industry: as a trainee pattern cutter, a seamstress, a silk screen printer. All were part of her master plan; to learn as much as she could about her chosen field.

The last job she had chosen was almost inevitable – at least that was how she saw it now. The area was renowned as the centre of England's textile industry – particularly the production of lingerie. Working at a local factory, Meredith had learned to fashion gloriously sensuous items from scraps of silk, satin and Nottingham lace. This, she decided quite early on, was her forte. And lingerie was to be her future. In a competitive market she could still see a niche for exquisite but affordable designs.

Shortly after reaching the decision to go freelance she realised that while Nottingham might be a good place to buy fabrics it was not a ready market for the finished products. Marketing herself in Nottingham was like trying to sell fridges to Eskimos. Thus, it quickly dawned on Meredith that London was the place to be. In the capital there were no end of boutiques and larger shops around which she could hawk her wares. And in London people had real money to spend.

It was after making her decision that Meredith found herself in a catch-22 situation. Only a generous loan by her parents enabled her to put down the deposit on her new flat and buy the materials and equipment necessary to get started. It wasn't quite the level of independence she had envisaged but she hoped she would be successful quickly enough to be able to pay them back. Then she truly would be self-sufficient.

And a grown up.

Meredith sat up straight, startled that the words had come into her head. Why was it, she groaned silently, that at twenty six, with a degree, a home of her own and heaps of talent, did she still feel as though she needed someone else to tell her what to do?

'I don't,' she replied aloud, the words shattering the oppressive silence of the shadowy room. 'I'm young, I'm not bad-looking and I've got what it takes. I don't need anyone or anything else.'

Wishing she could really believe her own hype, Meredith picked up the candle and carried it into her bedroom. If she was going to get started in earnest the following day she would need a good night's sleep.

From the depths of his leather armchair in front of the window, Alex watched the flickering light break the blackness of the window opposite. He imagined his new neighbour seated somewhere in that darkened room. Was she alone or entertaining a lover? Candle light was certainly the stuff of romanticism and sensuality.

He felt a familiar stirring in his loins and without hesitation unzipped his fly. He took his cock out and stroked it absently, as though it were a pet. He always found it comforting to stroke his cock. Like a child's dummy, or security blanket it pacified him. Sometimes he did it in the middle of choreographing a new dance sequence, when he was stuck for ideas. Only when he was on his own of course, not in front of other people. He had an irrational fear of being arrested for something he hadn't done – or at least didn't mean to do. It would have to be unintentional, he didn't have any criminal inclinations.

Christ, he thought, imagine the embarrassment of being had up for exposing himself. Would his girlfriends still be as compassionate and indulgent of him as they were now? Or would they nod sagely to each other and admit that they had suspected him of perverted behaviour for a long time?

Could what he was doing now be considered perverted? he wondered. Perhaps, in a lot of people's minds, the idea of someone stroking himself while watching out for his new female neighbour might be considered an aberration. He could see the headlines now: VILE VOYEUR IN MASTURBATION SENSATION . . . DANCE DIVAS TELL ALL!

Grinning inwardly at his ludicrous thoughts Alex glanced down at his lap. He couldn't help noticing how hard his cock had grown in spite of what was going on in his head.

'I always knew you had a mind of your own,' he said indulgently to his stiffening organ.

His hand movements quickened and as he felt the first real surge of excitement, he happened to glance up to see that the room opposite was now in total darkness. Swerving his gaze to the next window, which was obscured by a blind, he saw a silhouette illuminated behind it. There was no doubt the dark, sinuous shape belonged to a girl – *the* girl.

With her back to the window he couldn't help admiring the broad shoulders, narrow ribcage and an even narrower waist which flared out to hips that were quite generous in comparison. As he studied the tantalising vision he continued to arouse his cock with rhythmic, well practised strokes. He willed the girl to turn sideways. Although he could only see her outline he couldn't wait to discover the exact size and shape of her breasts.

There – yes – brilliant! She disappeared for a moment then returned to stand exactly as he wanted her to. With rising excitement he studied the generous mounds that thrust out in front of her. By her other movements he could tell that she was brushing her hair. Entranced, he watched the way the sideways-on breast rose and fell with each stroke of the brush.

Unconsciously, he copied the rhythm, matching her stroke for stroke. And gradually the reality of his own hand faded and was replaced by the fantasy of the girl herself. Kneeling in front of his chair she was the one who touched him. It was her nipples that tickled his thighs while her hand worked its magic on his desperately engorged cock. In his mind's eye he could see her long pale hair falling over her face. He pictured the childlike innocence in her expression, imagined himself as the maestro of her movements, orchestrating her rhythm to a final, glorious crescendo.

No, no, don't go! His hand worked faster as she began to move away from the window. There was a real urgency now in his technique. He had to get there. Had to . . .

She stooped forward and that brief glimpse of her gloriously dangling breasts and thrusting bottom pushed him over the edge. Then she moved right away, the silhouette and the light disappearing concurrently, leaving only a dark blankness at the window.

Feeling disappointed Alex looked down at his hand. It was sticky, thickly coated with his own semen. He had hardly noticed his climax. Now he would have to wait a while before he could do it again – properly. But at least, he reasoned, he had the full picture of the unknown woman now. By closing his eyes he would be able to put all the glimpses of her together, like a human jigsaw. Then she would become a real woman and around her he could weave a fantasy that would make his next orgasm a powerfully mind-blowing one.

Chapter Two

After nine days Meredith realised she hadn't yet sampled any of the nightlife that London had to offer. Nine days in one of the world's most exciting cities and she had spent every waking moment settling in properly and working.

Now, as she smoothed a swathe of pale blue silk across the top of her cutting table, she happened to glance out of the long window in front of her. As her eyes raked the crenellated vista of rooftops bathed in the heat mist that had yet to lift, and her ears caught the distant rush of traffic, she realised there was a whole world outside of her flat simply teaming with life and possibilities.

Turning away from the window for a moment she rested her bottom against the edge of the table and surveyed the interior of her flat.

In the short time she had been there, the bare-boarded, high-ceilinged living room had been transformed from an empty shell to a cosy seating area and efficient work space. Most of the large room was given over to work. She had positioned the cutting table in front of the French window to make the most of the natural light and to give her a nice view to contemplate when her back got too stiff and she had to straighten up for a moment. At either end of the cutting table stood high racks of wire baskets which contained all manner of things that she needed to keep handy: scissors, pins, scraps of fabric and lace to name but a few all carefully sorted and organised. In the far corner, currently to her right, was a second hand metal filing cabinet which she had painted purple. The top drawer held all her paperwork. The second her designs. And the third paper patterns.

The left-hand end of the room she had designated as the

relaxation area. There she had positioned her red velvet chesterfield and a couple of old armchairs. To disguise their shabby appearance they were draped with matching shawls which Meredith had picked up while holidaying in Spain. On a background of black silk, the shawls were a riot of huge red cabbage roses and trailing green stems. She loved the shawls, they pleased her aesthetic senses while the combination of silk and velvet as furniture coverings satisfied her sensual nature.

As a final gesture of dramatic creativity she had stained the bare floorboards a deep, majestic purple. If she was simply to describe the colour scheme to someone, she knew it would sound as though it clashed horribly, yet deep down she had known it would work. And she was right, she thought as she gazed around. Her surroundings were wonderfully bohemian, the deep rich colours lending the original featureless space a certain decadence and reminding her of a 1920's Parisian bordello.

Feeling satisfied with her efforts she got up and walked across the room.

'So Rhett, how are we today?' she asked, chucking the immobile figure under the chin. Tall and imperious, he stood alone against the backdrop of a blank purple wall. The response to Meredith's question was total silence and so she took a step back, cocked her head and regarded her taciturn companion thoughtfully. 'Why, oh why don't you ever answer me, you rogue?' she murmured.

Then she laughed at her own idiocy. Rhett was a shop window mannequin which she had discovered discarded in a skip in a back alley behind Nottingham's Flying Horse arcade. Even now she remembered the leap of delight she had felt as she rescued the dummy, pulling him from the skip, dusting him down and realising, as she gazed up at his perfectly chiselled face, what a startling resemblance he bore to her longstanding Hollywood heart throb, Clark Gable.

Ignoring the amused stares of passers-by she had stoically trudged along the streets of Nottingham, carrying Rhett – stiff as a corpse – in her arms. Back at her flat she had sponged him down and spent the next few weeks scouring antique clothing stalls until she had managed to kit him out in a severe but well tailored black suit, white shirt with stand up collar and stiff cuffs and adding the finishing touch, a black silk bow-tie.

Now Rhett was her sounding board. Her silent partner. In many ways, she thought, he made the perfect flat mate. He was clean, unobtrusive and handsome. He always listened to her without interrupting and never criticised her when she dressed in something outlandish, or came home in the early hours, blind drunk and with another man in tow.

Meredith reached up and stroked his dark hair fondly back from his high brow.

'You, my love, are gorgeous,' she murmured, gazing into the blank turquoise eyes. Inside she felt a familiar quickening of excitement and wished, for the umpteenth time, that something magical would occur and Rhett would suddenly come to life. In her imagination the first thing he would do was stoop down, sweep her into his arms and make delicious, endless love to her.

Just as rapidly, she came to her senses. She could feel the onset of a fantasy and had just enough self-possession left to realise that time was getting on and she had work to do. Moving back to the window and bending her head over the cutting table she resolved to go out that evening and continue her search for the man of her dreams. A real man.

Rhett wouldn't mind. He'd be quite happy here alone, watching over her flat while she went out and danced and flirted the night away. Even if she didn't meet her destiny, she hoped she would at least find someone she fancied enough to spend the night with. Her enforced celibacy was doing her no good whatsoever. If she couldn't find love she'd make do with the next best thing. Sex. Preferably of the hot and raunchy variety.

With a secretive smile touching her lips she happened to glance up. And it was then she noticed Alex for the very first time.

Alex was startled when the girl opposite suddenly looked up and stared right at him. Even with two panes of glass and a canal separating them he could feel the intensity of her gaze. Previously content to admire her from a safe distance, it now felt as though she were in the same room as him. So close he could feel the warmth of her body. Smell her perfume. Sense the latent desire surging in her veins. Her eyes and the expression on her small, heart-shaped face said it all.

His first instinct was to shrink back in his chair. He felt poleaxed. And not a little embarrassed. It was okay watching her and admiring her beauty from afar when she didn't realise he was doing it. It was quite another to realise he had been caught out. Metaphorically with his pants down.

Despite his shock he grinned inwardly. Her unexpected perception of him had left him feeling like a naughty schoolboy. It was as though she were the school mistress and he was twelve years old again, cowering shamefully behind the bike sheds, his hair tousled and his penis poking out like a frozen chipolata from his fly.

Without realising it he folded his hands protectively over his groin. He was sure she couldn't see him now but he still felt embarrassed. He was a pervert, he told himself and therefore deserved to be feel ashamed of behaving like a peeping Tom. All at once he felt the overwhelming urge to confess. But to whom and for what? For appreciating beauty when he saw it? For living a life that left him with so much unstructured time he had nothing better to do but sit and stare out of the window?

He hardly dared to glimpse back at the window. But when he did, when he peered cautiously around the soft leather wing of his armchair, he immediately felt let down. She wasn't still staring out of the window but had her head bent back over her work again. He wondered what it was she did exactly? He hadn't quite been able to figure it out, although he realised it was a table she was always working at and had noticed the occasional flash of metallic blades in her right hand. Perhaps she was a pathologist who took her work home with her?

The ridiculous thought made Alex laugh aloud. It echoed around the spacious room, which all at once seemed less like a home and more like an empty tomb. He decided in that instant to get up and go out. Somewhere. Anywhere. Staying cooped up in his flat was driving him mad. He'd go and see his agent, he decided, and perhaps call one of his lady friends, invite her out for lunch.

He checked his wallet. Inside he found a wad of receipts, three condoms, a couple of credit cards and a twenty-pound note. Well, that would do, he thought. He was adequately equipped to cover all eventualities.

Meredith's sixth sense told her to look up just as Alex emerged from the building opposite. Even though she had only seen his face for a split second, that moment seemed frozen in time. Everything about his face was imprinted on her brain: the finely sculpted bone structure, the thick beetling eyebrows, the full sullen mouth and the sable hair swept back from a high brow. It's him! she had thought at the time. Now, as she looked out of the window again, watching the lean figure stroll with easy grace along the tow path in the direction of the High Street, she was arrested by the same thought.

It was as though her dream had come true at long last and that the figure of Rhett Butler standing behind her had finally come to life. Feeling foolish, she glanced quickly over her shoulder to make sure he hadn't. Of course not, she berated herself for her fanciful notions. The mannequin was still there, as handsome and as immobile as ever.

Looking back to the tow path, Meredith experienced the singular pleasure of watching the living embodiment of her most ardent fantasy. She noted the broad shoulders beneath an unseasonal light coloured mackintosh. The unbuttoned coat almost reached his ankles and flapped out dramatically behind him as he walked. She saw the way his dark wavy hair just skimmed the collar of his coat. She saw him glance up at the sky and smile. Then all at once he turned the corner and was gone.

It took Meredith a few seconds to realise she was standing with her palm pressed against her chest. Beneath it she could feel the rapid pulse of her heartbeat. She felt breathless without exertion. Her erotic senses were not so much piqued as catapulted into oblivion. With her free hand she grasped behind her at thin air. All at once she felt desperate to sit down. Her legs were so wobbly she didn't think they would support her much longer. There was a grey tweed typist's chair just behind her which she used at her drawing board when she was designing. Feeling extraordinarily grateful for its presence she pulled it close to her and sank down upon it.

How come she hadn't noticed him before? She asked herself. Hot on the heels of his question came another: how long had he been watching her? She realised she owed part of her shaky feeling to the knowledge that she had been spied upon and perhaps on other occasions too. This new awareness made her feel vulnerable, unsure of herself. What had he seen exactly? In vain she tried to remember how often during the past nine days she had walked close to the full length window in a state of undress.

Walking around half-clothed, or sometimes completely naked, had become a way of life to her in Nottingham. But then her old flat had only had tiny – usually grimy – windows, not big or clear enough for a beady eyed pigeon to see through let alone another person.

She berated herself for her carelessness. London was not Nottingham. Good God, her new neighbours could be mass murderers and rapists for all she knew! It was just as well she realised it now, she thought, better late than never. As soon as she could she would go out and buy a blind for that window and a safety chain for the front door. There was no such thing as being too careful.

Alex arrived at the Chelsea mews which housed the offices of his agent, Alberta Naci, just after eleven. He made his usual cheery announcement into the intercom by the primrose yellow front door and was buzzed in immediately.

He entered Alberta's office and glanced around just once to acclimatise himself before sitting down on one of the yellow, petal-shaped designer chairs in front of her battered walnut desk. The fact that Alberta loved the colour yellow was evident by her surroundings. Decorated in shades of buttercup, lemon and primrose, her tiny office looked as though the sun lived there.

In contrast, Alberta was quite a dour, dowdy woman with short, carelessly shorn hair. Named after the Canadian province in which she had been born, her dark colouring was testament to her immigrant Italian parentage. True to form, Alex noted, she was dressed all in black. Today her choice was a long, unstructured sleeveless blouse worn over a pair of slightly too short palazzo pants. He guessed the grey nylons masking her sparrow-thin shins and bony ankles were pop socks.

Now in her late fifties, Alberta had once been a dancer of repute and the photographs of herself on stage, and with various celebrities, cluttering the walls and every available surface of her office bore testimony to this. Her most prized photograph, of herself standing between Wayne Sleep and Princess Diana at an awards dinner, took pride of place on her desk.

Alex picked up the photograph in its ornate gilt frame and smiled wryly at it before putting it down and turning his smile full on for Alberta's benefit.

'I can't get over how little you've changed since this photograph was taken,' he flattered smoothly. 'It must be what – ten years since—'

'Cut the crap, Alex,' Alberta interposed tartly. She glanced pointedly at the gold watch that was too loose for her scrawny wrist. 'I wasn't expecting to see you today and I've got a meeting in five minutes.'

Alex felt suitably chastened. Sometimes he had to struggle to remind himself that Alberta was supposed to be working for him, not the other way around. This was one of those times.

Nevertheless, he came straight to the point. 'I heard Liza Blair came to you for someone to choreograph her new video.'

Alberta regarded him over steepled fingers. 'This is true,' she said, 'but you are a dancer, Alex. A good one, I'll admit, but a choreographer you are not.'

Narrowing his eyes, Alex looked back at her, refusing to be phased by her put down. 'I need the work, Alberta. I'm going mad cooped up in my flat with nothing to do.'

'But you have your exercises and dance practice to occupy your time, my dear boy,' she responded, smoothly putting him down for a second time. 'You know how important it is to stay fresh.'

Alex sighed deeply and sat back in the uncomfortable chair. He crossed one leg casually over the top of the other and made it look as though he intended to stay a while.

'Have you planned your summer holiday yet?' he asked. 'Will it be back home to Canada again?'

Alberta looked suitably irritated, he noticed and ignored his question.

'I told you, I have a meeting in five, no, three minutes,' she said, sounding testy. 'There is no point in you making yourself comfortable, Alex.'

He wanted to retort, 'What, in this ridiculous chair?' but instead, said, 'Put me forward for the video, Alberta. I promise I won't let you down.'

Despite his intention to remain cool and give as good as Alberta dished out he felt his expression and tone of voice becoming pleading. It annoyed him and he had to force himself to keep an easy smile on his face.

She seemed to contemplate his suggestion for a moment. For so long in fact that Alex felt his resolve turn to watery hope. He was certain he could hear Alberta's watch ticking in the strained silence.

'Very well,' she said at last. 'I'll give Miss Blair's agent a call and see if I can get him to ring you.'

'When?' Alex was eager now.

Alberta clearly wasn't to be phased. 'When I get a spare moment. You are not the only dancer on my books, Alex. Charming though you may be, and possibly even extraordinarily talented, you'd do well to remember that I have at least a couple of dozen just like you.'

Alex felt mollified by Alberta's reference to his talent. It was the closest she had come in a long time to a compliment.

'OK,' he said easily, standing up. He saw the relief at his imminent departure wash over Alberta's face and felt tempted to sit down again just to wind her up. 'I'll be out for lunch but I'll make sure I'm back at my flat for three. Then I'll be in all evening.' Fleetingly, he wondered if there was anyone he could persuade to spend the evening with him.

'Don't hold your breath, Alex,' Alberta responded calmly. 'I told you, I'll make the call when I get a free moment. I'm a very busy woman.'

'Yes, Alberta. I know you are,' Alex placated her, 'but I know you'll come up trumps for me. You always do.'

He left her with a final, winning smile and a mental skim through the possibilities of a lunch companion. Halfway down the tiny cobblestone street that led away from Alberta's offices he made a decision. His next stop was the nearest phone box.

* * *

The basement bar Meredith had happened upon halfway along The Strand was large, yet the comfortable decor managed to lend it an air of intimacy. Ignoring the seating organised into groups around the perimeter of the room, she opted to sit at the central, horseshoe-shaped bar instead. The wooden chair was high, making it a bit of a struggle for her to climb onto elegantly, but it afforded her an excellent view of the rest of the bar and its patrons.

Straight away she noticed that most of the people drinking there appeared to have dropped in straight from work. Young career women dressed in sober colours chatted impersonally with their be-suited male colleagues. The polished wooden floor was awash with discarded briefcases.

Dressed in a bright red jumpsuit and carrying only a small black patent shoulder bag, Meredith felt horribly conspicuous.

The only female bartender – a small, sturdy blonde with a fierce face – took her time getting over to Meredith and taking her order.

'A white wine spritzer, please.' Meredith felt her smile waver then fade as the young woman gazed stonily back at her.

'With ice?'

'Yes, please, if it's no trouble.'

'Don't let her intimidate you, her glare is worse than her bite.' A deep male voice at Meredith's shoulder startled her.

Almost jumping out of her seat she dropped her bag. 'Oh, gosh, look what I've done now,' she twittered, watching helplessly as the catch on her bag sprang open and a motley assortment of coins and make-up spilled out. To her mortification a lone tampon rolled across the floor.

'Allow me,' the stranger said gallantly. Before Meredith could stop him he squatted down and retrieved all her belongings – including the tampon – and dropped them back in her bag. Then he handed it to her.

Meredith could feel her cheeks burning. It seemed his face had borne a knowing smile and his hand had lingered just a fraction too long before he let go of the tampon.

'Thank you,' she managed to gasp out as she took her bag from him. 'I'm not usually this clumsy.'

'No apologies necessary,' he said. As he spoke he waved away the five-pound note she held out to the bartender and paid for both their drinks. His was a bottle of designer beer. He took a long draught of the beer straight from the bottle then held out his hand to her. 'My name is Fergal, by the way.'

As she took his hand, Meredith found her eyes sliding up past the red and white silk scarf at his throat to a craggy face. Out of the deep brown creases of his eyes a pair of emeralds sparkled. His smile was as engaging as the boyish way his light brown hair flopped over his forehead.

Letting go of her hand he swept the hair back. It wasn't light brown, Meredith realised, but a darker shade deliberately streaked with gold. At the same time she also realised he wasn't particularly young. But she had to admit, he had a way with him. And, as she knew no one else in London, it might be pleasant to spend the evening chatting with him. *If* he wanted to, she reminded herself sternly. He might have other plans.

'I'm Meredith,' Meredith said. 'Are you here with anyone?' She glanced vaguely around and was relieved when he shook his head.

'Nope,' he said. 'I'm all on my lonesome, sweetness. Mind if I stick around for a while? Perhaps I could take your mind off your PMT.'

'PMT?' Meredith felt confused. Then she realised he was thinking of the tampon and had put two and two together. Her cheeks flamed. 'I'm not – I mean, I haven't emptied my bag out lately,' she stammered. Feeling horribly gauche she picked up her drink and gulped hastily at it.

'Except all over the floor.' His grin was engaging, wiping out her embarrassment in one fell swoop. 'Please forgive me for my faux pas. Can we start again?'

As she nodded Meredith found it impossible not to return his grin. She took another sip of the cold, slightly sparkling liquid from the glass in her hand and felt the remains of her tension magically disappear.

Turning in her seat she looked right at him. It was time to use her ace ploy. 'Fergal, that's an unusual name,' she said, deliberately adopting a dulcet tone. 'Tell me about yourself.'

* * *

Alex had rejected the notion of inviting Chloe back to his flat for supper and whatever. They had already enjoyed a long, boozy lunch during which Chloe had wasted no opportunity to crow about her latest casting as Pease Blossom in a modern dance version of A Midsummer Night's Dream.

It wasn't that Alex didn't feel Chloe deserved the part. She did. She was a bloody good dancer. And very attractive too in a typically Sloaney kind of way. No, the problem was she had a way of putting him down and making him feel inadequate without actually saying anything derogatory. It was a particular talent of hers, letting her unsaid words speak louder than her boasts.

Even the memory of her pert, 34B breasts and pincer-like vaginal muscles didn't deter him from putting her into a taxi after their lunch. Consequently, he spent the rest of the afternoon and evening alone.

At first he hadn't minded too much. The blank tape on his answering machine told him that he hadn't missed the longed for call from Liza Blair's agent – even though it was closer to four o'clock than three, which meant he still had that to look forward too. To kill time and work off some of the calories from lunch, he launched himself into a particularly gruelling exercise session. But by six he felt his energy and his spirits go into mutual decline.

Flopping down into the chair by the window, Alex glanced automatically at the window opposite. With a pang of disappointment he realised 'Juliet' as he had now dubbed her was no longer working but had disappeared into the deeper recesses of her flat.

He had picked the name Juliet because Chloe had left him in a Shakespearean mood, and for one brief moment he had contemplated the effectiveness of serenading his new neighbour from under her balcony. Too bad he couldn't play the guitar and was tone deaf, he told himself wryly. Executing a few dance moves out on the tow path was hardly likely to have the same effect. Most probably, instead of delighting her and gaining an invitation up to her flat, he would end up being carted away by men in white coats.

He had sat down with the full intention of willing her to look up at him again. Now he felt cheated. For about half an hour he waited for her to reappear but, when she didn't, he got up and went to run himself a mineral bath. Without the benefit of cool down exercises, his body had now started to stiffen up alarmingly.

Just as the delightful red-and-pink-streaked sky started to give way to the greyness of nightfall, he saw her return. To his dismay, he noticed that she had a man with her.

'Come in, make yourself at home.' Meredith led the way through the front door. As she paused to grope for the light switch, she recalled how natural it had seemed to invite Fergal back for coffee.

After their rocky start the evening had progressed surprisingly smoothly. Most of the time he had devoted himself to charming her with his ready wit and his stories about the Auld Country as he called it – meaning southern Ireland where he had been brought up.

Straight away Meredith had remarked on the fact that he didn't sound Irish.

'No, well I took elocution lessons when I came over here to study,' he explained.

'Study what?' Meredith had felt herself glowing with happiness, not to mention the several glasses of scotch which Fergal had persuaded her to move on to.

His crinkly smile delighted her all over again. 'Acting,' he said simply. Then, taking a step back he flung his arms wide and adopted a deep Burt Lancaster-type voice.

'You may remember me from such epics as *The Last of the Mohicans*, *The Pelican Brief*, *Mona Lisa* and *Highlander* to name but a few.'

Meredith shook her head regretfully. To her chagrin she had to admit she couldn't remember having seen him in any of those films.

'No wonder,' he said laughing and punching her lightly on the shoulder at the same time. 'They were only small, walk-on parts. Second Native American from the left, man drinking at bar, that sort of thing.' His smile crinkled and twinkled endearingly.

Laughing along with him, Meredith let her relief show. 'I'm not really much of a one for films anyway,' she said. 'I haven't even got a TV.'

Fergal pretended to look shocked. 'I could always get you a good deal on a second hand one,' he offered. 'In fact, I could come back to your flat and help you to decide where to put it.'

The intensity in his eyes told Meredith he had far more interesting things on his mind. His smile was both wolfish and heart-stoppingly attractive. Consequently, she felt her re-awakened sexuality soar to new and dizzy heights.

'You could,' she agreed, with a pert smile. 'And I could make you a cup of coffee for your trouble.'

They just about allowed themselves the time to finish their drinks before they were scampering up the stairs hand in hand. Out on the street Fergal flagged down a taxi and in no time at all they were pulling up outside the warehouse.

Back in the present, Fergal was looking around and nodding his shaggy head approvingly.

'This is a fabulous place,' he said. 'You've certainly got a flair for interior design.'

Meredith felt buoyed up by his compliment. She was never sure if her tastes were a bit too outlandish for normal folk. But then, she reasoned as she slipped off her coat and threw it over the back of the typist's chair, Fergal could hardly be described as normal.

She looked at him now, standing in the middle of the room, and realised that he seemed to take up quite a lot of space. It wasn't that he was a particularly large man – just larger than life. His style was flamboyant. If he hadn't told her he was an actor she would have guessed at that anyway, or perhaps an artist. Something creative at any rate.

He shrugged off the long tweedy coat he was wearing to reveal a loosely tailored brown velvet suit. The buttons on the jacket were not done up right and the matching brown loafers which he wore with red socks looked as though they had seen better days. Yes, Meredith thought, Fergal was definitely eccentric.

Making her excuses, Meredith fled into the kitchen. While she waited for the kettle to boil she asked herself if she was doing the right thing. Fergal seemed nice and easy going but he could be a sadist or something. For one brief, mad moment, she imagined him coming up behind her and slapping a pair of studded leather restraints around her wrists. Even then, she was ashamed to find that her body responded positively to the idea. What is the matter with you, girl? She asked herself sternly. You're sex-mad – get a grip!

Trying not to show how badly she was trembling, she carried two mugs of coffee back into the living room. But for all her efforts at trying to calm herself, she nearly dropped them when she saw Fergal.

Sprawled carelessly across her velvet couch, his head tipped back, eyes closed and his expression one of blissful contemplation, he was completely naked.

Chapter Three

Meredith took an involuntary step back. Then, when Fergal didn't open his eyes and she had recovered her composure a little, she tiptoed up to him. In front of the sofa was a wooden packing trunk – a junk shop find which she had bought the day before to use as a coffee table. Putting the mugs down on it she glanced over her shoulder and was startled to see that Fergal's apparently inert body now boasted a huge erection.

With cheeks aflame she glanced up at his face and saw that he had opened one eye and was peering at her.

'I didn't . . . what do you – ' she stammered, feeling lost for words.

As Fergal opened his other eye his face broke into a broad grin. He glanced down at his groin, automatically dragging Meredith's gaze to the same place.

'That's, er, very, er – ' Meredith muttered.

She cursed herself for losing her self-composure completely. Torn between embarrassment and wanting, she wavered. The thick cock rising from a wild bush of dark hair seemed to be yearning towards her. A small tear emerged from its tip and without thinking, Meredith leaned forward and swept it up on her fingertip. She rubbed her finger and thumb together, noting how the sticky blob of pre-ejaculate coated the whorled pads of her fingertips with viscous strands.

When she glanced down she noticed that Fergal was looking at her with darkened eyes. No longer emerald, his irises now appeared bottle green. Desire had definitely taken over from humour, she realised. The thought acted like a lightning bolt, filling her with a zingy, tingling sensation. She felt lightheaded. Breathless. Her heart was thumping nineteen to the dozen and between her legs she felt a telltale wetness.

'Now!' Fergal said.

Meredith didn't quite comprehend. She raised her eyebrows. 'Now?'

To her surprise Fergal suddenly leaped up from the sofa and grabbed her around the waist. Lifting her easily he carried her over to the wall and pressed her back against it. Her feet dangled a few inches from the ground. She felt limp and helpless, sensuality coursing through her at the speed of light as he kissed her. His hardness nudged at her pubic bone.

'How do you get out of this thing?' Fergal asked gruffly as he stopped kissing her and swept his gaze over her.

Realising he meant her jump suit, Meredith gasped out hoarsely that there was a zip at the back.

He put her down reluctantly. With one broad hand covering her right breast, he reached around behind her with the other and pulled down her zip.

She crushed herself against him, giving him room to manoeuvre and thrusting her breast further into his hand. The tight bud of her nipple chafed against the satin camisole she wore under the jumpsuit. She could feel the warmth of his hand enclosing her breast. His strong fingers squeezed slightly as though he were testing her breast for ripeness. A gasp of surprise broke from her lips as Fergal deftly pulled down her jumpsuit. His hand left her breast for just a fleeting moment, then it returned, the fingers massaging her pliant flesh eagerly over the thin layer of satin.

'Nice,' he murmured, flicking his eyes over her.

She wasn't sure if he meant her body, now clad only in oyster satin and a pair of cream leather high heeled ankle boots.

'It's one of my own designs,' she gabbled nervously. 'That's what I do for a living.'

She glanced around him to the cutting table on the other side of the room. It was then she realised that, with the light on and as yet no new blind, the French window afforded anyone outside the flat an excellent view of herself and Fergal. Across the way, she noticed with relief that the window opposite hers was a blank eye. Hopefully, the guy she had spotted watching her earlier was out.

'I wasn't talking about your undies,' Fergal said gruffly. 'I meant you. Your body.'

Quaking inside, she watched his expression darken even further as he took a couple of steps back and held her at arm's length while he gave her a more thorough appraisal.

Her mouth felt dry. She could feel her heart hammering and the crotch of her French knickers was clinging seductively to her damp sex.

'You look more naked like that than if you were wearing nothing at all,' Fergal said.

Meredith marvelled at his perception. It was the effect she always strived to achieve with her designs. Now, as she glanced down she saw exactly what he meant. Her nipples were thrusting hard at the fragile silk, the rest of the camisole clinging sensuously to her curves. Her slender, lightly tanned thighs disappeared under delicate lace-trimmed satin, which cleaved to her hipbones and the slight swell of her belly. Most shaming of all was the way the gossamer-light fabric moulded itself around her vulva, clearly outlining her labia and the groove between them.

Meredith's senses thrilled to Fergal's low growl of appreciation. His hands slid slowly from her shoulders, down the length of her arms. As his fingers caressed hers and whispered onto her thighs, he blew a stream of warm breath directly between her breasts. Like a stone tossed into a still pool, his breath rippled the satin over her sensitised flesh.

Unable to help herself, Meredith closed her eyes and let out a whimper of arousal. The caress of the satin on her fevered body was achingly seductive. Keeping her eyes closed, she felt her body sway as she concentrated on the featherlight touch of his fingertips. They coasted over the silken flesh of her thighs and up again, following the sinuous contours of her hips, her waist, her breasts.

At her shoulders they seemed to pause, softly stroking back and forth across the jutting hardness of her collarbone. Then, with the lightest of whispers she felt the thin straps of her camisole sliding from her shoulders. Slowly, so slowly, the fragile garment trickled down over her breasts and stomach to pool around her waist.

She felt the cool night air touch her febrile skin. She shivered, tiny beads of perspiration gathering at her throat. Her naked breasts felt as though they were straining towards something unseen. She craved his touch. Craved the most gentle or most brutal of caresses. It hardly mattered. She just needed to be touched.

'You are a beauty, sweetness,' Fergal murmured as his hands swept her breasts in that longed for caress.

Meredith whimpered again. She arched her back, thrusting her breasts forward. A moment later she gasped as she felt her nipples being pinched hard, then harder. They burned between his fingertips. Two throbbing, desperate buds of flesh. So sensitive and yet so receptive to his cruelty.

He laughed a dark, treacly laugh that thrilled Meredith to the core. 'Well, well,' he said, 'the lady likes it a little rough, does she?'

She shook her head. This sort of behaviour was new to her. And it shocked her to realise just how ardently her body responded to a bit of pain. In that fleeting moment she wondered whether she had made a mistake encouraging him. After all, his charming, easy going manner could easily mask the heart of a sadist.

His voice was soothing as he spoke again, making her wonder if he could read her mind.

'Don't worry, darling heart,' he said, releasing his grip on her nipples and stroking the stiff flesh gently instead. 'I don't get off on pain, either inflicting it or receiving it. I think the devil got inside me just then.' The last line was delivered in a broad Irish brogue, pronouncing devil as *deevil*.

Meredith laughed weakly, mainly from relief. She opened her eyes and found herself staring straight into his own.

'I'm sorry, I'm just a bit nervous,' she admitted. 'It's been a long time since—'

He pressed the pad of his thumb to her lips to silence her.

'Don't go apologising. I understand. I'll leave right now if you want me to. Just say the word and I'll go. Simple as that.'

Smiling, Meredith shook her head. 'You'll get yourself arrested if you do,' she said, glancing down at his erection. Her eyes met his again. 'Anyway,' she went on, 'I don't want you to go.'

To demonstrate the truth of her words she covered his hands

with hers and encouraged him to cup her breasts more firmly. Then she let her head drop back and let out a long sigh of pleasure as she rubbed her belly deliberately against his stiff cock. The warmth and hardness of that part of his body, as it slid back and forth across the thin film of silk that separated bare flesh from bare flesh, felt deliciously arousing.

Reaching down she gathered up the front of her camisole and wrapped it around his cock. Then she began to masturbate him, letting the warmth of her fingers seep through the silk to touch his straining flesh.

It excited her to hear his groans of pleasure and to see the way his expression slowly transformed from one of concern to that of blissful arousal.

'Don't stop,' he gasped, clutching at her hand and working it faster. Then, a moment later he whipped her hand away. 'No, no, not yet. I don't want to come yet. Not like this. I want to be on you, inside you, all over you—'

As he spoke he slipped his hands under the waistband of her knickers and slid them down over the curve of her hips and bottom. Inflamed by his words and desperate to have him inside her now, Meredith helped him to pull off the rest of her scanty clothing.

When she was naked he surprised her again by grasping her by the bottom and lifting her up. He pressed her back against the wall and she hooked her legs around his hips. She moaned with desire as she felt the tip of his penis nudging her vaginal lips apart and smoothly entering her moist tunnel.

He slammed up into her hard, his hands gripping her waist, moving her up and down as if she were a doll. She could see his shoulder and arm muscles working beneath the skin and realised at once how strong he must be to treat her as though she were no more than a featherweight. He hadn't looked strong in his clothes, nor even when he had been reclining on her couch. But then, she realised, she had been looking at Fergal the actor. The mild eccentric. Now she was experiencing Fergal the man.

Her vaginal muscles seemed to cry out with the joy of having something stiff and hard to cling to again. She could feel his wiry bush tantalising her sensitive inner folds. His pelvic bone rubbed remorselessly against her swollen clitoris as his cock plunged rhythmically inside her.

Desperate to feel more of him, Meredith wound her arms around his neck and crushed her breasts against his naked chest. The skin was hairless, as smooth as silk, and coated with a thin film of perspiration. Fastening her legs more tightly around him she urged her pelvis against him, meeting him thrust for thrust.

She felt hot and breathless, too consumed by pleasure to think of anything other than the torrid, liquid passion coursing through her body. When she came it was with a loud cry, of fulfilment and of triumph. Her vaginal muscles spasmed around his swollen cock, milking him so fiercely he was eventually forced to concede defeat. Slowly, they slid apart and sank down to the bare floorboards, their bodies too weak and depleted to do anything else.

As she cradled Fergal's head in her lap, Meredith glanced across the room to the window. There was a smile on her lips which quickly died. *He* was across there, watching. She didn't know how she knew it but she did. Though the flat opposite was still in total darkness she sensed the shadowy presence of her mystery man behind the pane of glass. Her cheeks flamed as she stared hard at that blank window.

She hoped he could see her. Hoped he could tell she knew he was watching her. Her eyes burned as she continued to stare. The heat in her cheeks faded away to nothingness. There was no room for shame now. More than anything, she wanted to teach him a lesson.

Alex sat in his chair feeling exhausted and gut-wrenchingly envious. He had watched the entire enactment of the scene that had taken place in the flat opposite. At first he had felt excited, especially when he realised what he was about to witness. Then, as he watched the naked man slowly undress the young woman he felt his mounting interest turn to frustration. He could hardly see a thing. The man was so big and so broad that his body almost completely obscured the object of Alex's desire.

The innately masculine bare back and buttocks very quickly became objects of annoyance to Alex. He could see the man's arms moving, his hands obviously stroking the sweet, womanly flesh that Alex could not see. Clenching his teeth, Alex willed the naked man to move to one side. Just a fraction would do, he thought. Was that too much to ask? Then he began to curse God for his cruelty. Didn't He, in His infinite wisdom, realise how wrong it was to deny one of his mortal creations the opportunity to admire the beauty of another?

'I'm not gay!' he ranted aloud into the oppressive silence of his surroundings. 'I couldn't give a damn about that guy's physique. I want to see *her*. I want to see her naked!' Consumed by the futility of his pleas he thumped his fists on the padded leather arms of the chair.

As if to tantalise him further he saw the crushing kiss, the slithering of clothes down naked limbs. A flash of slender leg here and of naked hip there merely added to his dissatisfaction.

Move, he urged silently. Turn around. Get away from her you bastard.

The guy opposite was seriously beginning to annoy him now. All Alex could think about was that he had his Juliet naked, acquiescent and steaming in his hands. Alex could almost feel the power of the young woman's arousal. He could tell the by the way she behaved that she was enjoying every minute of it. Like slides flashing quickly through a projector he watched her hands moving, caressing the naked guy. Then came a brief flick of her blonde head, a shapely leg curving around a masculine hip . . .

Slowmo, Alex thought. I want it in slowmo. He wished it were a video he was watching. He could slow down the action then, or pause it. What are you, some kind of control freak? The question came to him out of the pitch blackness of his frustration and taunted him. A girlfriend – young, bright, American, tits like melons – had demanded that of him once. Once when he had got carried away and ordered her down on all fours to crawl across the room she had stood naked and proud, hands on hips, and shot him down in flames with that question.

It's not me, he had wanted to say at the time. I saw it on a film. It worked for that guy, why not for me? Perhaps, he had asked himself afterwards, he had made a mistake not adding the words 'slut' or 'bitch' as the guy in the film had done. Years later, after other past lovers had asked him the same question, he began to wonder if it was true.

He didn't think he was alone in his fantasy of having a woman who would do anything – absolutely anything – she was told. No matter how humiliating or outrageous. Simple submission. That was what he wanted from his next girlfriend. If he could, he would give it a go; find out if the reality of being in control really did turn him on. Of course, it all hinged on finding the right woman in the first place.

Christ! He thumped the arms of the chair again. They were doing it now. Doing *it!* Up against the wall. And he still couldn't see anything unless you counted her arms and legs which were wrapped, limpet-fashion, around the guy who was screwing her.

You lucky bastard, Alex intoned against the glass, feeling like a kid outside a sweet shop with no money in his pocket. He saw his breath mist the pane in front of him and rubbed quickly at it. Best not to risk missing the moment. *The* moment. He watched the buttocks quiver. Noted the shakiness in the legs. He saw her clinging limbs slacken.

You lucky, lucky bastard.

Meredith woke in a tangle of sheets and confusion. For a moment she couldn't recall where she was, or who she had been with. Her thumping head reminded her of several glasses of scotch – not her usual, relatively healthy tipple. Then she remembered Fergal.

He was gone of course. Slunk away in the small hours like a thief in the night. She hadn't even got his phone number, or he hers. They had made no other arrangement. Chances were they would never see each other again.

Shit! She stared up at the ceiling, feeling strangely let down. Gradually she began to appreciate the softness of the pillows under her head and the fact that she had no appointments that morning. Who had used who? she asked herself with a wry smile.

A couple of hours after that, as she stood soaping herself in the shower, she remembered the voyeur – the guy in the flat opposite hers. A wicked thought sparked in her mind, making her tingle all over. Did she dare? She asked herself. Was she a daring young nineties temptress, or simply an idiot looking for trouble?

Idiot be blowed! She was going to go for it.

Stepping out of the shower she walked deliberately into the living room. She pretended it was purely accidental. She'd forgotten where she was for a moment. Forgotten that she should cover herself with a towel because her new living room had a tall window through which she could clearly be seen.

Dum, de, dum, dum, she hummed quietly to herself as she sashayed nonchalantly across the room. She could feel her legs shaking by the time she got to the middle of the room but she kept on walking, her skin prickling as it dried. Tossing her wet hair back with feigned casual aplomb, she paused in line with the window as if arrested momentarily by the thought of something. She risked a sideways glance. Was he there? Was he watching her?

With her heart hammering she turned and walked over to the cutting table. Idly, she moved pieces of fabric about, picked up a pair of cutting shears, put them down again. She glanced up and thought she caught a flash of something in the flat opposite. It could be him, she thought, or it could be someone else, his cleaning woman perhaps.

Just this thought alone stopped her from doing what she intended to do next. Instead she fled to the sanctuary of her bedroom where she stood behind the full-length blind, her chest heaving as she struggled to catch her breath. After a moment she reached for a pair of discarded leggings and a jumper. As she put them on she realised she had made the opening move in a dangerous game. What she longed to know the answer to was, did she have the courage to play the game out to the bitter end?

If there had ever been one heart-stopping moment in his life it was now, Alex thought. He had only wandered into the room to get yesterday's newspaper and there she was – strolling as bold as brass across the front of the window, totally naked.

He felt himself in awe of her beauty and the naturally graceful way she moved all those delicious parts of her around. The words 'at last' echoed inside his head as he admired the pert tilt of her breasts, the narrow waist, the long, lean length of her thighs. He could see her hair, divided into thick cords, dripping down the slender sweep of her back. He saw the curve of her buttocks and the surprisingly broad width of her shoulders.

'I have to have her,' he murmured to himself as he stood in a shadowy corner of his room, where he was sure he could observe her without being seen. Idly he reached under his bathrobe and stroked his stiffening cock. 'I have to find a way to meet her.'

It should be simple, he thought as he stroked himself. He could just go over to her flat and ring the doorbell. It wouldn't be difficult to work out which number she lived at. Hell, if it came to it he could ring every single bell until he got the right one. Her voice would be instantly recognisable, he was sure. But wasn't that a bit too easy – and too obvious? Might she not be put off by such a straightforward approach?

He sensed, though he didn't know why, that she was a woman who enjoyed playing games. The next move was down to him but what should it be? Something subtle definitely, he concluded. Their eventual meeting should appear to be accidental. As if it was fate that had brought them together, not pushiness on his part.

For once Alex, a man renowned for his creativity, was lost for ideas. Then the phone rang and all his mental machinations were scattered to the four winds. Glancing down he despaired at the sight of his tented robe. It was tempting to stand there and finish what he had started but he couldn't ignore the ringing – he had been waiting for it long enough.

Rushing into his bedroom, he dived across the bed and snatched up the phone, thinking, this had better be worth it. To his relief it was. And the caller was not just Lisa Blair's agent but the famous singer herself, wanting to talk to him about handling the choreography for her new video.

'These designs are fabulous,' the chic brunette said to Meredith. 'I'm sure we could take say a half dozen of each on sale or return.'

Meredith felt her initial leap of excitement pall a little. Sale or return was a nightmare. More often than not the returned goods ended up being soiled or damaged in some way, the ruined garments eating into any profit she might make.

'That's fine,' she heard herself saying. 'How soon would you like them?'

The brunette raised one finely plucked and arched eyebrow. 'Would a week be too soon?'

Meredith groaned inwardly. A week meant staying up all night to fulfil the order.

'No problem,' she responded, a fixed smile on her face. 'Do you have any colour preferences?'

When she got back to her flat she glanced around and realised that the welcoming surroundings had now become her prison. She would be stuck here, working her fingers to the bone, for the next week. There wouldn't be time to go out, or eat, or sleep. Every spare moment would be spent cutting and stitching.

This is what you wanted, Meredith, she reminded herself. This is what you've spent the past God knows how many years working towards. The boutique where her lingerie was to be sold was an exclusive one, in Bond Street of all places. By rights, she should be feeling over the moon.

'Contrary Mary' her mother had often called her and now she knew why. She wandered over to the cutting table and began to clear it in preparation for starting on the new order. As she happened to glance out of the window she was surprised to see a group of five young women walking along the tow path on the opposite side of the canal. The women were all lovely, long-legged and with angel faces. They stopped at the main door of the warehouse opposite and pressed the entry buzzer. A moment later, in a giggling huddle, they spilled through the open door.

'Someone's luck's in,' Meredith murmured to herself as she gathered up stray pins.

Without meaning to she glanced across to the window opposite. As far as she could tell the flat appeared empty. Then she saw him, walking in his graceful, gliding way across the room, dressed in tight black trousers and vest. With a tight feeling across her chest that she recognised as envy Meredith watched the room fill up with people. Or, to be more precise, women. The women on the tow path.

Well, that's just shattered your fantasy that he's obsessed with you, you silly girl, she said to herself. How could he be when he's already got a veritable harem?

'Come in, ladies, come in,' Alex greeted his visitors expansively. He held the door wide open and felt his interest stir as he watched the five young women enter his flat. A mixture of black, white, blonde and brunette, the dancers were all gorgeous. Of course, they had to be, he reasoned, watching their animated faces as they glanced around. Music videos were traditionally peopled by the young and lovely. 'Just put your bags over there,' he instructed. 'You can use the bedroom to get changed in.'

Alberta had handled the casting. He admired her efficiency. It had taken her less than three hours. 'The dancers I am sending you are the best,' she had assured him on the phone. 'They're young, mind you, but professional through and through.'

While he waited for the dancers to change into their practice gear Alex wandered over to his music centre and put on the demo tape which had been couriered over to him. He had already listened to it at least twenty times and had a few ideas floating around in his head. Now it was just a question of seeing if they worked.

He felt a rising excitement as the young women trickled back into the room. Not because their figures were perfect and their bodies strong and limber but because he was going to be directing their movements. Controlling them. The realisation made him hark back to his fantasy. All at once he found himself wishing he directed porn videos instead of dance steps. Now that would be a cause for excitement.

As he watched the young women bending and stretching in front of him, going through the series of warm up exercises that he had insisted upon, he found his imagination getting the better of him. Where was his professionalism now? He asked himself crossly, trying hard to think of those bodies executing perfect *plies* and *jetés*, instead of wild, uninhibited sex positions.

One young woman, a small half-caste girl with her hair braided into lots of little plaits, especially took his interest. This surprised him as he'd never had a particular penchant for black girls. Despite this, he found himself glancing at her time and again.

When she bent over, the ends of her plaits trailing the floor as she pressed her nose against her knees, he couldn't help appreciating the pronounced roundness of her bottom. For one mad moment he pictured himself grabbing her from behind and invading her nether regions. He told himself it was because he hadn't been able to finish masturbating that morning. After Lisa Blair's call he had been thrown into such a frenzy of excitement and activity he had even forgotten about the naked girl across the way. By the time he had remembered her it was too late. She had gone. And so had his erection.

Briefly, he outlined what he had in mind by way of the opening steps for the first few bars. The eventual video would be shot in an abandoned service station and its forecourt, he had been told. Lisa Blair would pull up in an old pink Cadillac and a couple of black male dancers – who hadn't been cast yet – would act as the garage attendants. Lisa had said that she hoped to get the whole thing in the can within six weeks. She agreed with Alex and Alberta that she would be pushing her luck but Alex had promised to do his best, which seemed to satisfy her. So much so in fact, Alex recalled with an inner flicker of anticipation, that she had invited him to meet her for dinner later in the week – time and place to be arranged.

He turned his attention back to the dancers and had to agree with Alberta that they were all very good. The black dancer, he was a bit disappointed to note, seemed, if anything, to be the least coordinated of the lot. Which knocks on the head that old adage about black people having natural rhythm, he told himself with a wry smile.

'What's the joke, honey?' The black girl surprised him by asking. 'Care to share it with the rest of us?'

'No. No, it was nothing,' he said, shaking his head in vigorous denial. For a moment his eyes rested on the sweet, round face from which two Malteser eyes gazed up at him. He felt a deep tugging sensation in the pit of his belly and knew, in that instant, that she would be staying behind for 'extra tuition'. Tearing his gaze away from hers, his glance took in all of them. 'I've just realised, we haven't done the name thing,' he said.

'Let's take five and I'll make us all some coffee.'

They sat around his spartan living-room; three girls on the sofa, two on the floor at their feet and himself in his leather armchair. As they sipped warily at their mugs of scalding coffee they offered up their names. The three on the sofa, two with shortish blonde hair and one brunette with a shoulder-length bob, introduced themselves as Karen, Philippa and Kerry. The two on the floor, another brunette and Alex's favourite, said their names were Pamela and Regina.

Regina? Alex thought immediately, rhymes with . . . He cut short the infantile thought and smiled. From her position on the floor, Regina caught his eye and grinned broadly. Thank God, he thought, she can read my idiotic mind and still be attracted to me. He found himself warming to her even more. Anyone who could live with a name like that and still be so cheerful had to be worth getting to know.

For the next ten minutes or so they talked about the video and about Lisa Blair's music in general. Most of the girls were huge fans but Philippa, who Alex thought was perhaps the coolest of the five, professed not to have much of an interest in contemporary music – outstanding or otherwise.

'I'm a classical person,' she said, smoothing back her blonde hair in an affected manner. 'Give me Tchaikovsky or Verdi any day.'

She made it clear, without having to say anything, that she would rather be dancing in a ballet production rather than a pop video. In that instant Alex knew that he and Philippa would eventually come to blows.

'Well, I'm not too proud to do anything as long as it means dancing,' Regina said, making Alex want to hug her. 'I mean, you uptight bitches really get me, man, you know?' She gave a laugh like trickling water and glanced around at the others for confirmation. Only Kerry dared to agree.

'Isn't it better to be working and to be seen, Philippa?' she asked in a husky voice. 'I mean, isn't that what we all strive for?'

Philippa's answer was a haughty toss of her head. She put her mug down, coffee untouched, and stood up.

'If you don't mind, I'm going to use this time to practise not sit around making inane conversation,' she said in an accusatory tone which made the others flinch and look guilty. A couple of them made to stand up and follow Philippa to the barre but Alex waved them back to their seats.

'No, you don't,' he said. 'Sit down.' He cast a sly glance across the room where Philippa was holding her right leg above her head. 'Don't you know, all work and no play makes Philippa a dull woman?'

Philippa dropped her right leg and glared at him over her shoulder. The others tittered nervously. Wonderful, Alex thought, cursing himself inwardly. One clever remark from me and I've managed to set the tone for the rest of this contract.

Chapter Four

Just as Alex suspected she would, Regina made an excuse to stay behind just as the dancers were all about to leave.

'Oops,' she said, pretending to rummage about in her holdall, 'it looks as though I've left my tights behind in your bedroom, Alex.'

'Well, you'd better go and get them then,' he responded with a smile.

He watched her dive into the bedroom in a fluster, then turned and waved goodbye to the other four girls. Inside he could feel his heart gathering pace with anticipation. A curvy little cutie in the bedroom was just what he needed as the end to a nigh-on perfect day.

Meredith happened to glance up from her work just as the dance troupe left the building opposite, though in her current frazzled state her brain didn't compute that there was one girl left behind. By looking across to the flat opposite several times that afternoon she had quickly come to realise that the group of young women did not comprise her mystery guy's harem but were, in fact, dancers. And by her amazing powers of deduction she worked out that he was a dancer too.

Feeling quite excited about this new discovery, she wondered if he was famous at all, though she couldn't honestly say she recognised him. It did explain his extraordinary grace however and, if anything, the knowledge that, like her, he wasn't an ordinary nine-to-fiver increased his appeal. She assumed that as a dancer he would be creative – like her – and possess a huge amount of drive and determination – again, like her.

This made her feel more kindly disposed towards him, as if she recognised a kindred spirit. It made sense to her now that she felt strangely drawn to him and her new found knowledge increased her desire to get to know him.

Without realising that she was still staring into his flat, Meredith watched him walk across the room. A moment later she saw a young, dark-haired woman join him. She was dressed in tight white leggings that showed off the pronounced jutting of round buttocks and muscular legs. On top she wore a hot pink cropped tee-shirt that showed a good expanse of deeply tanned stomach and a pair of large, bra-less breasts.

Those must be a bit of a handicap when she's dancing, Meredith found herself thinking. Then she giggled, imagining the young woman regularly giving herself two black eyes. With her own eyes popping, she watched the girl wrap herself around the guy and rub herself up and down him in a very feline way.

With a deadline hammering at her, the last thing Meredith felt like doing was stopping work to watch the two of them but she found she couldn't help herself. She saw the guy's hands linger on the tight round buttocks, his fingertips pressing and squeezing. Between her thighs Meredith felt an involuntary trickle. She clenched her own buttocks hard, imagining that it was her bottom his hands were exploring. In truth, she could almost feel his touch. And the tingling in her nipples when those same hands reached up and cupped the girl's swelling breasts, clad in hot pink stretchy cotton, was undeniable in its intensity.

Meredith realised she felt warm and a little lightheaded as she clutched the edge of her work table. She was desperate to move away from the window but felt rooted to the spot by her own curiosity. There was a sensual longing deep inside her that she could have understood better had it not been for her experience with Fergal the night before.

She wondered if she had to be some kind of nymphomaniac pervert to be standing there, getting turned on by watching another couple fondling each other. It was like watching a video, she realised, drawing her chair close so that she could sit down and spy on them in comfort.

All thoughts of moving away were long gone. With growing excitement she watched the girl pull her tee-shirt off over her head and saw the tiny plaits all bob about as she shook her head free of it. Carelessly, the girl threw her tee-shirt over her shoulder, simultaneously thrusting her breasts into the guy's waiting hands. Meredith hugged her arms around her body as she watched his fingers playing with the distended buds of the girl's dark nipples. Surreptitiously, she moved one hand, seeking one of her own nipples so that she could toy with it.

They can't see me, she told herself. And if they could they wouldn't be interested, they're too engrossed in each other.

Meredith was right up to a point. Regina hadn't noticed her sitting at the window opposite. But Alex had. He'd caught her out of the corner of his eye and kept the image of her face, with its glazed expression, uppermost in his mind as he began to plan how he was going to play this scene.

This was like choreography, he realised, with a feeling of exultation. The next move had been up to him and now was his chance to show her what he could do.

Murmuring a lewd comment in Regina's ear he waited for the expected giggle. To his delight it came in ripples that set her full breasts jiggling like jellies in his hands. Cradling her breasts in his palms he crushed them together and raised the nipples to his lips. With his head bent and his hair covering his face he could no longer see 'Juliet', not even when he glanced slyly sideways. But for the moment it was enough to have his tongue wrapped around those delicious flesh berries.

To his increased pleasure he felt the stiff nipples grow even bigger as his lips tugged at them. He nibbled gently and delighted in Regina's answering moan of delight. His cock grew huge inside his tight black practice pants as she squirmed against him. He could feel her strong, muscular thigh insinuating itself between his legs and rubbing at his groin. Her hands were all over his back, pulling up his tee-shirt and kneading his bare flesh.

Like sharp little blades her nails raked his skin. He backed off a little then, concerned that she would mark him. If she did, it could ruin his casting chances. The public didn't want to see a dancer's body sporting tramlines. Reaching behind him, one nipple clenched lightly between his teeth, he drew her hands away to do something more useful. He placed them over his cock and squeezed them over his obvious tumescence just in case she hadn't already got the message.

He needn't have worried. Regina had her hands down his pants in two seconds flat, her eager fingers working furiously at his stiff shaft. She slid his pants down over his hips, low enough for his fully engorged cock to spring free. Now he raised his head and glanced sideways. He had to. And there she was. His Juliet looking shocked and awestruck all at the same time.

At that point he almost winked at her but realised it would be a very crass thing to do. Plus, he didn't want her to know he was aware of her voyeurism, just in case he succeeded in frightening her off.

Instead he pulled off his trousers and sweat socks in one go. Then he dragged his tee-shirt off over his head. Proudly naked he watched Regina's face register his appearance and her pleasure at it. She didn't disappoint him. She looked like a starving woman faced with a whole roast suckling pig.

'Oh, baby,' she groaned as her eyes flicked over him. 'Oh, baby, this little momma's going to treat you so good.' As she spoke she sank to her knees in front of him, clasped his cock and guided it between her full plummy lips.

She sucked hard, as though she was trying to draw the very lifeblood from him. Then she changed tack completely and began to dab at his shaft and glans with the tip of her tongue before tantalising it with feathery little strokes.

Almost out of his mind with enjoyment, Alex heard himself groan and felt his fingers clutching at the little plaits. They were a bit disappointing, those plaits, he thought in a more lucid moment. What he wanted most was a nice thick head of hair to get hold of. But a moment later he was too lost in the wonder of her oral technique to bother about her hairstyle.

'Yes, oh, yes, that's good,' he encouraged her, trying hard to resist the urge to jam his cock right into her mouth.

He glanced at Juliet again and almost came there and then when he noticed that she was stroking herself blatantly. Admittedly it was over her clothes but he had the memory of her naked body still fresh in his mind from that morning. And Alex had enough creativity in his head to merge the two images into one.

With his last ounce of self-control he made himself pull back from Regina and tug hastily at her leggings. They came off easily, the wiry brush of dark hair at the apex of her thighs revealing that she was wearing nothing underneath.

As she thrashed her legs about, kicking off the leggings, Alex couldn't help noticing that the hair on her vaginal lips was beaded with her excitement. And the delicate lips between her outer labia protruded, looking as succulent and plummy in colour as her mouth.

Ignoring his own desperate need to come, he dived between her flailing legs, his mouth pressing hungrily at her moist sex. With his tongue he deftly parted her outer lips and lapped at the soft core of her. The bud of her clitoris was already swollen and he laved it with the flat of his tongue until she was crying out in ecstasy.

All his instincts were totally bestial now. He grasped her strong thighs and pressed them wide apart and back toward her chest so that her vulva was thrust into vulnerable prominence. He felt devilish as he teased her with his lips and tongue, bringing her to the point of orgasm so many times before retreating that she became almost incoherent with arousal.

'Fuck me. For God's sake, Alex!' she implored.

Alex deliberately ignored her. He felt her fingernails digging into his shoulders but even that didn't deter him. This was the performance of a lifetime, not just for himself and Regina but for Juliet. It was only when he glanced around for a third time that he noticed, with a desperate plummeting sensation behind his ribs, that she was no longer watching.

In the quiet sanctuary of her bedroom Meredith lay across her bed, arms and legs splayed, trying desperately to bring herself back to some semblance of normality. It was no good, she railed inside. Her arousal was so strong that the quick orgasm she had just given herself wasn't nearly enough. She was a woman in sexual torment.

It was with a feeling of finality that she put her hands between her thighs for a second time. She was still incredibly moist, she noticed as her fingers began to strum a familiar tune on her most secret flesh. Her desire was by no means satiated by the ten seconds of pleasure she had just experienced.

She thrust a couple of fingers inside herself hard, almost brutally, as the fingers of her other hand stroked expertly at her swollen clitoris. What made matters worse was that there was no way she could rid her mind of the images she had just witnessed. If it wasn't bad enough seeing the guy opposite in all his naked, well-toned glory, she had been forced to endure the sight of that long, delicious cock sliding in and out of the black girl's mouth.

Then . . . Oh, God, then – she rubbed more furiously as the recollection welled up in her mind – he had gone down on her. And in with such enthusiasm and relish that Meredith had been sorely tempted to strip off her clothes, fling open the French windows and yell, 'Me next!'

Please, me next, she moaned inside her head, feeling half delirious with wanting. If there had been one thing she had needed from Fergal and hadn't got, it was a good bout of oral. Christ! She cursed herself now for not insisting upon it. What was she, a wimp? Was she supposed to be grateful for what he had given her?

He, that guy over there, obviously knew what sex was all about. Give *and* take, she told herself, rubbing forcefully now, not just take. Five seconds later she came. And she came with such force that she surprised herself. Her mind hadn't even been on what she was going.

In that instant she realised her desire for that guy – her mystery man, someone she hadn't even met – was far greater than she could have thought possible. It had to be to provoke such a reaction.

Haven't met *yet*, Meredith, she consoled herself as she rolled over onto her side and curled up in the foetal position on the antique lace bedcover. Haven't met yet . . .

Alex couldn't deny that he enjoyed Regina's body that night. He fucked her every which way. On top, underneath, up against the wall, in the shower and straight afterwards, on the bathroom floor. It seemed the young woman was insatiable and her strength was such that she almost wore him out. Almost. But for him, the sudden departure of Juliet from the window had the same effect as a bucket of cold water being thrown over him.

It had almost robbed him completely of his passion, leaving him feeling that he had started something he was no longer sure he wanted to finish. However, he prided himself on being a gentleman and he could hardly ignore the sight of Regina's naked, curvaceous body thrashing about on the hard wood floor. By concentrating on her pleasure and the sweet, honeyed taste of her sex flesh, he managed to resurrect his wilting cock. After that, the rest had been plain sailing.

Or plain fucking, he told himself after Regina had gone. He hadn't relished the idea of her staying the whole night and so had gallantly paid for a mini-cab to take her home. His excuse to her was that they couldn't very well let on to others that they had something going.

'Imagine what Philippa's going to make of it,' he pointed out, though in reality he could care less what that silly bitch thought. 'She's going to accuse you of being teacher's pet and make life hell for you and the rest of us.'

To his relief, Regina saw the sense in this, though her face registered a disappointment that nearly made Alex cave in. Fortunately, a late telephone call from Alberta distracted him long enough for Regina to get her act together. By the time the call ended she was dressed again and standing in his bedroom doorway, holdall in hand.

'Thanks, Alex,' she said, smiling with a false brightness. 'It was great. Truly great.'

He nodded, feeling as guilty as hell, then annoyed with himself for feeling that way. Wasn't this the liberal nineties? He asked himself. And weren't they both adults? Who said sex had to imply some sort of commitment? Still, as he watched from the window while Regina walked down the tow path toward the yellow-and-white cab, he couldn't help feeling that by acting on impulse he had just made a rod for his own back.

This didn't stop him from immediately acting on another impulse, which was to glance across to the flat opposite. It was all in darkness save for a single pool of brightness which illuminated the intriguing figure of Juliet, seated at the window. The light came from a spotlight and seemed to imbue her lovely features with a magical quality. She was wearing something white and all encompassing, with long sleeves. Dressed in that way, she seemed even more like the beautiful heroine of an era long past.

To his delight she glanced up, her blonde tresses picking up the light and forming a nimbus around her head. She stared straight at him. And for a long time they remained, eyes locked, suspended in a moment in time that seemed eternal. Then, with something that appeared to Alex to be reluctance, she reached out and switched off the light.

He continued to gaze across the tow path, willing her to put the light back on again. But all he saw was her pale, ghostly shape hovering by the window for a moment before drifting away. As minutes passed and she didn't reappear Alex gave a long sigh. He shrugged his shoulders as he turned away from the window. If he couldn't have her in real life, at least he had his dreams of her to look forward to.

The urge to work had got the better of Meredith and drove her back to the cutting table. There she fought to ignore the temptation to look up and watch what was going on in the flat opposite. A sexual marathon by all accounts, she decided, when the lure of voyeurism got the better of her.

Having given herself several orgasms and a tepid shower – she couldn't quite bring herself to indulge in a cold one – and dressed in the Victorian-style nightdress that she dubbed her passion killer, she no longer felt such steamy, all encompassing desire. Now, she was able to view the activities across the way with a kind of detached fascination. But a fascination none the less.

She viewed the naked, coupling bodies with the sort of eye an artist might. The creative genius in her stirred at the sight of gleaming skin stretched over finely honed muscles. She could envisage its texture. Almost feel the silkiness of that skin. The perspiration-slicked covering that, in her imagination, she likened to rubber sheets smeared with baby oil.

Not that she'd ever experienced such a thing first hand, she reminded herself, smiling inwardly at the thought. But why not, in the future? The not too distant future, she hoped.

As she sat and cut and sewed and, from time to time, glanced up, she pondered on the variety of fantasies that sparked her imagination. Being tied up was one of her favourites, as was rolling around in the surf on a tropical island, propositioning a complete and totally unsuitable stranger and having half a dozen men cover her naked body with whipped cream then licking it all off.

Stop it! She admonished herself when she started to feel uncomfortably warm again. Leaning her elbows on the table top, she dropped her sewing and cupped her chin in her hands. The couple in the opposite flat were still hard at it – she giggled at the unintentional pun – with the black girl currently doing most of the work.

Just the faintest flicker of renewed interest licked at the soft flesh between her thighs as she watched the young woman bobbing up and down astride the guy – *her* guy as she thought of him now. There was no denying the girl knew how to enjoy herself and took the greatest pleasure in her sexuality.

One of the fantasies Meredith hardly dared acknowledge was that of herself with another woman. Half of her felt repulsed, the other half fascinated by the sensual possibilities of such an encounter. In Nottingham she had met a few bisexual girls and had responded to their lighthearted encouragement to her to try 'the real thing', as they put it, by laughing off their suggestions. Inside, however, she had felt a sneaking, growing curiosity about what it might be like to engage in an erotic liaison with a member of her own sex.

Now, as she tried to look at the young black woman with a dispassionate eye, she couldn't help noticing the full, rounded breasts jiggling up and down as she rode the guy beneath her, and the equally prominent curve of her bottom. With her palms pressed flat to the guy's chest, the girl's back was arched, her head flung back and her wide, full-lipped mouth open and grasping.

Without meaning to, consciously, Meredith found herself fantasising about what it might be like to run her hands over that dusky skin. To follow the delicious curves and contours. She shivered, imagining it and simultaneously envisaging other, feminine hands, exploring her body in a similar way. What would it be like? She wondered, glancing around for the glass of mineral water she kept by her elbow because her mouth had suddenly gone dry. More to the point, would she ever get the opportunity to find out?

It was the following day. The sun had risen early and now the fierce midday heat was gratifyingly tempered by a cool breeze gusting across the wide expanse of deserted forecourt. Around one of the disused, fifties-style, petrol pumps the dance troupe, along with two black guys Alberta had sent along, were chatting and laughing. At a discreet distance from them, Alex stood in close conference with Lisa Blair and the director of the video, Sam McNeill.

Alex recognised Sam's name as one of the leading lights in video direction — with various credits for music videos and advertisements under his narrow belt. He was a thin, wiry man, with a shock of red hair and goatee beard and, like all 'proper' film directors, he was clad totally in black.

Although he had seen her on TV, in real life Lisa Blair came as quite a surprise to Alex. She was much smaller than she appeared on film, Alex realised, probably only five feet three and a neat size eight. Her legs are about the same size as my arms, he found himself thinking. With shoulder-length chestnut hair that curved around the delicate oval of her face, she looked every bit as approachable as he had assumed she would be. She had seemed nice enough on the phone. However, he soon found out, after five minutes of conversation, that she was not going to prove to be the easiest person he had ever worked with.

Her opening gambit was a list of do's and don't's, followed by a catalogue of demands that amounted to a virtual straight-jacket on Alex's creativity.

'I don't want any arty farty stuff,' Lisa said bluntly, flicking a long column of ash from the end of her cigarette. 'No ballet steps. No airy fairy arm waving. What this has got to be is right-on and funky. I want the girls to come across as tough and assertive. A bit of Kung Fu would be good,' she added as an apparent afterthought. 'Some nice foot jabs to the head, that sort of thing. Yes, I really think that would work well.'

As her face took on a dreamy expression, Alex groaned inside. He listened to her speak and found himself wondering how she could smoke so much and still have such a great singing voice. The entire sequence of steps that he had planned were based on ballet moves, which meant he would have to rethink the whole thing. He despaired at the thought of the work he and the female dancers had already put in and which would now go to waste. And he knew the other female dancers would be none too happy about the situation either.

Naturally, Philippa – the true prima donna of them all – was the first to voice her complaints. 'Doesn't she realise I am an artiste,' she whined, waving her arms about theatrically, 'not a Bruce Lee type. Good God.' She shuddered, as though the very thought horrified her.

'Everything OK, folks?' Sam asked, coming up to the little group huddled conspiratorially around the petrol pump. He rubbed his hands together enthusiastically and beamed at them all with false gaiety.

'Not exactly,' Alex muttered, marvelling at the man's bad sense of timing, 'but we'll cope.'

Frowning slightly, Sam took Alex to one side. 'Look,' he began in a low voice, so as not to be overheard by the others, 'I know Lisa can be a bit of a – well, you know. I've worked with her before and she's always proved difficult. But—' He put up his hand to silence Alex who had opened his mouth to offer a comment. 'At the end of the day she gets results. There's no getting away from it, she's a lady who knows exactly what she wants. She's a perfectionist, but that's no bad thing. And the results are always fabulous. Plus, we mustn't forget *the* most important thing,' his added, his frown disappearing to be replaced by a wry smile.

'What's that?' Alex asked.

The smile on Sam's face grew broader as he slapped Alex on the back. 'She's the one paying our wages, old son. That's the bottom line.'

As it turned out, the day's session didn't go too badly after that. Alex was relieved that, presumably because she was satisfied everyone understood the ground rules, Lisa kept herself very much to herself and only tried to interfere on a couple of occasions. Philippa was the only one who made the day's work harder going that it needed to be.

'I can't do it, this is just not me,' she insisted from the low squatting position Alex had instructed them to adopt – they were then supposed to take three paces sideways, crab fashion and then three paces back, before jumping up and executing a one hundred and eighty degree turn. 'This position is not in the least bit ladylike.'

'Who said you were a lady?' Regina muttered under her breath. The others giggled and Alex flashed them a warning look which only made them giggle harder.

'That's it!' Philippa announced, straightening up and preparing to flounce off the set in a huff.

Alex rushed over to her and put his arm consolingly around her shoulders. He almost recoiled at the rigidity in her body. She was as cold and unbending as a lump of steel.

'Philippa, sweetheart—' He grimaced inwardly at the words and his sickly tone of voice. 'Please don't be like this. The show's the thing, isn't it?' He wanted to add, 'You say you're a professional, then bloody well act like one.' Instead he squeezed her unwilling body against him. 'Please, Philippa, this sort of temperamental behaviour isn't going to get any of us anywhere.'

For a moment she seemed intent on remaining steadfast in her refusal to cooperate, then all at once Alex felt the tension in her body ease a little. Nevertheless, she shrugged him off her as though he were a slobbering dog.

'Very well, Alex,' she said, smiling thinly. 'I'll do this for you. Not because I agree with it but because I admire your professionalism.' To Alex's surprise and horror, she gave him a look that could only be interpreted, in her case, as coquettish. 'Perhaps you would like to take me out to dinner this evening, Alex?' It wasn't so much a question as a demand and was accompanied by a disturbing glint in her green eyes.

When faced with such an enticing proposition, Alex thought wryly, I don't see how I can refuse. In all honesty he was just grateful that Philippa was going to cooperate at long last. Buying her dinner and spending an evening in her company seemed a small price to pay.

As the sun began to dip in the sky, Meredith put down her sewing and glanced with satisfaction at the set of lingerie she had already created. There were only three sets of bras, panties and suspender belts, all fashioned from the filmiest of fabric, but at least it was a start.

Bracing her hands against the edge of the cutting table, she pushed her chair back. Then she stretched, reaching her arms up as high above her head as possible. She felt the instant relief in her spine and cursed herself for spending so much time hunched over her sewing. The regular breaks she always promised herself never seemed to materialise. Once she got stuck into her work she invariably lost all track of time.

All at once she realised she hadn't eaten anything at all that day. Rising stiffly from her chair she wandered into her bedroom and began stripping off her clothes. I'll have a quick shower, she thought, then I'll treat myself by going out somewhere to eat.

As she rinsed herself under the warm jet of water, Meredith found herself wondering where the guy in the flat opposite had got to. It appeared that he had been out all day, since first thing that morning. And Meredith had felt a strange sense of loneliness as she sat there at her table, knowing that there was no possibility of glancing up and locking eyes with him.

Because she was treating herself, Meredith dressed up. As it was high summer and the evenings were warm, she opted for a calf-length halter-necked dress in a floral pattern. She let her hair dry naturally while she concentrated on making up her face. Then, when her hair was dry, she brushed it out so that it fell in a shiny curtain around her bare shoulders.

As she made her way down the tow path, Meredith pondered her eating options. She was in the sort of mood where, though she was starving hungry, she didn't know what she fancied to eat. I'll stop at the first likely looking place, she told herself, and hang the expense. She decided the meal would be a belated celebration for winning her latest order and for having the possibility of another on the horizon. That afternoon a woman had rung her saying that she had seen some of Meredith's things in a boutique and was interested in commissioning some one-off designs. She was due to marry in a few months time and wanted the lingerie for her trousseau.

Meredith had grinned at the old-fashioned notion of a trousseau. It seemed so upper class and indeed the voice on the telephone sounded it. Her name was Camilla something-something and she told Meredith a time, two days hence, when it would be convenient for her to call at the flat in person. Eager for the work, and the possible word of mouth recommendation that might follow, Meredith hadn't had the nerve to try and prevaricate. The woman's authoritative manner put her off a little but the thought of so much money in the bank, plus a possible 'in' with the moneyed set, forced her to keep her mouth shut and agree to everything.

The restaurant she finally happened upon was in a tiny back street just off Piccadilly. The food was Italian and the menu pinned to a lectern outside the restaurant was mouth-watering enough to make her decision an easy one. Taking a deep breath for courage she pushed open the door and entered the small bistro.

To her surprise it seemed jam-packed inside but the friendly maître d' led her downstairs to a much larger room where only half the tables were occupied. As soon as she sat down Meredith glanced around at the other diners. Most were couples, or groups of friends which made her feel horribly conspicuous in her single state. Her table was in a corner – a small square set for two and covered in rose pink linen, with a single pale pink carnation in a bud vase as the centerpiece.

She had difficulty deciding what to order but in the end she settled on fettucine with chicken and broccoli in a cream sauce. To go with it she ordered a half-carafe of Valpolicella. Just as the waiter had finished pouring her wine and moved away from the table Meredith happened to glance up. Directly in front of her was the staircase leading from the upper floor of the restaurant.

Just for a moment she felt transfixed as she gazed at the couple walking down the staircase. Her heart missed a beat. It was *him*. She was sure she wasn't mistaken.

Chapter Five

Although she had only ever seen him from a distance, Meredith had seen enough of her mystery man to recognise the dark wavy hair, the perfectly sculpted profile and the smooth easy gait. Feeling embarrassed without knowing why, Meredith picked up her wineglass and gulped hastily at the dry white wine.

She felt absurdly grateful that neither her mystery man, nor his companion, noticed her. And little wonder, Meredith thought. The cool, elegant blonde by his side was beautiful enough to command the attention of every man in the room.

Meredith felt herself sinking into the corner as they walked right past her table.

Just as they went by her the woman spoke. 'This is one of my favourite places, Alex. I promise you, the food is absolutely divine.'

Alex! Meredith thought, her mind reeling. His name is Alex. Feeling her heart fluttering excitedly behind her ribs, Meredith straightened up and stared at his retreating figure. With her eyes burning like laser beams into his straight back she willed him to turn round and, at the last moment, just before they reached their table at the opposite end of the room, he did.

He glanced over his shoulder long enough for a flicker of recognition to pass across his face.

Although her own face felt frozen, Meredith managed to curve her lips into a semblance of a smile and she nodded. It seemed like an age before he turned properly and gave her an answering nod. And the smile that followed was devastating. Even from a distance Meredith felt the warmth in his blue eyes. And there was no denying his powerful allure. It was so strong, sheer willpower was the only thing that stopped her from getting up and flinging herself at him.

The moment passed quickly. Alex and his companion sat down and a plate of food appeared in front of Meredith. No longer interested in her meal Meredith ate mechanically, not tasting a thing. Her whole body felt as though it were on red-alert, her erotic senses soaring. It seemed incredible to her that she and her mystery man – Alex, she must remember to think of him as Alex now – were actually in the same room together.

Even though he was seated some distance away she could feel his physical presence. Her cheeks flamed and her hands shook as she recalled the scenes she had witnessed in his flat and, worse still, her own provocative behaviour.

'Is everything to your satisfaction, madam?'

Meredith jumped. The waiter was at her elbow, looking concerned. She glanced down at her plate realising she had hardly touched her food.

'Yes, it is,' she said, forcing a tremulous smile. 'It's not that. I suppose I'm just not as hungry as I thought I was.'

'Would you like me to take it away and heat it up again for you, madam?' the waiter offered. 'It would be no trouble at all.'

Meredith shook her head. She realised that her appetite had totally vanished now. All that was left to gnaw at her stomach was a desperate hunger of a much different kind, made all the worse by knowing that her need for the man seated across the room was futile.

'No, thank you,' she said, feeling despondent but not having given up hope completely. 'But I wouldn't mind a cup of cappuccino instead.'

As the waiter nodded and removed the plate from the table, Meredith sat back. She re-folded her napkin and for once found herself wishing that she smoked. If ever there was a right time for a cigarette, it was now.

Meredith recognised a strange compulsion to torture herself unnecessarily. It was habitual and had her in its grip right now. As she sipped at a third cup of coffee she found herself wondering why she was so determined to prolong the agony. There was no way he, Alex, was going to leave the woman in his company to come over and talk to her. And it had been sheer folly to think he would. Perhaps the incredible erotic attraction between the two of them was all in her mind. The chances were he felt nothing at all. She was kidding herself as usual, she told herself sternly. Typically, she was romanticising a situation that was nothing more than a product of her overactive imagination.

Go now, she urged herself, you're acting like a total fool, and you're going to be hyper all night thanks to all this caffeine. She glanced ruefully at her half-drunk cup of coffee, yet as she signalled to the waiter to bring her the bill she decided a spell of hyperactivity would be no bad thing. She still had plenty of work to get through. Perhaps a few hours spent sewing would be the best thing for her right now. She needed something to calm her down and take her mind off a situation that was purely fantasy anyway.

As she left her table Meredith couldn't resist the urge to glance back over her shoulder. To her chagrin she noticed that Alex's attention was concentrated totally on the woman sitting opposite him. He didn't look up. There was no exchange of conspiratorial smiles. No zing of sensual electricity between them to send her on her way. Consequently, she left the restaurant feeling let down and totally inconspicuous. Even a wolf whistle from a young guy, who she careered blindly into as she stepped out of the restaurant onto the pavement, did nothing to lift her spirits and make her feel better about herself again.

By the time she got home however, Meredith felt a marked improvement in her spirits. Tonight had been a step forward. She knew her mystery man's name and knew that the attraction she felt for him was too strong to try to deny. She hoped Alex would continue to watch her through his window. And moreover, hoped he would somehow signal to her that her undeniable craving for him would be reciprocated. Only time would tell but, Meredith reasoned, that was a commodity she had plenty of.

A surprise shower had left the pockmarked streets of London strewn with puddles. As he walked home, Alex made a game of dodging them to pass the time. His reason for walking was that he hadn't wanted to share a cab with Philippa. Sitting opposite her in a restaurant all evening, listening to her catalogue of boasts about her dancing prowess and complaints about some of the other dancers they knew, had been enough to last Alex a lifetime and there was no way he wanted to prolong the agony.

He sensed that Philippa had been surprised by the way he ditched her. He had done it quickly and efficiently, with just the merest glance of a kiss on both cheeks. Then he had waved her away in the taxi. At the sight of the rounded back end of the cab moving away from him he felt the relief at Philippa's departure wash over him. Dismissing the idea of waiting for another cab to appear, Alex had turned in the direction of home. It was a long way to walk but he hoped it would give him time to clear his head.

What he couldn't shake off was the memory of her – his Juliet, as he had dubbed her – sitting there in the same restaurant that Philippa had chosen. Her presence had taken him by surprise and he had felt totally at sea when he clapped eyes on her. He cursed himself for grinning at her inanely. He felt like a complete fool and had gone out of his way not to catch her eye for the rest of the evening.

He found himself wondering what she was doing right now. She had managed to leave the restaurant without him noticing. Philippa had a way of demanding a person's full attention and so he hadn't been that surprised when he glanced over to Juliet's table and saw that it was empty. The sense of loss he felt at seeing that vacant seat had been profound. So much so that he had rushed Philippa through the rest of meal, hoping – though he knew it was futile – that he might catch up with his mystery woman out on the street.

Glancing idly at the shop fronts as he passed, Alex realised he was almost home. He felt excitement gathering inside him. All he wanted, he realised, was to get up to his flat, rush to the window and see if *she* was there.

Meredith was inserting a thin semicircle of underwiring into a blue satin bra when she noticed the light go on in the flat opposite hers. As if she were connected to the light switch in Alex's flat, a jolt of electricity stunned her. She dropped the bra, her heart missing a beat. Now she acknowledged that for the past hour or so she had been waiting for this moment.

With her gaze fixed to the illuminated window opposite she watched Alex walk towards her. At least that was how it seemed.

Even from such a distance she felt his eyes locked with hers and in that moment she realised that all her hopes were founded in something real after all.

As she continued to gaze at him she watched Alex walk right up to the window. He leaned forward, his hands resting on the ledge, until his forehead touched the glass. As if in a dream, Meredith stood up and leaned across the table. She placed her palms flat against the glass and gazed across the murky ribbon of the canal. Unlike the water below her, Alex's eyes were a bright, sparkling blue. Not that she could appreciate their hue from such a distance but that didn't matter, their sapphire brilliance was fixed in her memory.

She could feel her body coming to life inside the thick towelling robe she had changed into. Her skin tingled and her heart throbbed. Pressed against the glass, her fingers itched to move and caress herself. Ever so slowly she straightened up and moved around the table. She kept her eyes fixed to Alex's the whole time. Dragging the table away from the window she moved to stand right in front of it. Her right hand was at her throat, clutching at the collar of her robe. Her other arm was rapped around herself, the fingertips pressing into the indentation of her waist.

Slowly, she relaxed her grip on the towelling collar and allowed her hand to slide lower. It cupped her right breast, moulding it lightly over the nubbly cotton. From the distance that separated them she could feel Alex's interest. It was as though he were caught up in the same web of desire that held her in its thrall.

Even through the thick towelling she could feel her nipple harden. Naughty thing, she thought as she pinched it lightly. Then she grasped at it harder, rolling and tugging at the sensitive nub of flesh between her fingertips. Her breath was coming in short, sharp gasps now. It misted up the pane of glass in front of her, making Alex's image fuzzier, more surreal. The room behind Meredith was filled with such stillness that she felt as though she were standing alone in a desert. And in that desert she felt her body thirsting. Her desire longing to be quenched.

Feeling liberated by her own desire she rested her bottom against the table top and rubbed herself against it, moving her hips deliberately from side to side on the sharp-edged wood. The table edge dug into her bottom, marking it, she was sure, even through her robe. Strangely, she felt pleased by the idea of a red stripe across her bottom cheeks. Somehow it felt as though she were branding herself – for him.

Between her legs she felt her sex lips thickening with arousal, her vagina moistening in readiness for a coupling that could only exist in her imagination. The sheer frustration of it made Meredith bang her palms hard against the window in front of her. Bastard! She mouthed through the glass. You're doing this to me. You and your hard body and blue eyes. Why can't you stop looking at me? Why can't you move away from the window? Leave me alone!

Even as she railed against Alex's still, watchful figure she didn't take her eyes off him. Feeling demented with unsatisfied longing she tore at her belt, forcing the knot to loosen. The belt maddened her. Like a snake it constricted her, made her feel closed in behind the sexless shield of towelling.

'Come on, come on,' she muttered under her breath, until at last she felt the two ends of the belt come free and the front of her robe fall apart.

She sighed deeply with relief and threw her head back for a moment to luxuriate in the sensation of cool night air touching her fevered skin. She felt alive and abandoned. Goosebumps sprang up all over her, even on the covered parts. The bared portion of her felt all the more naked for the exhibitionist way in which she displayed herself – reclining against the edge of the table, thighs slightly parted.

Glancing down, her eyes followed the slim rectangle of the flesh she had just bared. The valley between her breasts was visible, though her nipples were not. The smooth line of her stomach curved over the slight swell of her belly. Below this, the inverted triangle of her pubic mound was framed by the satin textured flesh of her inner thighs.

Feeling a flush of shame warm her cheeks Meredith raised her eyes to meet Alex's steady gaze. He stared at her across the water, his eyes holding hers for a moment before flicking down to follow the same path her gaze had just taken.

Meredith felt her cheeks flame all the more as Alex's eyes

lingered blatantly on the exposed pouch of sex flesh at the apex of her thighs. She could feel her vulva pouting at him shamelessly. Her clitoris pulsed cheekily as trickles of moisture ran down the taut, sensitive flesh of her perineum. Sheer willpower kept her rooted to the spot even though her natural instinct was to cover herself up and make a dash for cover. Was it willpower, she asked herself, or was it more like a sense of daring, of wanting to do something totally out of the ordinary?

'OK, you – Alex – make of this what you will,' she muttered hotly as her desirous fingers started to twitch.

She grasped the edge of her robe and pulled them right apart, completely baring herself to his gaze. Her stomach did a double back-flip as she did so. She sucked in her breath hard as the night air caressed her breasts with the cool touch she normally associated with a doctor's hands. Her nipples sprang to attention, the hard little buds cresting breasts that seemed to swell and yearn towards something unseen. She lifted her ribcage, the shoulders of her robe slipping down her upper arms as she arched her back. With her breath coming in short gasps she felt her arousal mount as she slid her hands down her torso. Hardly caring any longer, her fingers eagerly sought the moist warmth of her vulva.

Trying all the time to restrain herself, Meredith caressed the soft bush of hair covering her mound. It was neatly trimmed and beneath the silky hair the swollen lips of her outer labia were parted, encouraging her to slide a finger down the slit between them. She felt the wrinkled flesh of her inner labia and recoiled as her fingertips caught the shamelessly swollen bud of her clitoris. It stood proud of its little hood of flesh and, though she could hardly bear the delicious intensity of it, Meredith couldn't resist stroking the tiny pearl at its tip.

The strength of her arousal was shocking, holding Meredith in its tightening grip. For a few moments she was so self-absorbed that she forgot all about Alex. Only when she happened to glance up again, to stare out of the window through eyes heavy-lidded with lust, did she remember that she was not completely alone in the private domain of her own pleasure.

He was watching her still – of course. But now he was stroking the front of his trousers. Still caressing herself,

Meredith stared back at him. Feeling as though she were in a trance she slid a finger into herself and watched as he unzipped his fly. Deliberately slicking a thin film of her own juices over her inner sex flesh she gasped aloud as his cock sprang out. It was so ramrod straight it almost hit the glass. A smile flickered across her lips and she smiled coquettishly at him as he caught his erection and held it in both hands. Be careful, her expression conveyed to him, mind you don't damage the goods.

As she slid her finger in and out of herself, occasionally lubricating her slit, she rubbed her clitoris with the pad of her thumb. Her other hand roamed freely over her breasts, cupping and squeezing them alternately. Although her breasts were not that large she delighted in the sensation of all that flesh oozing between her fingers. All this could be yours, she thought with unashamed delight.

Meredith directed this thought at Alex and in the next moment she fancied she caught an answering flash of intense lust in his eyes. Of course, it had to be a trick of the light, she realised. There was no way she could see him that well, even though the distance that separated them was maybe only twenty metres at the most.

She started to moan aloud as she felt her orgasm building. Across the water, Alex's hands were rhythmically squeezing and pulling at the meaty length of his cock. Who is going to come first, him or me? She wondered. Deliberately, she slowed her finger movements until her middle finger simply rested, motionless, inside the wet channel of her vagina and her thumb was pressed against the pulsating bud of her clitoris.

Instead of stimulating herself she watched Alex intently, her gaze fixed to his hands and cock. She imagined she could feel his energy, the virility coursing through his veins. Building. Building.

'Come on,' Meredith breathed against the glass. 'Do it for me, Alex. Give it to me. All of it. Yes. That's it.'

Without realising it, her finger and thumb had started to move again. They probed and circled her sex flesh, driving an intense heat through her loins. In moments the heat flooded her pelvis at the exact same time a thin jet of semen arced from the tip of Alex's cock. The impressive sight surprised Meredith.

She felt herself shaking, rocking against the table, the vibration of her spasming body sending things crashing from the table to the floor. Scissors, a tape measure, an open tin of pins, all of them fell onto the bare boards, the pins scattering so volubly that Meredith was reminded of the silence otherwise contained within her abode.

As her fingers worked furiously, extracting every last ounce of pleasure from her throbbing sex, all Meredith could hear was the jagged hiss of her own breath and the sound of the empty tin rolling away across the floorboards.

Triumph! she thought as she slid her finger from her vagina and raised her gaze to meet Alex's. Simultaneous orgasm. As their eyes locked she deliberately pursed her lips and raised her honey coated finger. She sucked deeply, wrapping her tongue around her finger and relishing the sweet taste of her own juices.

Alex's expression was filled with wonder and longing. That much was obvious to her. There was no mistaking the message transmitted by his body language. He stood there, right in front of the glass with his cock still semi-erect and poking out from his fly.

In response, Meredith withdrew her finger and smiled. Then she turned her hand and waggled all her fingers at him. He waved back, slightly more tentatively than her, she thought. This was followed by a broad smile which spread across the face. The smile, coupled with the innocent appearance of his depleted cock made Meredith want to weep with longing. He was so, so beautiful. And the sensuous, orgasmic moment they had shared had been beautiful too, in its way.

Slowly, with regret but knowing it was the only thing to do, Meredith gathered her robe about her and covered her nakedness again. She smiled back at him. The moment felt pregnant with poignancy. Meredith wanted Alex. He wanted her. Was there a future for them, or would they eventually tire of their game playing and go their separate ways? Meredith didn't know the answer and suddenly felt too tired to care. There was plenty of time for them both, she thought as she backed away from the window, negotiating the table as she receded farther and farther into the depths of the spacious room.

For a moment she felt her feet skidding on the scattered pins.

She glanced down and when she looked up again he was gone. As simple as that. For once Meredith didn't bother about making sure everything was neat and tidy before she went to bed. That could wait until the morning, she decided. Right at that moment there was only room in her life for one thing – her dreams.

The tall brunette who entered Meredith's flat the next morning was as intimidating as she was beautiful. With her glossy hair coifed into a neat chignon and her reed thin body sporting a black and white check Chanel suit, Camilla Braxton-James was the epitome of chic.

She extended a slim hand with long fingers tipped with purple painted nails toward Meredith.

'Pleased to meet you, Meredith,' she said in a low, well modulated voice that carried far more weight than her body. Her eyes flicked around the room, taking it all in with an attitude that – to Meredith's relief – was interested rather than disdainful. 'I must say, I am looking forward to this,' she went on. 'I love lingerie and simply cannot wait to see what you have to offer me.'

Meredith felt herself shrinking as Camilla's keen-eyed gaze came to rest on her. There was something lurking behind the young woman's words that Meredith couldn't quite fathom. Whatever it was, it sent a thrill of excitement through her.

Of course she should feel excited, Meredith reasoned with herself as she gestured to Camilla to sit down on the red velvet chesterfield. Her new customer had the sort of money, social standing and contracts that could propel her to instant success. Yet, as she busied herself making a pot of coffee and arranging her best bone china cups and saucers on a tray, Meredith couldn't quite shake off the feeling that there was more to her sense of anticipation than the thought of making her mark in London.

'Here we are,' she said with false bravado as she marched in with the tray and set it down in front of Camilla. 'Do you prefer it black, or with cream?'

'Thank you, I'll take it black,' Camilla replied, leaning forward and pouring herself half a cup of steaming liquid.

Meredith wasn't in the least surprised that Camilla drank her coffee black. As she eyed the way Camilla crossed one long slim leg encased in sheer nylon over the other, Meredith felt sufficiently demoralised to pour too much cream into her own cup.

For a few minutes they sat and chatted about the glorious weather and Camilla's forthcoming wedding. 'You must come to the wedding,' Camilla said generously. 'Everyone will be there. You might make some useful contacts.'

Meredith felt a leap of gratitude and found herself stammering as she answered. 'Th–thank you, I'd love to.' Then she added, 'But you haven't seen my stuff yet. I mean–' She glanced up to realise that Camilla was watching her with a steady gaze.

Her eyes were as beautiful as the rest of her, Meredith noticed, almond shaped and slightly slanting above well-defined cheekbones and perfectly arched brows. Framing the hazel irises, which were delightfully flecked with gold and green, were long, curling black lashes.

In her confusion, Meredith put her cup and saucer down with a clatter. 'I'll go and get you some samples,' she said, jumping hastily to her feet. 'Then I'll take your measurements.'

All at once she realised she was not going to find it easy to treat Camilla's body with the dispassionate eye she usually reserved for personal clients. The thought of asking the other woman to undress, and to wrap her measuring tape around the exquisitely proportioned breasts and hips was as exciting as it was intimidating.

Apparently oblivious to Meredith's nervousness, Camilla smiled easily. Her plum coloured lips parted to reveal the ivory tips of small, perfectly aligned teeth. She reclined back and re-crossed her legs.

'Whatever you say, darling,' Camilla said. 'You are the expert. I shall bow to your wishes.' She made a slight inclination of her head, the amused smirk on her lips and the sparkle in her eyes telling Meredith – in no uncertain terms – that she would only ever concede to another person if it suited her.

Feeling thoroughly discomfited, Meredith beat a hasty retreat to her bedroom where she had arranged a small selection of items on hangers. Picking them all up in one go she brought them back to Camilla and laid them neatly over the back of a chair. Then she held up each set of lingerie individually for the other woman's inspection.

After appraising each one for a moment, Camilla nodded. Sometimes her brow furrowed a little, or she pursed her lips, making Meredith feel increasingly worried that her work was not up to scratch after all. She concluded her small display by holding up a slinky, full length nightgown in the finest black moire silk. It was cut on the bias so that it clung to the torso, then draped the hips and legs with the fluidity of oil.

Forgetting her nervousness for a moment, Meredith held the night gown against herself and for a moment felt herself transported into a fantasy. She was in a luxurious boudoir, clad only in the gown and reclining on a chaise longue as she waited for her handsome, dark-haired, blue-eyed lover to arrive.

She was startled out of her reverie by the sound of Camilla clapping her hands. 'Bravo!' Camilla enthused, much to Meredith's surprise. 'Your designs are wonderful. I love all of them.'

When Meredith looked at Camilla she noticed that the other woman was leaning forward eagerly. Gone was the cool, dispassionate expression, to be replaced by the bright sparkle of excitement. All at once Meredith's fears dissolved.

'These are only examples,' she said, 'I intend to make a few special, one-off designs for you as well.'

Camilla stood up and took the hanger from Meredith's hands. She held the gown against her own body, stroking the fine silk with a tenderness approaching adoration.

Or was it the image of herself draped in the gown that Camilla found so entrancing? Meredith wondered. If that was the case, she wouldn't be wrong to have such a narcissistic view of herself. Meredith could clearly imagine how sensuous and sophisticated the other woman would appear in luxurious lingerie.

'Let us have our own little fashion show,' Camilla suggested, surprising Meredith all over again. 'We cannot possibly appreciate your designs properly while they are still on hangers.' She picked up a set of camiknickers in pale rose satin and handed them to Meredith. 'Put this on,' she ordered crisply, 'I shall try this delightful gown.'

Taken totally by astonishment, Meredith wavered. Then she

remembered that the customer was always right.

'You can use my bedroom to change in,' Meredith said in a voice that was hardly more than a whisper.

'Thank you.' Camilla flashed her a smile and, clutching the black night gown in her arms, swept imperiously out of the room. At the doorway she paused and glanced back over her shoulder. 'This is so exciting, isn't it, darling?' She said. 'I can't wait to see the transformation.'

Camilla's departure left Meredith with no choice but to get changed in the living room. Glancing down at her jeans and tee-shirt – her usual working gear – she couldn't help reflecting on the other woman's use of the word 'transformation.' Though clean and smart, Meredith realised her outfit was hardly what one could describe as chic.

Glancing at the window, Meredith rued the fact that she still hadn't got around to getting some curtains or a blind. Are you there today, Alex? She wondered as she stripped hastily. She hadn't noticed him this morning. Though she had been a little preoccupied, she remembered. Then she laughed to herself. How ridiculous, in view of the display she had made of herself the night before, to worry about Alex catching a glimpse of her getting undressed now.

When she was ready, she perched nervously on the edge of one of the armchairs, waiting for Camilla to reappear. Without thinking she glanced toward the window and began to stroke a breast absently through the fine silk. The nipple stiffened and she jumped guiltily and snatched her hand away when Camilla suddenly walked back into the room.

Embarrassed though she was, Meredith couldn't help exclaiming, 'My goodness, you look lovely,' as the other woman glided serenely across the room toward her.

Just as it was meant to, the black moire clung to every curve and indentation of Camilla's slender body. Though it was cut to fit her, Meredith couldn't help noticing how the garment looked almost as though it were tailor-made to Camilla's dimensions. On second glance she realised that the hem was a couple of inches too short and that it was a little loose around the bust. But not to any great detriment. Meredith felt a glow of inner pride at the realisation that this was *her* work on display. It was the first time she had ever seen it on someone other than herself. All at once she envisaged a proper fashion show of her designs. With real models and a catwalk and flashbulbs popping everywhere.

'What do you think?' Camilla asked. She twirled around so that the hem of the gown billowed up around her knees. 'Isn't it just divine?'

Brought back to earth by Camilla's question, Meredith found herself envying the woman's amazingly slender calves. They were well toned but without the muscular definition of her own.

Meredith nodded. 'Absolutely,' she said, forcing a tremulous smile. Then she glanced down at her lap before looking back up at Camilla. 'I'm sorry. I think I just feel taken aback at seeing that design on someone else. And you look so lovely in it. Much better than me.' Her smile strengthened as she realised the foolishness of her reaction. Some sales woman you make, she admonished herself.

To her surprise Camilla threw her head back and laughed a real laugh – not the false trill that so many women in her position used.

'Darling, you are such a sweetie,' Camilla said. She reached up and made a swift adjustment to a couple of hairpins which had worked themselves loose of the chignon. 'You simply don't realise how gorgeous you are, do you?' She shook her head as though amazed by Meredith's naivete.

'I wouldn't go that far,' Meredith demurred, blushing. 'But thank you for the compliment anyway.'

Camilla shook her head again, this time making a tut-tutting sound. 'Come on silly bones,' she said. 'Stand up. I want to see how you look.'

Feeling incredibly conspicuous, even though there were only the two of them, Meredith got to her feet. Her legs felt shaky, she realised, as she followed the path that Camilla's finger sketched out imperiously in the air. By the time Camilla held up her hand to stop her, Meredith felt hot and light headed, her lungs constricted so much that she could hardly breathe.

Chapter Six

Meredith felt her legs trembling. She was so weak she had to put out a hand to steady herself against the back of the chair. The rapid clamouring of her heart meant she had to force herself to calm down a bit by breathing in deeply through her nose and letting the breath out slowly through her mouth.

There was no way she could dispute her reaction was one of arousal and sparked wholly by sensuality. She couldn't ignore how good the rose silk camiknickers felt against her skin; the luxurious fabric was cool whereas she felt feverish. Nor could she contain the frisson of desire that leaped up in her every time she glanced at Camilla and saw she way she looked in the black moire gown – as though she had just stepped from the pages of *Vogue*.

The one thing Meredith couldn't establish was whether Camilla felt the same erotic charge as her. The other woman looked as cool and composed as an alabaster statue, the expression in her eyes assessing as she appraised Meredith's body clad in the silk lingerie.

Without thinking, Meredith glanced down at herself. The camiknickers had thin shoestring straps, doubled on each shoulder and joined together just above the bust with tiny bows in matching satin. In the centre of each bow was a tiny seed pearl. The same pearls were echoed in the form of buttons which ran from cleavage to waist, fastening loops of rose satin. At the crotch, another three loops and pearls provided a useful opening.

'Turn around, darling,' Camilla said in a slightly husky voice. 'Let me see all of you.'

Meredith thought the other woman should have referred to the garment rather than herself and felt a fresh wave of dizziness overtake her. She was loathe to let go of the back of the chair but had no choice. Slowly, she turned. When she had her back to Camilla the other woman asked her to stand still. A moment later Meredith felt an unfamiliar pair of hands sweeping over the curve of her hips. Their touch was light yet commanding, letting Meredith know that their owner was experienced in appreciating the female form and perfectly in control of the situation.

'Lovely,' Camilla said, the single word a caress of warm breath between Meredith's shoulder blades.

Meredith shivered in response. She felt the hairs on the back of her neck prickle. Beneath the fragile silk camiknickers her nipples stiffened and she couldn't ignore the immediate rush of moisture that soaked into the insubstantial crotch. Oh, God, she moaned inwardly as she swayed and caught the back of the chair to steady herself again, this can't be happening.

As her pulse began to race she felt Camilla's hands slide over her bottom and then up again. They curved over her hips, into the indentation of her waist and then up and around her torso to stroke her breasts.

'Naughty, naughty,' Camilla admonished in an amused tone as her fingertips encountered Meredith's erect nipples. She teased them skilfully until Meredith let out a soft whimper of pleasure. 'That's it, darling,' Camilla crooned in Meredith's ear, her hands moulding her breasts over the silk, 'let yourself go a little. I hoped you would be like this. I can always recognise another sensual being when I see one.'

Meredith couldn't help noticing how pleased Camilla sounded with herself. Not only that but she was obviously delighted with the way Meredith's body was responding to her caresses. As Meredith squirmed and whimpered, Camilla's touch quickly became a little less exploratory and more assured. Taking the hard buds of Meredith's nipples between her fingers Camilla began to pinch and tug at them until they peaked proudly at the fragile silk.

'Beautiful,' Camilla said as she glanced over Meredith's shoulder and saw the effect of herself. 'What wonderful breasts you have, darling. So full and so gorgeous.'

Meredith felt herself growing weaker and weaker with lust

as Camilla smoothed her palms over her silk clad torso, investigating her body in a deliberately tantalising way. The hands slowly worked their way down to the lace trimmed hem of the camiknickers, then slid up under the loose silk to caress the tops of Meredith's thighs.

Feeling another rush of moisture soak into the silken crotch, Meredith let out a low groan. If Camilla were to investigate farther she would be sure to encounter the shaming proof of her arousal.

'So you like that do you, darling?' Camilla murmured. 'Tell me what else you like.'

Unable to speak, Meredith merely let out another whimper as Camilla's hands began to stroke her buttocks.

'Well,' Camilla went on, apparently unperturbed by Meredith's inability to communicate, 'if you won't tell me, I shall just have to find out for myself won't I?' She laughed lightly and teasingly.

Meredith wondered what Camilla would do next and blushed hotly when she felt the other woman's fingers prising her buttocks apart. A nail scratched tantalisingly at the sensitive puckered membrane surrounding her anus. Instinctively Meredith tried to clench her muscles but once again she found she was no match for Camilla's delicately enticing caresses.

'No, oh, God, please don't–' Meredith gasped, groping blindly for Camilla's wrists. She wrapped her fingers around the dainty wands of flesh and bone, completely encircling them, trying to prevent Camilla from exploring her nether regions any farther.

Marvelling at how fragile the other woman's wrists felt, Meredith tentatively exerted a little more pressure. Even so she was forced to concede defeat. It was obvious that the other woman's exquisite exterior masked a steely determination. There was no way another mere mortal could deter Camilla from her chosen quest. And today that quest is me, Meredith realised with a wild surge of anticipation.

As comprehension finally dawned, Meredith felt herself yield completely. Her body sagged, her flesh appearing to melt in Camilla's hands. She felt her juices flowing freely, her skin warming and becoming tingly with arousal.

Then all at once it occurred to her that where she stood she was in full view of the window, facing it. Her stomach flipped as her upward glance met a familiar uncompromising gaze. Her worst fears were realised. Alex was there, blatantly watching.

'No, oh, quick, please stop,' Meredith gabbled, grasping wildly at any part of Camilla she could reach.

'Relax, darling,' Camilla soothed. 'You don't need to feel embarrassed. No one need know. This can be our little secret.'

Meredith could hardly tear her gaze away from Alex's. Right at that moment she felt like dissolving into hysterics. No one need know, Camilla said, yet there was Alex to witness every caress. She wished desperately that she had more experience. If only she could handle this situation with casual aplomb instead of feeling as gauche as a teenager.

'My neighbour,' Meredith gasped, finally. 'He's watching us. Over there. Look.'

To her consternation, though Camilla did look out of the window, she merely laughed huskily.

'Well, well,' she said, sounding – if anything – more pleased than ever, 'an audience. What fun.' As she spoke her hands moved around Meredith's hips to stroke her pubis.

Meredith wriggled in the circle of Camilla's arms. The other woman's touch was as arousing as it was shaming and despite her panic Meredith felt her sex responding. After a moment she dared to glance back at Alex and found, to her increased mortification, that he had pulled up a chair and was sitting and watching them with such unequivocal boldness that Meredith felt a frisson of excitement. Right at that moment she felt as though she were no longer a person but a sex toy. A living thing made purely for the enjoyment of others – of Camilla and Alex. They were both taking pleasure in her body, though in different ways.

In an odd way this realisation made Meredith feel liberated. Wasn't it enough, she asked herself, to feel desired by others? Surely it was way past time she stopped worrying about how things looked or how they 'should be', and simply learned to enjoy herself. Latching on to the moment and seizing unexpected opportunities for pleasure such as this would be a step in the right direction.

'Isn't he naughty?' Camilla said, referring to Alex and breaking Meredith's train of thought so that she was dragged back to the stimulating present. 'Fancy him watching us as blatantly as that. Do you think we should call the police or something?'

The teasing note in Camilla's voice told Meredith that her question was merely rhetorical. In fact, Meredith realised, Camilla was probably getting just as much of a buzz out of the situation as she was.

'It's not the first time he's watched me,' Meredith admitted. Her voice was hardly more than a whisper. She felt a blush suffuse her cheeks as she added, 'I watched him too. The other evening, with a black girl. It's become a sort of game. A challenge.'

Camilla's fingers continued to rake through the light covering of blonde fuzz on Meredith's pubic mound.

'Really?' she said. 'How fascinating.' She slid her hands out of the camisole and placed them lightly on Meredith's shoulders, turning her around. 'I'm afraid we are going to have to disappoint him for now.'

Meredith could hardly think straight as her bewildered gaze concentrated on the movement of Camilla's plummy lips. They formed a slightly mocking smile, while above them the gold and green flecks in the other woman's irises glittered like jewels.

'Why?' Meredith asked simply, feeling slightly let down.

'Because, darling,' Camilla said, taking her by the hand and leading her to the sofa, 'I want you seated. Sit there on the sofa,' she encouraged as Meredith hesitated.

Feeling confused, Meredith groped behind her for the seat and lowered herself on to it gingerly. Just as she was about to cross her legs Camilla stopped her.

'No, not like that,' she said. 'I want you to spread your legs for me, darling. Go on, wider, wider–' She waved her hand as she spoke, waiting patiently but with a commanding air until Meredith had complied with her wishes.

When Meredith's legs were splayed wide apart Camilla moved the makeshift coffee table out of the way and dragged one of the armchairs around until it was placed in front of the sofa, about a foot away from where Meredith sat.

'OK, darling,' she said, sitting down and arranging the gown neatly before looking directly at Meredith. 'Now I want you to unfasten the buttons. No, not those buttons,' she added quickly when Meredith's hands automatically moved to the ones at the front of the camisole. 'The ones at your crotch.'

'Oh, no, I couldn't—' Meredith protested, feeling her cheeks flush with embarrassment for the umpteenth time that morning.

'Yes, you can,' Camilla said firmly. She leaned forward and looked archly at Meredith. 'Or would you rather I did it for you?'

Meredith shook her head quickly. 'No, that's all right. I'll do it.' She let out a breathy sigh of compliance, murmuring, 'I'll do it,' once again. There really was no point in arguing. Or in denying her true feelings. She was as excited as hell and wanted to follow Camilla's lead.

With trembling fingers she undid the buttons, sliding them carefully through the looped satin. When she had finished, the top flap of silk still covered her vulva.

'Pull it up, darling,' Camilla said, looking directly between Meredith's thighs. 'Tuck the crotch out of the way. I want to be able to see all of you.'

Meredith's instinct to disobey Camilla was chased away by a powerful wave of lust. Her excitement was so great as she fumbled with the silk that she felt the wetness increase between her legs to the same degree that her mouth dried. She swallowed deeply and licked her lips, trying to recreate some moisture there.

'Look at me,' Camilla said gently but firmly. 'Come on, darling, let me see the desire in your eyes.'

Feeling her cheeks burning with shame, Meredith raised her head and looked directly at Camilla. The other woman was gazing straight at her, her eyes transmitting a message of such powerful eroticism that Meredith could hardly breathe. Then, to her overwhelming embarrassment, Camilla lowered her gaze. She did it slowly and deliberately, her eyes fixing on the plump flesh that pouted at her indecently from between Meredith's thighs.

Camilla let out a long sigh of satisfaction. She nodded appreciatively, cocking her head slightly to one side, then the other, as though she were a connossieur considering a work of art.

'Perfect,' she said at long last, clapping her hands lightly together. 'Simply perfect.' A smile followed. Then it disappeared to be followed by a distinct darkening of her irises. 'Do you realise how wet you are, darling?'

'No, I – yes, I think so,' Meredith gasped out. She felt the velvet cushion under her hands and clutched at it as though she could draw strength from it somehow.

'Well,' Camilla went on, reclining back casually and crossing her legs, 'I think you should put on a little show for me, don't you think?'

'A show?' Meredith's mind whirled at the suggestion.

The smile returned to Camilla's lips. 'Yes, darling. I want you to touch yourself. Imagine you're all alone. You do touch yourself when you're alone, don't you?'

'Yes, of course.' Meredith almost felt affronted and sounded it. 'But that's private. I don't—'

Camilla leaned forward slightly, her gaze flicking up to Meredith's face. 'Surely you have masturbated in front of someone before. A lover—'

'Yes,' Meredith cut in, 'but that's different.'

'Different?' Camilla laughed. 'Why was that different, my darling – because your audience was male? Don't you think I will enjoy watching your fingers caressing that lovely pussy of yours? Or perhaps you think it inconceivable that a woman could enjoy the same things as a man.'

'Of course not,' Meredith responded, knowing that she had just managed to back herself into a corner.

'Then, what's stopping you?' Camilla waved a hand airily. The smile returned and with it a tone of voice that was almost hypnotic in its persuasive cadence. 'Come on, my lovely girl. Show me all your secret places. Allow me entry into that private pleasure palace of yours. Let me see you come.' To Meredith's surprise Camilla paused and stroked her hands lovingly over her own breasts. Beneath the thin fabric Meredith saw the nipples harden and peak at the black moire. 'Grant me this pleasure, darling,' Camilla went on. 'You don't realise quite how beautiful and desirable you are, do you?'

Dumbly, Meredith shook her head, though it wasn't quite true. Various men had told her much the same thing. She was used to being complimented on her looks. But her mind told her this wasn't the same. Not at all. To be seduced by another woman was so extraordinary that she wondered why she didn't feel repelled by it. *Because you want to be seduced by her*, she told herself. *You wanted it from the first moment Camilla started coming on to you. And you desire her too. Admit it. You want her. You're enjoying all this.*

'Very well,' Meredith said hoarsely, knowing when she was beaten.

She paused to clear her throat, as though she were about to deliver a speech but instead of saying anything else she unclenched her hands and moved them to the tops of her thighs. In that instant – as she stared right at Camilla and saw how the other woman's gaze immediately dropped to that lewd part of her she thought so beautiful – Meredith realised that before she could carry on she would have to close her eyes and pretend she was all alone.

While Meredith slowly began to pleasure herself, Alex glanced at his watch then reluctantly got up from his chair. He had a twelve thirty appointment with Lisa Blair. They were due to meet at Alberta's office and he knew neither woman would tolerate him being so much as five seconds late.

His was almost a physical pain as he thought about leaving his flat, or rather his chair by the window. The sight of Juliet being caressed by another woman had been a welcome surprise. After the night before he thought his new neighbour would have gone into hiding for a while. After all, her most recent erotic exhibition had been unexpected and uninhibited enough. Surely, he thought, in the cold light of day, she would be feeling a little embarrassed.

Not a bit of it. Obviously.

Walking down the tow path, Alex couldn't resist glancing back up at her window time and again. He had been disappointed that today's show – which had got off to such a promising start – should have been cut short just when he was beginning to feel seriously aroused.

He laughed to himself then. Who was he kidding? He'd felt aroused the instant he saw her in the other woman's arms, his desire gathering momentum as he watched the woman's hands caressing Juliet's lovely body under the alluring silk thing she had been wearing. And perhaps it was just as well they hadn't carried on right in front of him. If they had he would have had a very difficult decision to make. Whether to stay put and risk putting his job on the line, or go and regret it forever after.

He glanced back at the window on the third floor and executed a mock salute. Thanks ladies, he thought, for not putting me on the spot like that. Then he laughed aloud. What a terrible life he had, he mocked himself, when the only decisions he had to make were largely trivial. Money or pleasure. Those were his choices. And, very often, the two came together – in the form of Regina and countless others like her. Not a bad life, Alex old son, he said to himself as he glanced back for one last time before he turned the corner. Not a bad life at all.

Meredith's breath was coming in short, sharp gasps as she stroked the sensitive bud of her clitoris. It was pulsating madly and whenever she trailed her fingertips down her slit to circle the sensitive outer rim of her vagina she could feel how awash she was with her own juices.

She had got used to the idea of Camilla watching her. Well, just about, at any rate. It had been difficult to block out her presence at first but as Meredith spread her outer lips apart and began caressing herself with reassuring familiarity, so she was able to lose herself in that other world of pure sensation.

Gradually, as she felt herself drawn down deep into the realm of her sensual desires, Meredith was able to let Camilla back into the picture. Firstly, by allowing her eyelids to flicker open for moments at a time. Then by accepting the stimulating knowledge that just a short distance away sat a woman who was getting as much enjoyment out of her self-pleasuring as she was.

If nothing else, Camilla's occasional murmurs of encouragement could hardly fail to remind Meredith that she was not alone in her erotic pursuits.

'Come on, baby girl. Yes, that's it. Lovely. Do it for me. Yes, darling, get that lovely pussy nice and hot.'

Meredith shivered with arousal every time Camilla spoke, yet her caresses never wavered. She was too far gone now. Too lost in her quest for pleasure to allow anything – or anyone – to put her off. A moment later she heard a gentle rustling sound and when she opened her eyes again, it was to see Camilla kneeling in front of her. The gown was spread out around her like a pool of black ink and Camilla's expression was rapt as her gaze lingered on the bloom of flesh between Meredith's open thighs.

'Don't stop,' Camilla urged in a breathy voice. 'I won't touch you. I just wanted to watch you in close up.'

'What are you thinking?' Meredith asked, surprising herself with her question. For a moment her fingers stopped moving. Then she went back to stroking the delicate petals of her inner labia.

Camilla glanced up at her face for a brief moment. 'I'm thinking how lovely you are. How shamelessly, wantonly beautiful. I can't help wanting to taste you. To run my tongue over that dewy flesh and delve right into your little honey pot.'

A shiver of elation ran through Meredith. Never before had she wanted to feel the touch of another's mouth upon her most secret flesh so badly. And yet if she succumbed to temptation, she asked herself, where would it all lead? Would she be able to return the compliment? Could she really imagine herself caressing another woman intimately? Even though she desired the other woman, she couldn't help wondering if she would actually enjoy stroking and licking the soft folds of Camilla's vulva. It was all so strange and alien to her that she felt afraid.

'I'm scared to let you,' Meredith admitted, once again surprising herself. 'I've never done this sort of thing before.'

Camilla looked back up at her face and smiled. 'I understand,' she said.

Meredith reacted to the smile with a rush of tenderness and desire. Gone was the Camilla who had entered her flat earlier that morning. It was as though all the hard edges of the other woman had been blurred by an eraser. Instead of appearing hard and brittle she was now so soft and achingly feminine that

Meredith felt her heart fill up with something akin to adoration. This was a woman who had many things to offer her, she realised. With Camilla's help she could unlock another door to her psyche and explore her innermost desires.

'Help me,' Meredith pleaded. 'I don't know what to do.'

Slowly, Camilla reached out and stroked her hands along Meredith's inner thighs.

'You don't have to do anything at all,' she said soothingly. 'Let me guide you. All you need to do is trust me.'

'I do,' Meredith gasped, feeling a hot rush of wanton lust surge through her as the other woman's fingertips brushed the pouting lips of her outer labia. Her own fingers fluttered out of the way as Camilla moved forward and pressed her mouth upon the fleshy mound of her pubis. 'Oh, God, yes—'

Alex arrived at Alberta's office with a few minutes to spare. He winked broadly at Suzie, Alberta's receptionist, as he entered, then he glanced back at her with an enquiring expression when he noticed there was someone else waiting in the outer office.

'An actor,' Suzie mouthed back at him. Then she raised her eyebrows and added aloud, 'Alberta's running a bit late I'm afraid.'

'Typical,' Alex said with a smile as he sat down on one of the squashy chairs and picked up the latest copy of *Variety*. 'And there was me panicking about being late. Has Lisa Blair arrived yet by the way?'

Suzie nodded. 'Yes, she's in conference with Alberta now.'

At this piece of information Alex made to stand up again. 'Should I go straight in?'

'No, not yet,' Suzie said, 'Alberta asked me to tell you to wait until she buzzes for you.'

Alex reclined back in the chair and pretended to study the magazine while really appraising the other figure in the room. Obviously male, he was tall and rangy with collar length fair hair. He was standing looking out of the window so Alex couldn't see his face. Nevertheless, he couldn't shake off the feeling that he recognised the other guy from somewhere.

In the end Alex's curiosity got the better of him. He got up and wandered over to the window. 'Hello, have we met before?' he asked.

The other guy turned and smiled and in that instant Alex realised he was mistaken. There was nothing recognisable about the rugged face in which a pair of brilliant green eyes glinted with unselfconscious friendliness.

'I don't think so,' the guy said, extending a hand which Alex shook briefly, 'but don't be embarrassed about it. People often think they know me because they recognise me from a play or film. My name is Fergal by the way.'

'Alex,' Alex said, returning Fergal's easy going smile. 'That's probably it then. Are you very well known?'

Fergal laughed. 'No, not really. I've never done anything more challenging than walk on parts but Alberta has high hopes for me.'

'Yes, Alberta can be very encouraging,' Alex said wryly, 'when you're in her good books that is. Otherwise she can be a real tyrant.'

'Taking my name in vain again, Alex?'

Alex jumped at the unexpected sound of Alberta's voice. He hadn't realised she was standing in the doorway. When he turned he had the grace to look abashed. Much to his surprise Alberta laughed. It wasn't a sound he was used to hearing and he smiled warily, like an animal coming face to face with one of its natural predators.

'I didn't want your latest protégé to be under any illusions about you,' he said lightly, while his insides quaked. Though she was his agent, Alex could never shake off the feeling that he worked for Alberta rather than the other way round.

'Well, there's certainly no danger of that with you around, is there, Alex?' Alberta's smile didn't quite touch her eyes. They held Alex in their steely grip for a moment, then Alberta appeared to relent. 'Oh, come on you,' she added, glancing back over her shoulder in the direction of her office, 'Lisa Blair wants to discuss a few things.' She flashed a quick, though genuine smile at Suzie. 'Would you mind bringing some coffee through?'

'No problem, boss,' Suzie said with her usual irreverence. 'Just as soon as I've finished typing up these contract amendments.'

With a shrug of acceptance, Alberta turned and led Alex through to her office where Lisa Blair sat waiting for them. She stood up when they entered and shook Alex's hand as if they had only just met.

'Nice to see you again, Alex,' she said with a warm smile. 'I just wanted to bring you up to spec on my latest ideas for the video.'

Alex groaned inwardly. No more changes. He couldn't hack all the hassle and was beginning to wonder if working with the famous Lisa Blair was worth the effort. A moment later, as he watched her lower her perfectly shaped bottom on to the seat of her chair and cross her equally perfect legs – bare and very much on view below a short white skirt – he wondered who he was trying to kid.

He glanced at her speculatively as she smoothed the pelmet of her skirt over the tops of her thighs and briefly fantasised about ravishing her across Alberta's desk.

'Alex, are you with us?' Alberta's voice surprised him for the second time that day and jolted him back to unwelcome reality. 'We have a lot to get through and I hardly have to remind you that time is money,' the other woman added, glancing pointedly at her wristwatch.

'Sorry, I was miles away,' Alex responded, taking the chair next to Lisa. He gave both women what he hoped was a disarming smile. 'Of course, Alberta, please carry on.'

When Alex finally left Alberta's office an hour later he was surprised to find Fergal still waiting in reception. He had his head buried in the copy of Variety that Alex had discarded but glanced up as Alex walked past him.

'Hold on, old chap,' Fergal said.

Alex glanced down at him. 'Yes?' Then he added, with a touch of surprise, 'Have you been waiting for me?'

Fergal lowered his voice to a conspiratorial whisper. 'I can't deny it. I want the lowdown on Alberta and realise that you're just the fellow to oblige. Mind if I waylay you for a while. We could go for a drink.'

Alex smiled. Though he had met a lot of actors in his time, for some reason he couldn't fathom, he felt drawn to this one in particular. Perhaps it was his strange, theatrical way of speaking.

Or maybe he realised it didn't hurt to have an ally in the ongoing battle which was his relationship with Alberta. On the other hand it could be that he simply craved a bit of male company. He didn't have any friends of his own sex. Invariably, the only men who showed an interest in getting to know him turned out to be gay. By now he had come to accept that it was the price he had to pay for being a dancer – no doubt his graceful mannerisms and physique sent out the wrong messages.

'OK, why not?' he responded with a casual shrug. 'I must admit, I could do with one. Where shall we go?'

'I know just the place,' Fergal said, unravelling himself to his full height as he eased himself out of the squashy sofa. 'Full of fabulous chicks. I met a real stunner there not so long ago. I'll tell you all about it if you twist my arm.' He grinned engagingly and Alex felt himself warming to the other guy even more. There was no doubt this Fergal character was totally hetero and if there was anything that got Alex's juices flowing it was the prospect of some salacious gossip.

'You've just sold me,' Alex said. 'Let's go.'

Just as he reached the door he glanced back and winked at Suzie and it was only then – when the young woman licked her glossy red lips in response – that Alex remembered the scene he has witnessed that morning from his window.

Buoyed up by the recollection, he rushed after Fergal who was already striding away up the street. 'By the way,' he said, when he managed to catch up with his new companion, 'if you like scandal, I've got a real prick-stirrer of a story to tell you—'

Chapter Seven

Meredith couldn't remember the last time she had felt so thoroughly aroused. So far Camilla had played her like a violin, her skilful hands drawing the beauty from her sinuous body, producing the most exquisite notes of ecstasy. And now she lay on her stomach on the sofa, her spine tingling to the sensation of Camilla's fingertips as they delicately stroked the length of it – from the nape of her neck to the uppermost swell of her buttocks.

'Such sweet little dimples,' Camilla murmured, her finger straying to lightly encircle the twin indentations either side of the base of Meredith's spine. 'I can't resist them.'

Meredith shivered with pleasure as Camilla pressed her mouth to the tiny dips, first one then the other. The pointed tip of her tongue followed the paths her fingertips had just made causing Meredith to whimper softly. She wondered fleetingly how long she and Camilla had been making love to each other now. Was it an hour? A day . . . ? Though through the window she could see that the sun still hovered as brightly as ever in the clear blue sky, it seemed to Meredith as though she and Camilla had already spent a lifetime together. There had been so much to learn. So much to discover.

There still was, she realised with a fresh thrill of pleasure as Camilla's fingers trailed between her buttocks to the wet place between her thighs. Languidly she rolled over, trapping Camilla's hand between her legs. She smiled gently, her eyes exhibiting the way her body felt. Relaxed. Replete.

'My turn,' she ventured boldly after a few exquisite moments had passed.

Lazily Meredith let her thighs fall apart, allowing Camilla to remove her hand. Then she turned over and grasped the same hand. She took it all the way to her mouth where she licked greedily at the honey coated fingers and across the soft, pink-skinned palm where skeins of her own juices glistened.

Camilla returned her smile, her eyes meeting Meredith's in a profound gaze of complicity. After a moment their expressions changed. Unlike Meredith's insolent expression as she licked her lips the look in Camilla's eyes was alert, expectant. Until this moment Camilla had called all the shots and yet she seemed prepared, if not eager, to hand total control over to Meredith.

'Lie here,' Meredith murmured huskily as she moved to make room for Camilla on the sofa. 'I want to repay the compliment.'

Camilla gave a gracious nod of her head. 'As you wish,' she said, with just the merest ghost of amusement touching her lust-laden eyes.

Meredith cursed her inelegance as she scrambled to her knees and watched Camilla recline languidly in the space she had just vacated. She envied the other woman's poise as she watched her arrange herself, not deliberately but with accomplished beauty – one leg bent, revealing the soft pouch of her sex, slender arms flung carelessly over her head.

A moment later, as if dissatisfied with the image she presented, Camilla moved her arms. Instead of being flung back one arm crossed her smooth forehead and simply rested there, palm upwards, fingers slightly curled but relaxed. The other arm snaked under the back of her head to cushion it. The expression in her eyes also changed. Now they were dark pebbles. Watchful. Expectant. Desirous.

Feeling a flicker of nervousness, Meredith bit her bottom lip. Her gaze raked Camilla's supine body, noting with pleasure the narrow ribcage with its small, perfectly rounded breasts. The nipples were gorgeously prominent. Hard red buds surrounded by generous circles of puckered, darkly pigmented areolae. Her gaze travelled down, following the slim yet sinuous lines of the other woman's body. Envy mingled with desire as her eyes came to rest momentarily on Camilla's concave belly which was suspended between jutting hip bones.

Feeling as though her fingertips were crossing a precarious rope bridge, Meredith reached out and tentatively traced a path from one hipbone to the other. The skin was smooth and cool to the touch. It was unblemished yet, almost to Meredith's relief, she realised she could just make out the faintest line of dusky hairs. They arrowed down from the base of Camilla's navel to the neat triangle of much darker hair which graced her pubic mound and shadowed the secret place between her legs.

Meredith felt transfixed by the sight of Camilla's sex displayed in such a blasé manner. Her heart hammered behind her ribs as she felt the onrush of pure lust. Even so she felt unaccountably afraid to touch the other woman intimately too soon. Instead, Meredith allowed her hands to travel the length of Camilla's outstretched leg.

Wonderingly, her fingers followed the curves of the slender, nicely toned thigh and calf. As she reached the trim ankle Camilla flexed her foot, then pointed her toes as though to display the fine arch of her foot in its best light. Meredith was suitably impressed. There was not one single thing about Camilla that wasn't perfect. Her foot was no exception. It seemed so narrow and delicate. The perfect finishing touch to a body that appeared to be sculpted by the finest artist.

Drawing in her breath Meredith began the upward journey with her hands. As her palms and fingers travelled over terrain that was becoming ever more familiar she couldn't help marvelling at the silky texture of Camilla's skin and the much softer flesh of her inner thigh.

At the top she paused.

'Yes. Oh, yes please,' Camilla sighed. She flexed her thighs, parting them more and raising her hips just a fraction.

Meredith recognised the silent plea and hesitated no longer.

As the backs of her fingers brushed the hair which covered the wine red pouch of Camilla's vulva, Meredith was surprised by its springy texture. Camilla's pubic hair looked as soft and silky as her skin and yet was quite prickly to the touch. Tentatively Meredith spread open the plump outer lips to reveal the blushing folds of her inner labia. As delicately as though she were peeling away layers of tissue paper on a much wanted gift, Meredith gradually revealed the core of Camilla's desire. And there it was, she mused with a frisson of excitement as she drank in the sight of the other woman's clitoris, pink and slightly swollen, its pearly tip hidden under its protective cowl of skin.

Knowing just how she liked her own clitoris to be touched Meredith brushed the soft pad of her thumb across the taut bud. An answering sigh of pleasure from Camilla encouraged her to repeat her action. Then she dipped her head and gently touched the coy little swelling with the tip of her tongue. Camilla began to churn her hips in time with the rotations of Meredith's tongue and after a few moments Meredith raised her head again and replaced her tongue with her fingertips so that she could watch the changing expressions on Camilla's face.

The other woman's head was flung back, her face contorted in serious concentration of her own pleasure. The taut muscles in her belly rippled as Meredith continued to circle her clitoris with her fingers. Just below the hard nub of roseate flesh a mouth gaped, begging attention. Meredith smiled to herself as she wiggled the fingers of her other hand. This was the moment for internal exploration.

She eased her middle and index fingers in, taking care not to scrape the delicate flesh with her fingernail. A tiny thrill ran through her. The sensation of her fingers inside the pulpy softness of a vagina was not a new one – she had explored herself often enough. Yet this was so so different. For one thing she had no direct knowledge of the feelings suffusing the body that squirmed with pleasure at her touch, though she could easily guess at them. And for another, she was able to experience the incredibly arousing sight of her fingers buried deep inside another woman's body.

All at once, as her ears picked up the thrilling sound of Camilla's ecstatic moans and whimpers and she felt the hot, wet body grinding away in mindless abandon, she became suffused by a strange and totally compelling notion. That she was no longer Camilla's servant – a simple seamstress bowing to her client's wishes – but a puppet master, or should that be mistress? She smiled inwardly then and increased the rhythm of her caresses. A moment later she was rewarded as Camilla's internal muscles spasmed around her fingers. Glancing up she noticed how the smooth belly tightened and bowed outwards as the muscles tensed. A scream of pleasure graced her ears and after a minute or so the other woman relaxed and instantly became limp.

Meredith's confidence soared and her inner smile broadened. If Camilla though that was the end of it then she, Meredith Baxter, had other ideas. Now the one in control, she wouldn't withhold her caresses until the other woman climaxed at least one more time.

Alex hadn't intended to ask Fergal back to his flat for coffee. He had a million and one things to get on with, not least yet another unwelcome revision of his carefully choreographed plan for Lisa Blair's video. This was her instruction. The one she had given him in her usual forthright and succinct manner a couple of hours earlier at Alberta's office.

His aim had been to have a quick sandwich and one, maybe two, drinks with the charismatic actor and then regretfully make his excuses. But he hadn't reckoned on Fergal's lively personality, his ready store of amusing and often titillating anecdotes, nor his remarkable ability to persuade Alex into accepting 'one more for the road...'

Consequently, when the barman was forced to practically expel them physically on to the street, Alex had forgotten all about his original plans. His head swam when the fresh air hit it and he felt himself tottering slightly as he raised his arm to shield his eyes from the over bright sun.

'I feel like a vampire,' he joked as he squinted at Fergal.

The other man grinned in response. 'I know what you mean, old mate. This sun's a killer, isn't it? All I want to do is scurry into a darkened room and simply flop.'

Fergal's wishes echoed Alex's exactly. He nodded. 'Me too,' he said. 'Fancy a coffee. My place isn't too far from here.' He couldn't help noticing that his companion flashed him a suspicious glance.

'Here, you're not gay are you?' Fergal asked bluntly. 'I daresay being a dancer and everything... But I think it's only fair to tell you right now that I only get hard when I see something in a skirt. And I don't mean a transvestite either,' he added quickly.

Alex's whisky-softened expression broadened into a grin. His blue eyes sparkled. 'Rest easy, my man,' he reassured Fergal. Even so sheer devilment encouraged him to place a hand on the other man's shoulder and give it a squeeze. 'Just teasing,' he said when Fergal flinched from his touch. 'Not all dancers are gay. I'm certainly not, though I don't mind mixing socially with them.' He chuckled. 'In my line of work I can hardly avoid it.'

'No. Nor me.' Fergal squared his shoulders as though trying to look as macho as possible. 'But I don't think the sight of some other guy's cock could ever have the same effect on me as a juicy pussy.' He licked his lips and rolled his eyes expressively, making Alex laugh aloud. 'Come on then, show me this place of yours,' he added. 'But you'll have to forgive me if I end up nodding off. I seem to have fallen into the habit of enjoying a little siesta these days.'

Chance would be a fine thing, Alex mused as he steered Fergal in the direction of the wharf. He seemed to have so much on his plate at the moment and it showed no signs of letting up. Alberta had hinted that straight after the video she had another project lined up for him.

For a moment he felt sorry for himself. He was a hedonist at heart and yet barely seemed to have five minutes to himself. What he longed for was the time to completely relax and unwind, preferably in the company of a beautiful woman. Just for a little while – as he and Fergal strolled along the city streets – Alex allowed himself to indulge in a fantasy which primarily involved making slow delicious love to someone who truly appreciated his desire to pamper and indulge. And his partner mustn't be averse to moments of downright dirty sex, Alex reminded himself, feeling an answering tightness in his groin. His ideal woman was both a goddess and a whore – an angel with a 'fuck me' expression ever present in her eyes.

'Would you believe it, I know this place?' Fergal exclaimed, breaking through Alex's thoughts.

They had turned the corner and were just about to walk down the tow path that edged Alex's building. Having walked there on automatic pilot, Alex glanced around in surprise.

'Do you?' he said. 'Not many people know about this place unless they actually live here. I always think of it as one of London's best kept secrets.'

'That girl I was telling you about.' Fergal said cocking his head in the direction of the opposite building. 'The blonde I picked up in Smollensky's . She lives over there.'

Alex felt a quickening sensation inside. All at once he realised his heart was beating rapidly and his mouth had gone completely dry.

'Oh, yes,' he offered casually and swallowing hard, 'which floor?'

Fergal gave him a quizzical look. 'Third, if I remember rightly,' he replied. 'But then again I wasn't really concentrating on my surroundings at the time.' He looked across the canal and let his glance travel up the building. 'Yes, it must have been the third floor,' he said. 'I remember there weren't any more stairs.' He pointed to the top windows overlooking the canal. 'That must be her flat, up there, because I remember she had these big windows that looked across to the other building. And she didn't have any curtains. Still doesn't by the looks of it.'

'What did you say her name was?' Alex asked, still trying desperately to sound nonchalant.

Inside his mind was whirling with the realisation that the old adage 'It's a small world,' held true. It seemed inconceivable that his newfound friend and the owner of the broad back and taut buttocks that had so irritated him by obscuring the object of his voyeuristic interest all those nights ago, were one and the same. The knowledge filled him with an overwhelming mixture of envy and outrage. Right at the moment he would have loved nothing better than to push Fergal into the sparkling waters of the canal. Perhaps the shock would wipe that cocky look of the bastard's face, he thought angrily.

It irritated him even more that his companion-turned-adversary seemed to be struggling to remember Juliet's name.

'Meredith,' Fergal said at last, shattering the last of Alex's illusions about his mystery woman. 'Don't recall if I even asked her her surname though. If I did I can't remember it.'

Yet it will be etched in my memory for all eternity, Alex thought. Inside his head a cauldron of passion and furious jealousy simmered. He wasn't used to feeling this strongly about a woman and it shook him greatly. It wasn't as though they had even met for Christ's sake, he reminded himself. She was nothing to him and he nothing to her.

In a burst of self-reproach for his murderous feelings toward Fergal, Alex held the front door open wide for the other man to pass through. He even managed to force a smile.

'We'll have to make this coffee a quick one,' he said, trying to sound regretful as he led the way up the stairs. 'Thanks to today's meeting with Lisa Blair I've got a whole new set of steps to work out.'

Fergal shrugged. 'Oh, don't you worry about me,' he said, clearly oblivious to Alex's attempt at a brush-off. 'I'll most probably fall asleep. You do what you have to do, old mate.'

It seemed ages later before Alex was allowed to get on with his planned schedule. Despite his insistence that he would most likely nod off before his coffee had even reached drinking temperature, Fergal had stayed resolutely awake. To make matters worse, now he realised that Meredith's flat was directly opposite, he seemed determined to resurrect the story that he had already recounted to Alex in the pub and add a few more embellishments.

'She was gorgeous,' he said. 'A real stunner. Great tits. Fabulous legs. And her bum was—'

'Yes, I know, you told me,' Alex interrupted. He glanced pointedly at his watch. 'I really must get on.'

Again, much to Alex's annoyance, Fergal had simply shrugged and waved his hand dismissively.

In the end Alex had forced himself to get up and go into his bedroom to change into practice clothes before going over to the barre and starting on some warm-up exercises. In the end, much to his relief, Fergal seemed to get the message and eventually stretched out on the sofa. A moment later he was snoring, rather loudly and irritatingly.

It took Alex a while to realise that his heart really wasn't in his work today. It was only when a flurry of activity in the flat opposite caught his eye that he paused, ankle poised on the barre, his leg perfectly straight at right angles to his body. He turned and as he did so his eyes widened. Juliet – no Meredith, he corrected himself hastily – was standing right in front of her window. Though it was late afternoon she was displayed in all her naked glory. And, as Alex's eyes eagerly drank in the sinuous curves of her breasts and bottom, it took him a moment to realise that another figure hovered in the shadowy recesses of the room.

When the figure revealed itself to be that of another woman – this time tall, boyishly slim and as dark as Meredith was fair – he felt an indescribable excitement well up inside him. She too was completely naked and by the way the two women moved together and held each other, it was clear that they were lovers.

'Oh, my God!' Alex's hoarse exclamation was immediately drowned by another loud snore from the sleeping Fergal.

He glanced at the inert form of his companion and thanked his lucky stars that the other man wasn't awake. An oaf like him didn't deserve to witness what he was seeing. Feeling as though it was crucial not to make a sound, Alex slipped his leg from the barre and made his way silently across the room to the window. There he slipped into his favourite chair. This time though he didn't relax into it as he normally did but remained upright, alert to the scene taking place across the canal.

The brunette moved to stand behind Meredith, her hands immediately seeking the lush globes of Meredith's breasts. With an ache in his chest as well as his groin, Alex watched those slender hands gently caressing the taut flesh, the fingertips – with their scarlet talons – tweaking and pulling at the hard little nipples. Meredith threw her head back against the other woman's shoulder, her mouth opening and closing in – what was to him at least – wordless ecstasy.

He marvelled at the sight of their naked bodies pressed so close together. The brunette's skin was so pale in comparison with Meredith's, her figure much more slender than Meredith's womanly curves yet none the less lovely to look at. Glancing warily over his shoulder, Alex was relieved to note that – if anything – Fergal seemed to have slipped into a much deeper sleep. He had turned over onto his side and now had his face pressed into the back of the couch.

With a low growl of anticipation Alex relaxed more into his chair and moved his hand to his crotch. He couldn't, and wouldn't, deny himself this opportunity to enjoy the spectacular scene taking place in front of his eyes.

* * *

Something, a sound from outside or perhaps just her sixth sense, made Camilla turn her head towards the window. She was startled momentarily to see the young man seated at the window of the apartment directly opposite. Even as her surprise registered on her brain she couldn't help taking in his swarthy good looks and insolently appraising expression on his finely chiselled face.

She was astonished to find the warmth of a blush stealing over her and turned quickly back to glance down at Meredith, or rather the delicious sight of her breasts cupped in her palms.

'Don't look now but he's back again – your voyeur,' Camilla whispered, as though she imagined they could be heard as well as seen.

Naturally, Meredith glanced toward the window. 'So he is,' she said, as if it were the most normal thing in the world to be watched by a neighbour as she made love to another woman. The knowledge that Alex was watching them sent a thrill of arousal through her. She turned in Camilla's arms and smiled up at the older woman. 'Should we give him a bit of a show? Or would you rather we continued in my bedroom? There's a blind.'

Pausing, Camilla glanced back across the canal. A smile curved her lips. 'Far be it from me to be coy,' she said. 'Certainly not at this stage in my life.' Deliberately she took Meredith's face between her hands and brushed the younger woman's lips with her own. 'A short but erotic display would be the perfect end to a perfect day, I think,' she added. Then she sighed. 'I hate to say this but I must go shortly, darling. Though I anticipate that our arrangement will require another fitting or two before my wedding.' Her words ended on an inquiring note.

Meredith nodded. She returned Camilla's smile and felt an incredible churning sensation inside her. 'Absolutely,' she said, before venturing boldly. 'And perhaps after you return from your honeymoon you'll need other things – more items of lingerie especially designed for you? I could do so much if I only had the time–' Her voice tailed off. It was an open invitation and one, she was pleased to note, Camilla took up with alacrity.

'Of course, darling,' the older woman agreed. 'I've always found that once one acquires a taste for the finer things in life, one simply can't get enough.'

Time passed in a blur for Alex. He lost count of the number of times he climaxed and hardly noticed the clammy sensation of his semen-soaked sweat pants sticking to him. As usual he wore no underpants and, though he only dared caress himself over the top of his trousers, the sight of the two women kissing and pleasuring each other was enough to make him come without touching himself at all.

He felt a keen sense of loss when he watched them eventually break apart and disappear into the deeper recesses of the apartment opposite. Half an hour later he saw the tall brunette, now fully dressed but every bit as beautiful clothed as she was naked, leave the building. Surprisingly, Meredith was with her, though they parted company at the top of the tow path. A moment later Fergal woke up prompting Alex to grin to himself. The man's timing was impeccable.

Buoyed by renewed bonhomie brought about by the notion of having enjoyed more of Meredith than Fergal was ever likely to, Alex invited him to stay to supper.

'I can't, old mate,' Fergal responded to the offer with a regretful shake of his head. If he thought it odd that Alex didn't get up from his chair he didn't show it. 'I promised to meet a couple of guys for a drink. One is a director and the other, apparently, has a shit-hot script that I'm just right for.' He grinned engagingly. 'Fingers crossed, eh?'

'Yes,' Alex said, grinning back. 'Some other time perhaps.' Just as Fergal was about to leave Alex remembered something he had meant to ask his new friend. Still wary of getting up and revealing his soiled trousers, Alex turned in his chair.

'By the way, Fergal,' he called out, 'any chance of Meredith's phone number?' He said it so casually he marvelled at his own acting abilities.

His elation was short-lived.

'Sorry, old mate,' Fergal replied, 'I didn't bother to get it off her. I daresay her number's in the book though.'

'Yes,' Alex said. 'Don't worry about it. It was just a thought.'

'Good luck,' Fergal said as he opened the door. 'I've got to go.'

Only after the door closed behind Fergal and Alex glanced back to Meredith's empty flat did he feel a sense of despondency. Despite the coincidence of bumping into Fergal, learning Meredith's Christian name and having it confirmed that she was a fabulous fuck, he was still no further forward.

The last thing he expected therefore, as he hurriedly changed and dashed downstairs hoping to get to the corner shop before it closed, was a face-to-face encounter with his fantasy woman.

Chapter Eight

The enticing scent of fish and chips wafted towards Meredith on the warm current of air as she strolled happily along the bustling street. She glanced about her as she walked, enjoying the window displays in the shops, the greengrocery displays spilling out onto the pavement and the free and easy atmosphere.

Office girls on their way home from work walked jauntily, their jackets slung over one arm and hips swinging under short skirts. Meredith couldn't help noticing how pale their skin seemed in comparison to her own – though she had spent precious little time outdoors lately – and how eagerly they turned their pretty faces up to the sun. Some, those who had obviously managed to slip out to a park or some similar open space at lunchtime, displayed a touch of nasty looking sunburn on their shoulders and throats.

It wasn't the first time Meredith had experienced the sharp and uplifting contrast between the pattern of her own working day and that of her peers. She appreciated how lucky she was to be her own boss. Not for her the nine to five slog, or the hour each way commuter run. She could choose when to work and when to play. And today, she mused, thinking about the wondrous hours she had spent with Camilla, she had chosen to play.

A smile touched her lips as she hugged her secret to her. All right, she reminded herself, so she and Camilla weren't the only ones who shared their secret. There had been Alex, of course, watching them from his window across the canal. A thrill ran through Meredith as she recalled the expression on his face and the blatant way she and Camilla had caressed each other while he watched. Rather than make the two women feel self conscious, his voyeurism had merely served to increase their passion for each other.

The recollection immediately prompted a question which Meredith had frequently asked herself of late: was there something wrong with her? Was it right, she wondered, to actively enjoy flaunting herself and behaving in such a sexually provocative way?

The answer, as always, eluded her.

The scent of salt and vinegar once again touched Meredith's nostrils, diverting her from her uncomfortable thoughts. This time it came from a paper cone of chips which was held by a man who ate as he walked. As he hustled past her Meredith stared wistfully at the chips, wondering if she should give into temptation and retrace her steps; the fish and chip shop was quite a way behind her now. No don't, she warned herself, think what they'll do to your figure. Do you imagine Alex would be quite so entranced by the sight of bulging hips and a couple of spare tyres wobbling around your middle?

The imagined vision was enough to make Meredith continue in the direction she was going and put temptation firmly behind her. Her last planned stop was the newsagents, for the latest issue of Vogue, and then she could go home and enjoy the delicious mackerel salad she had already planned for her supper. At least, she thought, she would be having the fish if not the chips.

'Good afternoon, Mr Malik,' she said cheerfully as she entered the shop.

The doorbell pinged as she opened the door, summoning the swarthy Asian from the stockroom at the back of the shop. Now he stood, panting heavily as though unaccustomed to the heat, and rubbing his pudgy hands together in expectation of a sale. The sleeves of his beige and cream striped cotton shirt were rolled up to the elbow revealing arms thickly matted with black hair, while the stomach that bulged over the waistband of his brown slacks boasted of his prosperity.

He smiled as he nodded to her displaying two rows of white, even teeth. 'Good afternoon. My goodness, it has been a hot one today hasn't it?'

To her surprise Meredith found herself blushing as she

nodded. It had been a hot day for her but not in the way Mr Malik meant.

'Is the new *Vogue* in yet?' she asked, looking away hastily and scanning the packed shelves of magazines instead.

As if to add to her embarrassment she found her gaze accidentally coming to rest on a row of soft-porn magazines. All that blonde hair tumbling over huge naked breasts and those glossy scarlet mouths seemed to taunt her. Once again she had to quickly avert her gaze and was relieved when she spotted the cover she sought. It depicted a woman with dark hair coiled into a sleek chignon and wearing a chic red evening dress. Not surprisingly the model reminded Meredith of Camilla and she felt an instant pang of desire as she mentally transposed the model's face with one that was much more familiar.

'Ah, thank goodness, here it is,' she said shakily. Her trembling hand reached for the magazine and she snatched it up. She scanned the rest of the magazines on display while clutching the copy of *Vogue* to her breast. Presently she felt her pulse return to normal.

The doorbell pinged again but she didn't bother to look round. A body brushed past her though she hardly registered it. Even the gruff sound of a man clearing his throat didn't divert her attention from the rows of glossy fashion magazines. To her they were like manna from heaven and she only wished she could afford to buy them all.

'Hi, Sam, how's it hanging?' a man's voice said.

Meredith heard the Asian chuckle before replying, 'So, so, Mr Alex, you know how it is for us poor, overworked shopkeepers.'

'Yeah, yeah,' the other customer responded in a jovial tone. 'Don't give me all that sob stuff. Have you got an *Evening Standard* left by any chance? I meant to come in earlier but I had other things to, er, do.' The voice trailed off uncertainly.

Alex? The name suddenly registered on Meredith's brain. Could it possibly be *him*? She swung round quickly. Too quickly. In her haste she caught a freestanding display of hosiery and sent it crashing to the floor.

The shopkeeper was by her side like a shot. 'Oh, my goodness. Look at this.'

97

He swept a disbelieving hand across his brow which was beaded with perspiration. Then, huffing and puffing, he stooped down and began to gather up all the scattered packets.

Flushing hotly, Meredith tried to help him. 'I'm sorry,' she muttered, 'I didn't see it there.'

'No problem. Don't worry about it,' the shopkeeper assured her. 'I keep meaning to move the display. I think I will put it in the corner over there by the counter. You mustn't fret about it.' The kindly Asian smiled at her then glanced over his shoulder.

As Meredith automatically followed his glance she unwittingly found herself staring at a familiar pair of legs. Her eyes travelled up and up until she felt herself drowning in a couple of deep blue pools. It was him. Alex. There was no mistaking that slim, wiry body. The dark wavy hair. The casual insolence of his expression.

All at once Meredith felt her body flame then turn to water.

I'm melting, she thought helplessly, feeling herself to be in the grip of something beyond her control. Desire had never flared in her so strongly before. Just when she thought she had calmed down she felt her cheeks burning hotly again.

Somehow she managed to straighten up but then stood rooted to the spot while it seemed her mind was intent on hurtling into fantasy hyperspace. In her imagination the shopkeeper disappeared in a puff of smoke and Alex threw her across the counter and screwed her senseless.

'Do you need a hand with that, Sam?' Alex asked the Asian who was struggling with the unwieldy stand.

'No, no, that's all right, Mr Alex,' the shopkeeper said, shaking his head emphatically. 'I can manage.'

Coming back to reality, Meredith realised she had never felt so embarrassed in her life. The times she had tripped over a broken paving stone while trying to walk nonchalantly past a building site full of catcalling men. Or, even worse, the one occasion she had been waiting for a train and her knickers slipped down to her ankles seemed nothing in comparison with this. She was, as her mother had often said to her, a walking disaster area. And this latest faux pas just went to prove what she'd been brought up to believe – that her mother was always right.

'I'll pay for any damage,' she offered weakly, the image of her mother reminded her of her manners. Somehow she managed the few paces to the counter.

At her offer the shopkeeper turned and gave her the benefit of his toothy smile. 'Please, Miss Baxter. I told you. It is nothing. No problem.'

He held out his hand and for a long moment Meredith simply stared at it, her eyes taking in the deeply etched lines on the palm before she realised he was waiting to take the magazine.

'Will that be all?' he asked her.

Meredith nodded dumbly. She couldn't bring herself to look at Alex again, though she was acutely aware of his presence just six inches or so to her left. She could even smell his aftershave and instantly recognised it as Gaultier. Reaching in her shoulder bag for her purse Meredith almost pulled out the small wrapped package of mackerel by mistake. Thank God, she thought as she handed the shopkeeper a five-pound note, I nearly made an idiot of myself again then.

With a trembling hand she took her change and simply dropped it into her bag. She couldn't face trying to fumble with the catch on her purse. In all truth her fingers felt numb and tingly, as did the rest of her body. In fact she wondered how her legs were still managing to support her.

Just as she turned to leave Meredith managed to flash a tremulous smile at Alex. His answering smile was as devastating as it was confident. The blue eyes crinkled at the corners, the effect almost knocking the breath from her body. Feeling as though she were using someone else's legs, she stumbled across the shop and out through the door.

It was only when she reached the safe haven of her flat and closed the door behind her – with the relief of someone being chased by a pack of wolves – that she realised, in her confusion, she had left her magazine behind on the counter.

'Shit, shit, shit!' she cried aloud. She slapped her palm against her forehead and sank down on the bare boards in despair. After all that. What an idiot. There was no way she could go back to the shop. Not yet at any rate. Alex might still be there and she didn't dare risk bumping into him again. Who knew what further embarrassment lurked around the corner.

What is it with that man? she asked herself sometime later, after two-thirds of a bottle of wine had succeeded in calming her down. She sat at her cutting table, nursing a plain goblet of wine and staring across the stretch of canal to the blank window of Alex's flat. And what is the matter with me? Why have I let him get to me like this?

A light suddenly went on in Alex's flat, startling her out of her reverie. Worried that he might come over to his window and see her sitting, there, Meredith jumped up and almost ran into her bedroom.

It took several hours deliberate mediation of the work she still had left to do for Camilla's trousseau, not to mention the rest of the bottle of wine, before she was able to drift off into a fitful sleep.

In contrast to Meredith's unconscious state, Alex was a mass of nervous energy. Having come face to face with the object of his voyeuristic activities, he felt unable to handle the quixotic mix of emotions that gripped him. That he desired Meredith even more for meeting her in the flesh – he shuddered at the very thought, his cock instantly hardening as he recalled the softness of her hair and the sweet scent of her silky skin – was worryingly apparent.

I don't need this right now, he told himself forcibly. I've got too much on my plate and enough women chasing after me to start my own harem. So why this one – what's so special about her? Sod it, I can't even think straight any more let alone work properly.

He stared at the phone by his side, daring himself to call someone – anyone – and invite them over to keep him company. A diversion was what was called for here. A few hours of horizontal aerobics with a nubile young beauty would be the best cure for his current malaise.

Determined to do something to take his mind off Meredith he flicked through his filofax, his eyes alighting on names that conjured instant, raunchy memories. Yet somehow, as his fingertips touched the numbered buttons on his phone, he found himself dialling directory enquiries instead.

'Name please?' the disembodied voice inquired.

'Baxter,' Alex said, his voice gruff. 'Heron House, Princes Wharf.' He added the postal district and waited as instructed.

It was only after he had written down the number that he realised this was exactly what he had intended to do all along.

Meredith woke instantly to the sound of the phone ringing. She reached groggily for the cordless handset on her bedside table and managed to utter a terse, 'Yes?' only to be rewarded by the sound of silence.

There was someone there though, on the other end of the line. She could hear breathing – but quiet breaths, not the heavy kind.

'Camilla?' she said, thinking her new friend the most likely candidate for something so bizarre. 'Is that you?'

Still no answer.

'Look, who is this?' Meredith heard her own voice rise. Calm down, she told herself, don't get hysterical. If it's not Camilla then the caller is probably just a crank.

All at once annoyance took over.

'Listen, you stupid pervert, if you don't get off the line I'll put my husband on. He's a policeman and—'

A soft chuckle interrupted her tirade. 'Meredith?'

Meredith stopped in her tracks. The voice was male. It sounded vaguely familiar yet she couldn't quite place it.

'Who is this?' she asked again but more softly this time.

A brief pause. Then, 'Alex.'

'Alex?' Her pulse began to race.

'Yes. We met. Sort of. Earlier this evening. In the newsagents.'

All at once Meredith felt as though she were a maverick horse broken free of its constraints. Her whole body galloped at a frenzied pace. Yet somehow she managed to keep her voice neutral.

'Yes, I remember.'

She gripped the phone tightly. There was so much she wanted to add. So many questions she needed to ask him.

'I just wanted to let you know I think you're the most beautiful woman I've ever laid eyes on.'

Against her will, Meredith blushed. She felt the warmth

stealing slowly over her entire body. Between her thighs a trickle of moisture told her she was melting all over again. Damn him!

'Thank you,' she managed to gasp out. 'But I don't – I mean I—'

'Shush. Relax. Let me do the talking.' Alex's voice was gentle. Hypnotic.

Allowing herself to drop back against the pillow, Meredith held the phone to her ear and closed her eyes as his voice began to lull her into another world. One where sensuality and eroticism resided, to the exclusion of all else.

When she woke up the following morning Meredith sprang out of bed feeling excited and invigorated. She felt more alive than she had in a long time and sang merrily along to the radio as she showered.

Afterwards, wrapped in a towelling robe, her long hair freshly washed and turbanned in a matching white towel, she made herself a huge breakfast. Her confusion the night before had made her forget all about supper and now she felt ravenous.

Don't forget you'll need all your strength for later on, she reminded herself as she poured cereal into a blue and white china bowl. She pondered the suggestion Alex had made to her the night before and welcomed the surge of anticipation its recollection gave her. Granted it was a strange situation to put herself in but exciting too. And she knew, despite her misgivings, that she would go along with it. After all, she mused as she sat down to eat, wasn't it the next logical stage of the game?

Alex too was full of vim and vigour. His phone call to Meredith had served as an exorcism of sorts. Though he hadn't banished the ghost of her. Far from it. Now he had made the next, most crucial step, the game they had started was finally underway in earnest.

That was provided Meredith didn't back out, he reminded himself.

I don't think she will, he said to his reflection in the shaving mirror. She's not that type of woman. He had guessed at her hidden desires the very first time she had allowed him to watch her. It was true what he'd told her the night before – about her being beautiful. And he'd been thrilled that she had continued to listen to him while he outlined his ideas for tonight's game play.

But for now he had to get down to the garage lot and on the way come up with a whole new set of steps. Time and Lisa Blair waited for no man – least of all him.

The dancers were already there when he arrived.

'Hi, Alex.' Regina was all smiles as she broke away from the group and came up to greet him. 'I've missed you. Where've you been?'

'Working,' Alex said shortly. Then he softened his tone. It wasn't Regina's fault that she assumed she had some kind of hold over him now. If anything the fault lay with him. He should have remembered that most young women her age thought a simple fuck meant something much more. 'I've been really busy,' he explained. 'Lisa demanded that I come up with a whole new set of steps.'

'Oh, poor you. What was wrong with the old ones?' Regina asked sympathetically.

Alex shrugged. 'Beats me. But she's the one paying the bills.' He broke off to clap his hands briskly together. It was Regina's dismissal and his signal to the others that they should stop chattering and take their places.

Taking a long stick which had a piece of chalk on the end he began to sketch out a series of step marks on the concrete forecourt. Presently he sensed another feminine presence by his side. Unlike Regina this woman emitted all the warmth of a boa constrictor.

'Philippa,' he said, arranging his face into a smile as he turned. 'How are you this fine morning?' He kept his tone deliberately light and jovial.

Philippa's demeanour, however, remained icy. She stood, arms tightly folded and looked at him through narrowed eyes. As he gazed innocently back at her Alex was struck by the realisation that Philippa was not beautiful at all but ugly. As ugly and forbidding as gargoyle.

'I've been expecting your call, Alex. Why have you been avoiding me?' she demanded. Clad in pale cream kid, the toe of her right foot tapped impatiently on the dirty concrete.

'I haven't been avoiding you, Philippa,' he responded evenly. 'I told you, I've been busy.'

'Too busy to show me a bit of courtesy?' By her raised eyebrows and incredulous expression it was obvious that Philippa couldn't quite grasp the concept.

'Yes, that's right,' Alex said.

Deliberately ignoring her he continued to trace out his hastily reworked set of steps on the concrete. After a moment's strained silence he was rewarded by the sound of Philippa's frustrated sigh. Though he didn't dare glance up, from the corner of his eye Alex was relieved to notice her striding back across the forecourt to rejoin the others.

Despite Philippa's frosty demeanour she managed to cooperate grudgingly with Alex's instructions, while the others – all well aware of Lisa Blair's exacting disposition and consequently sympathetic with Alex's plight – threw themselves into the new routine with enthusiastic fervour.

Alex was elated at how quickly things were coming together and by the time they broke for lunch he was all smiles. He congratulated all the dancers effusively then slipped away to a quiet corner to make a call on his mobile phone.

Meredith threw down her sewing and snatched up the phone the moment in rang. Determined to make the most of the sun, she was seated outside on the tiny balcony instead of indoors. And she had swapped her usual shorts and tee-shirt for a bright canary yellow bikini.

'Alex?'

'The one and only,' Alex responded jokily. He glanced swiftly around to make sure there was no one close enough to eavesdrop on his conversation. Then he dropped his voice an octave. 'How are you feeling – are you still on for tonight?'

Meredith's fingers tightened around the cordless phone. 'Yes,' she said. She paused to clear her throat which had suddenly gone dry. 'I think I made myself clear last night. I'm not going to be the first one to back out of this game.'

Alex felt a frisson of anticipation. She was one hell of a woman.

'I just thought,' he said, 'that maybe in the cold light of day—'

Meredith's giggle interrupted him. 'Haven't you noticed,' she said, 'the sun is as hot as it gets in this country. And so am I,' she added in a huskier tone.

An unexpected tightening sensation in Alex's groin made him gasp. It took all his willpower not to give into the temptation to call off the rest of the days' rehearsals and dash round to Meredith's flat.

Instead he asked, 'What are you doing now?'

Meredith smiled. She was tempted to tell him that she was masturbating. Indeed, the image of herself reclining on the old fashioned deckchair on the balcony, with her hands caressing her near naked body, was so arousing that she sighed and stretched luxuriously. She flicked her hair away from her shoulders and glanced down to the bronzed mounds of flesh swelling over the cups of her skimpy bikini top.

'I was working,' she said softly, still gazing down at the beguiling sight of her own body. 'I'm out on my balcony so that I can soak up the sun at the same time. But since you called I've felt this overwhelming urge to pleasure myself.'

Alex groaned inwardly with desire. Oh, God, why did he have to be stuck in this Godforsaken place when he could be at home, watching her?

'Do it,' he urged, gripping the phone, 'Stroke your breasts. Will you do that – for me?'

'No,' Meredith teased him, with a throaty chuckle. 'But I'll do it for me.' She slipped the fingers of her free hand inside her bikini top and began to toy idly with a nipple. It hardened instantly. Then she moved her hand to her other breast. 'I'm doing it now,' she went on after a moment. 'I'm playing with my nipples. God, they're hard and swollen. Like organ stops. I wish you could see them. But perhaps you can imagine them, Alex? What do you think – can you? Can you see them all red and swollen with my fingers pinching and pulling at them?'

'Yes.' The single word was torn from Alex's dry throat. He could hear her breathing. It was soft and rapid, punctuated occasionally by a sigh. The thought of her playing with her hard, thrusting nipples made his cock swell. After a moment he dared to ask, 'What are you doing now?'

Meredith breathed softly into the receiver. She wedged it

between her ear and her shoulder and parted her legs. Then she allowed her hands to travel slowly and tantalising down the length of her torso. Covered liberally with sunscreen, her skin was slick and oily. As her fingertips rested lightly on the gently swelling mound of her belly she hesitated. Then she took a deep breath and inched her fingers beneath the taut fabric of her bikini bottoms.

'I'm touching myself between my legs now, Alex,' she said after a moment spent caressing herself. 'I'm spreading my labia wide apart. And, oh, God ... my clitoris is so swollen already. I can't tell you how horny I'm feeling, Alex. I'm so wet I've got to put a finger inside myself. Ah, that's better. Oh, yes, much, much better.'

Her breathing became more ragged and Alex felt a wave of dizziness sweep over him.

'Put two fingers in,' Alex urged, when he found his voice. A whimper of pleasure told him she had complied. 'Now rub that little clit as well. Finger fuck and rub ... Finger fuck and rub ...'

'Oh, God, yes I'm doing it!' Meredith gasped as she rubbed her swollen clitoris furiously and jabbed two fingers deep into the slippery depths of her vagina.

Lust flamed instantly and she wished, right at that moment, that Alex was there with her, touching her with fingers that she knew would be clever and knowing. They were bound to be, he knew her so well already.

'Are you coming?' Alex asked, furtively rubbing himself. He had turned to face the wall and slid his hand down the front of his pants. His cock felt as stiff as a baton.

Meredith's frantic gasps and whimpers told him that she was.

Suddenly Alex heard a voice behind him.

'Alex, could I talk to you for a moment?' It was Lisa Blair.

'Sorry,' he mumbled into the phone. 'Got to go.' He snapped the mouthpiece shut, cutting off the call and whirled around.

Lisa stood, hands on hips and smiling. When she swept an appraising glance over him however, her expression froze.

All at once Alex remembered he was sporting a bloody great hard on. In his tight lycra sweat pants there was no way he could conceal the tell tale bulge.

'My, my,' she said eventually, 'it looks as though I interrupted something. That must have been some phone conversation you were having.' She shrugged her shoulders and smiled sweetly. 'Sorry.'

'That's, er, all right,' Alex mumbled, as a loss for words.

He clasped his erection with both hands and willed it to go down. Surprisingly and embarrassingly, it stayed exactly as it was. Then he realised his body was responding to the very fetching sight of Lisa clad in a skimpy white thong leotard over purple lycra shorts that left very little to the imagination. Whether he liked the woman or not, he had to admit she had a very fit body.

To his alarm he realised Lisa was walking towards him. Instinctively, he backed away until he found his spine pressed against the back wall of the forecourt office.

'Don't be shy, Alex,' Lisa crooned as she came right up to him and moved his hands, replacing them with her own. Deftly, she slid her hands inside his pants and clasped his erection. 'I think I can help you out with this. That's if you want me to?' she added, raising her eyebrows inquiringly. Her smile mocked him though her olive green eyes blazed with lust.

Dumbstruck, Alex gazed back at her. Did he want her? His cock did apparently. He could feel it growing even larger between her more than capable fingers. And no matter how badly she had treated him up to now, he couldn't ignore the temptation of the wet, pink lips, parted so enticingly and just centimetres from his own. Nor could he resist putting his arms around her and running his hands down her slender back and over the firm mounds of her buttocks. As tiny as she was, and with her silky brown hair caught up in a ponytail, she looked less like a woman and more like jail bait.

'Yes, I want you to,' he gasped hoarsely. Grasping her by the ponytail he yanked her head back roughly and began to lay a trail of kisses down her throat.

Chapter Nine

With a harsh gasp Lisa arched her spine and thrust herself against Alex. He could feel her small breasts and hard ribcage pressing against his chest and his body thrilled as she rubbed herself up and down him like a cat. Her movements were lithe and sensuous, her merciless fingers massaging his straining cock in a frenzy while a wild light danced in her eyes.

Groaning harshly with pent-up lust Alex let go of her hair and at the same instant Lisa sank to her haunches, pulling his pants down as she went. With a leap of joy his cock sprang free. Completely erect it stuck out at right angles to his body. The veins stood out from his rigid shaft and a small tear of fluid oozed from the slit at the tip of his swollen glans.

Though he knew he was with Lisa, somehow all Alex could think about was Meredith. When he looked down he saw a silky blonde head, not Lisa's chestnut locks. The fingers coiling avidly round his cock were Meredith's, as was the tongue which darted out and flickered experimentally over his glans. And when he acquiesced to the full ministrations of Lisa's mouth he imagined they were Meredith's lips engulfing him.

'Yes,' he moaned hoarsely, his legs trembling as he felt a lightening bolt of desire hit him. 'Oh, God yes.'

The image of Meredith's naked breasts sprang to mind. He saw her sprawled on a deckchair, her fingers buried deep inside herself and an expression of pure ecstasy on her face. In reality Lisa was gripping him hard, her wet tongue flickering around his glans and laving his stem. He could feel the pleasurable sensations, feel the virility surging through him, but the sensuality of the moment held a dreamlike quality. It was as though he stood apart from himself. His body responded yet all he could think about was the wet, feminine place between

Meredith's thighs and her practised caresses of self pleasure.

More torturous was the expression of pure bliss on Meredith's face. He pictured her eyelids half closed with arousal, her lashes casting feathery shadows over her soft, pink cheeks. The same lustful blush spread down her throat and over the generous contours of her breasts. Again he could picture the nipples, hard and rosy, jutting out proudly from her magnificent globes. And the similarly swollen flesh was echoed in her clitoris which pulsated under her stimulating fingertips.

Clutching mindlessly at Lisa's head, forcing her harder against his goin, Alex didn't think about who she was. He was intent only on ramming his cock as deep into her throat as possible while he fantasised about Meredith alone on her balcony. And when his cock jetted a seemingly endless load of hot jism he thought little about the owner of the mouth into which it spurted.

Afterwards he felt ashamed of himself and made a half-hearted, if outwardly convincing, offer to Lisa to return the compliment.

'No time,' she said, glancing at her watch as she straightened up. Her eyes sparkled with triumph as she wiped the back of her hand across her mouth where traces of his semen still glistened. 'We have work to do. But perhaps we can take a raincheck?' she ended on a hopeful note.

Alex forced a smile. Though he couldn't envisage a day when every spare moment aside from his work wouldn't be spent on Meredith, he nodded. 'Yeah, sure. Just tell me when.'

Lisa grinned broadly as she began to repair the damage to her wrecked pontail. 'Don't worry, I will,' she said, 'and I can promise you somewhere a bit more salubrious than this place.' Her glance took in the shabby office with its bare whitewashed walls and peeling paint.

All at once Alex was struck by the incongruity of the situation. He had just had his cock sucked dry by one of the country's leading female vocalists. And in a shabby deserted garage, of all places.

'Anywhere would be better than this,' he agreed, his smile for real this time. 'But thanks for – you know – everything.

Lisa gave a pert toss of her ponytail. 'Think nothing of it,' she said. 'I only hope I haven't depleted your energy too much. We've got a lot to get through.'

Alex had to admire the way Lisa pleasantly but effectively reminded him of their individual roles – he as the employee and she as the one who called all the shots. As he followed the young woman back out into the sunshine he fervently hoped she would allow a five minute break later on. He had to ring Meredith back, for one thing to apologise for cutting her off and for another, to make sure she was completely certain about her instructions.

The East end pub was typically noisy and shabby. The outside sported peeling paint on the window frames, grime smeared panes of glass and poorly tended hanging baskets. The narrow street was lined on both sides with cars, some parked askew, with a front wheel on the pavement. The obstacle course of a road made the taxi driver's job difficult and he moaned like hell.

Meredith willed him silently to shut up. As a London cabby surely it wasn't the first time he'd come up against this sort of problem, she mused crossly. His constant carping about the heavy traffic throughout the journey had made her head ache and she was tempted to tell him to turn round and take her straight home. It was only the thought of having to spend more time with him that stopped her.

And Alex of course. How could she forget Alex and what awaited her? She smiled despite her anxious state.

'Just drop me off here,' she ordered tersely, interrupting the cabby's muttered oaths as he tried to negotiate his way around the back end of a white Honda which was sticking out.

'I don't know what these bleedin' nutters think they're doing, parking like this,' the taxi driver complained as he accepted her payment. 'I shudder to think what they'll be like on the roads later, when they've got a belly full of beer inside them.'

Meredith sighed. 'Yes, it's awful isn't it? Keep the change.'

Before going into the pub she struggled to pull down the hem of her dress. It was far too short. And tight. But those had been Alex's instructions. She found herself wondering what he would think when he saw her and whether he would mind because the dress was pink and not black as he'd asked.

A blast of hot, smoky air assailed her as she pushed open the door to the saloon bar. On the threshold she took a deep breath. It seemed that everyone turned to look at her as she entered. And was it her imagination or did the cacophony of loud voices die a little when she made her entrance?

The interior of the pub was packed. Each of the tightly packed tables was filled by a clientele who mostly looked as though they had arrived straight from some building site or other. Meredith scanned the room as she walked up to the bar, pointedly ignoring the stares of the men seated all around her and avoiding eye contact with any of them. She couldn't see Alex yet but a glance at her watch told her she was a good ten minutes early.

The only female present – a big, blowsy woman with bleached hair and a beauty spot on her left cheek – turned to smile at her.

'Hello, chick,' she said in a vaguely northern accent. 'You want to watch yourself here in that get up.' She gave Meredith a swift appraisal as she spoke then gestured to the empty bar stool next to her. 'You'd better sit here. Let me take care of you.'

'That's very kind,' Meredith muttered, slipping on to the seat and pulling down her hem again. 'My friend should be here in a moment actually.'

She couldn't help noticing the shared, conspiratorial smile between the woman and the barman. Though she felt nervous she gave an inward shrug. Yes, I'm totally out of place here, she wanted to say. But this wasn't my idea. Glancing around, hoping in vain to see Alex, she gave up and ordered a gin and tonic.

The woman gave her empty glass a meaningful glance.

'Can I buy you a drink?' Meredith offered dutifully. She felt trapped by the woman but was unable to think of a way to back out graciously. Her only alternative was to sit alone in another part of the pub and she fancied that idea even less. At least, she thought, as she ordered a Pernod and lemonade for her new companion, there's something to be said for safety in numbers.

As she sipped her drink she couldn't escape the fact that all the men present were eyeing her up. Or, more precisely, her legs which, on Alex's instructions, were clad in sheer black nylon. The black clashed horribly with the sugar pink shade of her dress and she couldn't help feeling distinctly tarty. But then, she reminded herself, wasn't that the object of the exercise? Her only concession to herself had been to wear tights instead of stockings. There hadn't been time to go out and buy a pair specially and now she was glad because, no matter how much she tugged at it, her short hem revealed an awful lot of thigh.

'Your friend,' the woman said unexpectedly, 'is it a man?'

'Yes,' Meredith responded, trying to sound noncommittal. She kept her eyes averted as she sipped her drink. After a moment she realised she was being very ungracious and against her better judgement asked, 'Are you from the North?'

The woman's huge breasts wobbled as she threw back her head and laughed. 'Oh, aye, you can tell then?'

'It's your accent,' Meredith said, blushing, 'I used to live in Nottingham.'

'Well I've lived here for the past twenty-odd years,' the woman said, 'and no one's said anything about my having an accent. Don't I sound like a Londoner then?'

Meredith stifled a smile as she shook her head. 'Not really.' Then she added, 'I suppose I've got an ear for accents.'

'You don't sound as though you're from Nottingham,' the woman said.

'I'm not,' Meredith replied, 'I just lived there for a few years. I originally come from Surrey.'

'That figures.' The woman nodded sagely and she and the barman shared another conspiratorial smile.

Meredith wished fervently that Alex would hurry up and arrive. She knew the woman and her friend, the barman, were taking the rise out of her but was powerless to prevent it. It seemed that whenever she opened her mouth she managed to compound her crime of being middle class. Surrounded as she was by scruffily dressed men with greasy hair, nicotine stained fingers and loud voices, she was cleary out of her depth.

All at once she wondered how on earth she was going to carry out Alex's instructions to the full. There wasn't one single man present who appealed to her even in the slightest. The very thought of one of them putting his grubby, calloused hands on her, let alone . . .

She broke off her thoughts hastily and shuddered. Now she wished just as fervently that Alex wouldn't turn up at all. Hopefully, he would be the one to renege on the deal.

As luck would have it he arrived a few moments later, though Meredith missed his arrival because Liz – the woman at the bar – had just started to regale her with a long, convoluted story about her landlord problems.

'He's a total git,' Liz was saying. 'Told me if I couldn't pay my rent in cash I'd have to pay in kind. As if.' She raised her eyebrows then winked at Meredith.

Just at that moment Meredith was startled by the touch of warm breath on her left ear.

'Mind if I buy you a drink?'

Prepared for the owner of the breath and the voice to be someone totally abhorrent, Meredith swung round, her face set in an irritated expression.

'No thank you,' she began primly, 'I – oh – it's you.'

Alex grinned broadly at her. 'Yes, it's me,' he concurred. 'Sorry I'm late.'

'Pleased to meet you I'm sure.' Alex and Meredith were interrupted by Liz. She stretched her arm across the bar in front of Meredith and chuckled throatily when Alex kissed her hand as opposed to shaking it.

Realising she would have to go through the rigmarole of introductions Meredith groaned inwardly.

'Alex, this is Liz,' she said, glancing from one to the other. 'Liz, my friend Alex.'

She yelped as Liz jabbed her sharply in the side with her elbow. 'He's a stunner ain't he? You lucky girl.'

Meredith was pleased to note that Alex flashed her a warm and shockingly intimate smile.

'Yes,' she managed to gasp out. 'He is. Well,' she added brightly, turning her back deliberately on Liz and returning Alex's smile, 'shall we go and find a quiet corner somewhere?'

With a nod, Alex held out his hand and helped her down from the bar stool. As she slithered from the seat Meredith's dress rode right up to the tops of her thighs. She tried to cover them hastily but not before she caught a certain look in Alex's eye.

'Tights!' he admonished, yanking her away from the bar with little finesse. 'I thought I said stockings.'

'I didn't have any. There wasn't time . . .' Meredith realised she was gabbling. Her cheeks started to flame and as she shook Alex's hand off her arm. Her expression was one of anger and confusion.

'I'm sorry,' Alex apologised immediately. He began to rub gently at the red marks his fingers had left on her arm, 'I didn't mean to be so rough.'

With a rueful smile Meredith looked down at the sensitive flesh on her inner forearm where his thumb still caressed her. Then she glanced up at his face. Her expression dissolved when she saw how contrite he looked.

'It's OK,' she said, 'No real harm done. I suppose I should apologise for the pink dress as well.' She was disappointed when Alex stopped stroking her arm and put his hands in his pockets instead.

He rocked back on his heels and for the first time gave her a proper appraisal. It was true, he thought as his eyes swept over her sinuous body, she wasn't dressed at all as he'd instructed. Yet he had to admit the colour suited her. And the dress was very tight and revealing. It's low cut neckline showed the softly swelling mounds of her upper breasts and a generous cleavage to perfection, while the body hugging material enhanced her other curves in a very tantalising way.

He swallowed deeply, feeling the tightness in his chest. Christ, how he wanted her! What man in his right mind wouldn't? For the first time he wondered how long he would be able to keep the game going. His assumption had been that Meredith would be the one to call a halt to it all. Now he wasn't so sure.

'Go and take the tights off,' he said gruffly, glancing at her legs, 'and your panties. Bring them back and give them to me.'

Feeling a tremor of excitement assail her, Meredith hesitated. Then she flashed him a quick, outwardly confident smile and turned toward the ladies' lavatory.

'All right,' she said, 'I'll just be a moment.'

She came out of the Ladies' to find Alex leaning nonchalantly against the wall, hands still thrust deep in his pockets. He was wearing a loose cut sage green jacket and trousers. Underneath the jacket a black cotton T-shirt hugged his torso.

Without saying a word he held out his hand and, blushing furiously, she handed him her tights and panties. He stuffed the tights into his trouser pocket straight away but, as if to add to her embarrassment, he turned the flimsy pink lace knickers over in his hands before pocketing them as well.

'Very nice,' he commented.

She smiled a half smile, feeling the warmth in her cheeks flare again. 'Thanks. I made them myself.'

Alex gazed at her for a long moment. He had heard of women making their own clothes but what sort of woman made her own underwear?

'That is my speciality,' she explained, realising his confusion. 'I design and make lingerie.'

'So that's what you do seated at that table in front of the window all day and half the night,' he said. Taking her hand he began to lead her through the pub.

'Yes, I've got quite a few orders to fill,' she said proudly.

As they negotiated a couple of particularly jam packed tables Meredith felt someone pinch her right buttock. She squealed instantly and glanced around, wondering if she could spot her assailant.

Alex glanced at her over his shoulder. 'What's the matter?'

'Someone just pinched my bum,' Meredith said.

Alex's glance automatically fell to the taut, rounded curves of her buttocks under clinging, shocking pink.

'I'm not surprised,' he murmured.

As he raised his head her gaze met his and, for a long moment, time seemed suspended as they simply stared wordlessly at each other.

Then, right beside them, a couple of men got up from their table and made for the door. Their departure shattered the electrifying atmosphere which surrounded Meredith and Alex.

Alex acted swiftly. 'Here we go, this'll do,' he said, pulling her down on to one of the empty seats. He opted to sit beside her, rather than opposite. Their backs were to the wall affording them a good view of the saloon bar and its patrons.

Meredith was uncomfortably aware of his closeness. He was wearing the same aftershave, she noticed, and she could feel the warmth emanating from his body. His trouser leg brushed her bare skin making her shiver with expectancy.

'They're a pretty average lot, aren't they?' he commented after a moment.

Meredith pursed her lips. 'That depends on what you call average,' she said.

'In view of the circumstances I'll be magnanimous and allow you to choose,' Alex murmured.

To Meredith's amazement he raised his hand and managed to summon a young woman who seemed only too glad to take his order for drinks.

'I didn't realise pubs like this provided a waitress service,' Meredith commented dryly. 'Can I take it you're used to living a charmed existence?'

Alex laughed. 'But of course. Women fall at my feet all the time.'

Meredith made a disbelieving sound and pretended to ignore him. She glanced around, ostensibly looking for a suitable 'target'. In reality she felt suffused with a desirous warmth. Alex was so sure of himself and too charming for words. Yet there was nothing false about him. And his pretence at arrogance displayed more than a hint of self-mockery. There and then she decided that she liked him. Truly liked him. His looks weren't simply window dressing. His persona was definitely charismatic. And she didn't doubt that when she got to know him better she would find that his handsome exterior harboured a great sense of humour.

The thing that affected her most deeply was his sensuality. His suggestion to her the night before had been blatant and purely erotic. Why she had chosen to agree to it was something she had yet to fathom. And whether she could actually keep up her end of the game was something she was seriously beginning to doubt. By the looks of the men surrounding her and knowing the way she usually approached sex, she couldn't help feeling that she was going to fall at the first hurdle.

'Have you made your decision yet?' Alex asked gently.

Meredith blushed again as she shook her head. Her hand

trembled as she picked up the glass of gin and tonic which had just been put in front of her.

'No, they're all horrible,' she said.

Alex inclined his head to a couple of young men who had just entered the pub. 'What about them?' he asked.

Glancing across to the door, Meredith saw that the men were not nearly as bad-looking as the rest of the pub's clientele and much more smartly dressed. In fact one of them looked to be a distinct possibility.

Somewhere in his mid twenties he was fairly tall and had long, light brown hair which was streaked with gold and fell well below his shoulders. To Meredith's eye it looked well cut and, more importantly, squeaky clean. Again on the plus side his physique looked muscular. His chest and shoulders appeared broad beneath the cream cotton-knit sweater which he wore tucked into black leather trousers.

As she watched him stroll over to the bar, his tight buttocks undulating beneath the black leather, Meredith felt her stomach tighten. She could feel her breasts swelling in anticipation of sex. Her nipples chafed at the tight covering of her dress. Swallowing deeply to clear her throat, she crossed her bare legs purposefully and smiled at the young man when he turned his head in her direction.

'That's the one,' she said in a low voice.

Even as she spoke she marvelled at her ability to appear outardly calm. Inside she was a churning mass of emotions. The thought of approaching a strange for sex scared the hell out of her. Yet at the same time she couldn't deny the way her body betrayed her, putting her innermost desires on show.

Alex was clearly tuned into her, she realised as he gazed knowingly back at her. His blue eyes seemed as deep and fathomless as an ocean and Meredith felt herself drowning helplessly in them. What had started out a not so innocent game was rapidly turning into something else far more profound.

Hastily, she grabbed her glass and downed the rest of her drink. She needed all the courage she could get, she realised, and the sooner she got this ordeal over and done with the better. Rising shakily to her feet she bent down and murmured to Alex that she was going to get another drink.

He smiled his comprehension back at her and nodded. By God, he thought, she was actually going to do it. What a girl.

Though she tried to look nonchalant, Meredith felt as if she were going to faint. It was only now that she became fully aware of the way her tight dress clung to her breasts and buttocks, leaving little to the imagination. And the cool air snaking up the hem and between her legs reminded her of her naked sex. The sensation was so strange Meredith felt a strong urge to rush back to Alex and demand that he return her knickers. And her dress felt so tight she was constricted by it. Her whole body, it seemed, was in full bloom and desperate to burst free. In her overactive imagination she pictured the thin fabric of her dress splitting under the strain and rending wide apart to reveal her shameless body to the whole pub.

It was almost with relief that she found herself standing next to the object of her lewd intentions. She pretended to jostle for space at the bar, her arm deliberately nudging him.

'Sorry,' she murmured, glancing up at him from beneath her lashes, 'it's so packed in here.'

He smiled easily displaying white, slightly crooked teeth. His eyes were grey-green she noticed and his features were pleasantly craggy. Up close she realised he must be quite a bit older than she'd originally assumed, probably in his late twenties or early thirties.

'No problem,' he said, adding, 'Here let me get that for you,' when the barman set yet another gin and tonic in front of her.

She nodded in what she hoped was a grateful, acquiescent way as he took a ten pound note out of his wallet. As her fingers curled around the cold glass she noticed that his hands were tipped by short, clean nails. Thank God for small mercies, she breathed inwardly. With a deep breath she turned to face him again, holding the glass to her lips. She made her eyes twinkle provocatively and she wrinkled her nose as she took a sip of her drink. She was not used to 'pulling' as such and hoped that all these ploys, which she had read about in magazines, were going to work in practice.

She needn't have worried. The man introduced himself as Wizz and even spelt it out for her.

'That's an unusual name,' she commented, for something better to say.

'I'm in a rock band.'

Meredith nodded sagely. 'Ah! That explains it then.'

Wizz pretended to look hurt. 'You mean I'm cliché man?'

Laughing, Meredith shook her head with such vigour that a trendril of her hair ended up in her drink. She fished it out of the glass and sucked its sodden tip while gazing up at him. He was quite nice really, she found herself thinking. In a sort of rugged, macho way that was.

'The reason people call me Wizz,' he began patiently, 'is because people say I'm a wizard on the guitar. Not,' he added, 'because I do a lot of speed.'

'Just a bit then,' Meredith teased.

'No,' he assured her, 'not even a bit. I can't afford to. I've seen too many of my mates get wrecked on that stuff, and worse. I admit to smoking a bit of weed though.'

'That's nothing, is it?' Meredith said. She felt her breath catch as he reached out and gently drew the hair away from her mouth.

'You are though,' he said, his fingers stroking her cheek. 'Something, I mean.'

She smiled. 'Thank you. So are you. I couldn't help noticing you when you arrived.'

Now it was his turn to look pleased. Taking his hand away from her cheek he postured proudly. Then he glanced around.

'I don't know what's happened to Chris, my mate,' he said.

Meredith shrugged. 'Who cares?'

She couldn't help noticing that her unconscious gesture immediately diverted Wizz's gaze to her breasts. She took a deep breath, forcing herself not to hunch her shoulders in an effort to shrink away from his probing gaze.

'Not me,' Wizz declared, dragging his eyes back to her face at long last. 'I couldn't give a toss now I've met you. Fancy another?' He nodded at her half empty glass.

'No but I fancy you,' Meredith responded with a boldness that surprised her.

'Well, well, this must be my lucky day,' Wizz said.

All at once it seemed, the atmosphere between them changed

noticeably. What had started out as an innocent conversation, progressing into mild flirtation, was now rapidly approaching something else entirely. His darkened gaze told Meredith that her advances weren't about to be rebuffed.

'Let's go somewhere else,' he said, taking her drink away from her and putting it down on the bar.

Meredith's heart galloped wildly. She snatched her glass back up and downed the rest of her drink in a couple of hasty gulps. This time the alcohol hit her and she rocked unsteadily on her spiky black heels. This was it then, she told herself. If she was going to do it, if she was going to play her part in the game, this was the point of no return.

'OK, where do you suggest?' she asked.

Wizz appeared to ponder her question for a moment. Reaching up he ran a hand distractedly through his hair.

'How about the pub garden?' he said.

Meredith knew she looked surprised. 'This pub has a garden – where?' She hadn't noticed one when she arrived.

'Out the back, of course,' Wizz said. He grasped her gently by the elbow and steered her to a door at the side of the bar. 'We'll have to go through the public bar.'

Feeling panicky, Meredith glanced around. Her eyes sought Alex and she noticed with relief that he was already rising to his feet.

'OK,' she agreed, shrugging again.

The garden, as it was optimistically called, was more a patch of uneven paving stones, a couple of wooden benches and tables and numerous broken earthenware pots containing wilting plants. Obviously, Meredith thought, it wasn't used as a garden all that often because most of the space was taken up by stacks of aluminium beer barrels.

'The cellar's not that big either,' Wizz explained, gesturing toward the barrels. 'Come on let's go and sit over there.'

He led her over to one of the benches and they sat down next to each other. Meredith looked up at the sky as a way to distract herself from the uncomfortable pounding of her heart. Out of the corner of her eye she noticed Alex skirting the garden and taking a seat in the farthest corner away from them. Wizz seemed oblivious to Alex's presence, a fact which made

Meredith feel extraordinarily relieved. If he had he might have insisted on taking her somewhere else, somewhere where Alex wouldn't be able to go. Not only would that be dangerous, she mused, but it would totally defeat the object of the exercise.

'It's a lovely clear night isn't it?' Wizz said moving closer to her and putting an arm around her shoulders.

'Uh-huh,' Meredith muttered.

She felt his fingers squeezing her bare upper arm and when she glanced sideways she noticed how good he looked in profile. He had a good bone structure and his jaw and chin were strong and shadowed by an attractive growth of stubble. Without thinking she reached up and traced his jawline with the backs of her fingers. The stubble prickled her skin and she shivered.

Turning his face slightly he caught her hand and held it tightly.

'Cold?' he asked.

She shook her head. 'No. Very warm as a matter of fact.' She gazed at him meaningfully.

He moved her fingers to his lips and he kissed the backs of them while holding her gaze. After a moment he glanced down at her heaving breasts and gave a low groan.

'Christ!' he muttered hoarsely, dropping her hand and crushing her to him.

His mouth sought hers and in moments he was kissing her deeply, his tongue exploring her mouth while his hands roamed her back. Roughly he pulled her onto his lap. His left hand cupped the back of her head and his right immediately moved down to her buttocks. Massaging her left buttock fiercely he pulled his mouth away from hers and began to kiss his way down her neck and along her shoulder instead. When his lips came to her shoulder strap he pulled it to one side and cupped her exposed breast lifting it to his eager mouth.

'Oh, God!' Meredith couldn't help herself. His passion for her was inflammatory.

She threw back her head and arched her spine, thrusting herself against him. As he continued to massage her buttocks he managed to work the hem of her dress up so that the bare flesh was exposed. When he realised she was wearing no knickers he suddenly stopped what he was doing and stared hard at her.

'You really are a hot little bitch, aren't you?' he said. 'Bare bum and all.'

The way he spoke the words, combined with the wolfish expression on his face made Meredith feel as though she were the rudest, lewdest woman on earth. Unable to help herself, she rubbed her naked vulva shamelessly against his bulging black leather-clad crotch.

The leather was warm and stimulating. Skin on skin it aroused her to greater heights. She felt her juices flowing out of her and she gripped his hips hard with her inner thighs as she continued to grind herself against him.

Chapter Ten

As Meredith churned excitedly away on top of Wizz she happened to glance in Alex's direction. He was watching the two of them intently, she noticed, his chin supported by his fist, elbow resting on the table to the side of him.

Though it was too dark to see the expression on his face she imagined that he was getting a great deal of pleasure from her performance. As if he was the only one, she mused, groaning with enhanced arousal as her latest conquest slipped a couple of fingers inside her and caressed her g-spot. There was no denying, she found this encounter every bit as daring and erotic as she'd imagined.

If she needed physical proof she only had to feel how wide open she was. Her body admitted Wizz's fingers easily. Her juices were copious and she could detect their sweetly musky scent. In response she began to fumble with the zip on Wizz's leather pants and when she had made a big enough opening she slipped a hand inside.

Straight away she felt the satisfying length and girth of his erection, he was not huge but certainly large enough to give her a great deal of pleasure.

'I'm not very comfortable,' she admitted to him a few moment later. 'Do you mind if I move?'

With obvious reluctance, Wizz slipped his fingers from her vagina and nodded.

She got up awkwardly, feeling her cramped legs immediately give way to pins and needles. With her dress hiked up around her hips she paced back and forth until the feeling returned to her legs. Glancing at Wizz she noticed he was watching her intently. Then she glanced over Wizz's shoulder to Alex and saw that he was doing exactly the same.

The knowledge that she was putting herself on display for not one but two men and that anyone could come outside and catch them, added an extra dimension to the erotic charge that zapped through her. She could feel the cool night air caressing her naked belly and buttocks. Like balm it soothed the moist, swollen flesh between her legs and dried the trickles of feminine honey that clung to her inner thighs.

Feeling thoroughly wanton she pulled the neckline of her dress right down so that both her breasts were fully exposed. Then she stood, legs apart, directly in front of Wizz and began to caress herself openly.

'Jesus!' he cried, leaping to his feet. Grabbing her he turned her around and bent her forward over one of the beer barrels.

The aluminium was cold under her palms and Meredith trembled with anticipation as she felt Wizz positioning her the way he wanted. He muttered to her to spread her legs and briefly reached under her to caress her dangling breasts. His main interest though seemed to be her upthrust bottom and the shamelessly exposed pouch of her sex. He thrust a hand between her legs, his fingers inexpertly seeking her clitoris.

Moving one hand, Meredith guided him. She worked her fingers on top of his in a steady rhythm until she was gasping and moaning incoherently with undisguised pleasure.

From a few yards away Alex sat and watched Meredith and her 'pick up' in absolute amazement. He had not for one minute thought she would go this far. Arousing though it had been to watch events unfold, the sight of her bent over the aluminium barrel, with her gloriously rounded buttocks gleaming in the moonlight, was almost too much for a red blooded guy like himself to bear.

He could clearly see the puffy, reddened lips of her sex. They had blossomed between her thighs to reveal her moist, pink inner flesh and the achingly inviting opening of her vagina. Alex felt as though he could hardly blame the long haired guy for not being able to keep his hands off her superb breasts, nor his fingers away from all that succulent, honeyed flesh. Her body was like a banquet, he thought. Delight after delight displayed in the most tempting and delectable way possible.

When the guy unzipped his trousers and took his erection in his hands, preparing to enter her waiting body, Alex felt like pushing him out of the way and spearing her delightful flesh himself. It would be like pushing himself into a ripe fig, he thought, licking his lips at the evocative imagery.

He cursed himself now for suggesting this new dimension to their game and not simply taking her himself. It was what he wanted, what he longed for, so why was he so intent on torturing himself this way?

Because the more I want her and the more desirable she becomes, the greater the ultimate pleasure will be, he told himself. This was his *modus operandi*. From the very first moment he had realised that a simple fuck would not be enough. Meredith was too special for that. He wanted to tempt her and test her in the same way he wanted to test himself. Like a cruel form of foreplay, it seemed imperative that he push them both to the limit of their endurance.

Stifling an anguished groan he prepared to watch Meredith's conquest consummate their brief liaison.

At the first thrust Meredith gasped aloud. She had been relieved when Wizz paused to don a condom – if he hadn't she would have had to mention the pack she had prudently obtained from the machine in the pub. Even though she knew he was about to take her she was still surprised by the suddenness and force of his entry.

His passion was fierce. She could feel his fingers gripping her hips hard as he rammed into her. There was little finesse about his technique but that in itself was arousing. This was undiluted sex. Hot, raunchy and explosive. Their desire was purely carnal and, as Meredith felt his pelvis slamming against her, driving his cock deep inside her hungry body, she gave herself over to the pulsating desire that swamped her.

That first explosive force did nothing to dissipate her desire. If anything she felt as though her body had just been primed. It had been the appetiser before the entrée.

'Don't stop yet,' she gasped when Wizz prepared to pull out of her.

She reached behind her and grasped at thin air, seeking a

part of him to hold on to. She wanted desperately to keep him there. Buried deep inside her. Thankfully, she felt his body movements start up again. She could feel his pelvis grinding against her and she churned her hips, matching his rhythm to perfection.

After a few achingly delicious moments she murmured to him to stop. Straightening up she caught and held his gaze. He looked slightly mesmerised now, as though the release of his initial passion had the effect of doping him up. Smiling to herself Meredith turned around and sat on the barrel. Ignoring the cold aluminium under her bare bottom she parted her legs invitingly and beckoned to him to come closer.

'Put it in me like this,' she muttered hoarsely.

Wizz gave a half groan. Whether it was in defeat or with renewed arousal Meredith couldn't tell. His cock had started to wilt slightly though, she noticed. Taking pity on him she reached out with both hands, removed the used condom and began to caress him. After a moment she took one hand away and began to stroke herself.

'See, I haven't nearly finished with you yet,' she said, smiling wickedly in the moonlight.

To prove it she slid a couple of fingers inside her gaping vagina and smeared the resultant juices up the exposed pink flesh of her slit and over the throbbing bud of her clitoris.

Throwing her head back she groaned. The effect of her actions, she was pleased to note, was evident by the growing stiffness between her massaging fingers.

'Oh, that's nice,' she murmured when his fingers joined hers on her swollen sex. 'Mm, yes, just there. That's it.'

They caressed her together and she caressed him until she was able to stretch out her legs and wrap them around his hips. She felt her elation mount as Wizz knelt down and took another condom from his pocket. With a half smile he handed it to her. Ripping open the packet she put the condom on him as though it were a caress. She smoothed the rubber down his stiff shaft, her touch gentle yet arousing.

She gripped him hard with her legs, drawing him toward her until the tip of his cock nudged the entrance to her body.

'Yes, yes!' she cried. 'Fuck me now. Do it!'

Wizz responded with a groan and a hard thrust. Once he was inside her he cupped her aching breasts and buried his face in them.

Grasping his hair, Meredith urged her body against his with greater and greater desperation. Now fully inflamed, her passion was all consuming. Mindlessly scrunching handfuls of his hair in her hands she thrust her breasts at him, her whispered words encouraging him to suck her nipples, squeeze her breasts hard, fuck her harder, faster . . .

Their interlude was finally cut short by the sound of someone calling Wizz's name. By this time he and Meredith were both satiated. They sat side by side on the bench, sharing a cigarette. Meredith looked almost demure with her dress once again concealing her cooling body.

'That sounds like Chris, my mate,' Wizz said.

Meredith smiled lazily at him and she took the cigarette from him for another puff. She didn't usually smoke but just occasionally she enjoyed a few puffs of someone else's cigarette. She supposed it was a bit of a cliché but a smoke after sex always seemed to her the most enjoyable way to wind down. Just like in the films of the sixties and seventies, she mused as she exhaled slowly. Before smoking in front of the camera became politically incorrect.

'You'd better go and see what your friend wants,' she said, offering the cigarette to him.

'No, that's all right. Keep it,' he said. 'Are you sure you don't mind?'

She shook her head and grinned up at him. He was already on his feet and she could see he was at a loss as to what to do about her now.

'No,' she replied honestly, 'I'll just sit here for a minute and finish this,' she waved the cigarette in the air. 'Then I'll go home. I've got a lot to do tomorrow.'

'Here, let me take your number on something.' Wizz patted his trouser pockets agitatedly as though looking for a pen and paper.

'That's OK,' Meredith assured him. 'I expect we'll bump into each other again sometime.'

Wizz still looked doubtful but Meredith assured him that she didn't expect anything else from him. He stooped down and gave her a brief kiss and a few moments later he was gone.

For some time Meredith simply sat and gazed at the stars. She finished the cigarette and ground it underfoot.

'Alone at last.' Alex's sudden presence surprised her. She had been so lost in her contemplation of the night sky and a review of the events that had just taken place, that she had almost forgotten him.

'So it seems,' she murmured. With a slight shrug of her shoulders she turned to smile at him. She didn't want Alex to think that she was unhappy about Wizz's departure.

For a long moment Alex was silent. He leaned forward, hands loosely clasped between his knees and contemplated the ground.

'That was some performance,' he said finally, without looking up.

Studying the back of his head, Meredith had to fight hard to resist the urge to stroke the dark hair that curled over his collar.

'It was what you wanted,' she said. 'What we both wanted. Wasn't it?' She was surprised to find her voice was hesitant, as though she doubted herself as well as him. She shivered and wrapped her arms around herself.

Still with his head bent, his gaze averted, he nodded slowly. 'Oh, yes,' he said in a voice so soft it was barely a whisper, 'it was exactly what I wanted.'

Later, as they drove home in a shared taxi, Alex found himself uncharacteristically lost for words. There was so much he wanted to learn about this young woman. He had witnessed her in her most private moments and yet he hardly knew anything about her. A thousand questions hovered on the tip of his tongue but he felt unable to voice any of them.

As the taxi drew to a halt he came to a sudden decision. Putting out his hand he covered Meredith's hand which rested on her knee. Her skin was cool to the touch and a brief flicker of imagination caused him to wonder what it would feel like to have her hands running over his body.

'I want to thank you,' he said hoarsely, trying to ignore the image of her exploratory caresses. He paused to clear his throat. 'There's no need for us to continue with the game any more if you don't want to.'

If he was surprised by his own depth of feeling, the passion blazing in Meredith's eyes was even more startling.

'Oh, but I want to,' she declared in a tone that brooked no argument. 'This was one of the best nights of my life. I'm not joking,' she added when Alex looked doubtfully at her. 'What you don't seem to understand, Alex, is that I want to do this. Very much. What started out as a bit of teasing has become – oh, I don't know.' She broke off and fell silent. Looking past his shoulder she stared out of the window at the blank night.

'Last night, when you phoned me,' she went on hesitantly, as though she were choosing her words carefully, 'was *the* most exciting night of my life. To meet a complete stranger, knowing that he had watched me indulge in some things that would normally be kept very private, was the most incredible experience. Then to have him call me up and seduce me with soft words and erotic suggestions. Well, I can't tell you how that made me feel.'

'No don't,' she added quickly when Alex opened his mouth to interrupt. 'You helped me to realise that I harbour a lot more than most women. Or maybe not, who knows how many others there are like me out there. But that's not the point. The thing is I am enjoying this. It's only just started and yet I feel as though I was born to it. As though this is the real me and all the time before I was just acting a part. Does that make any sense?'

Raising his head this time, Alex nodded. He gazed deep into her eyes and wished there was some way of letting her know that this was more than just a game to him, or simply self-indulgent erotic titillation.

'Anyway, enough of this idle chatter,' Meredith joked. She nodded in the direction of the taxi driver. 'The cabby must be desperate to get rid of us by now and I need my beauty sleep. It's been a hard day.' Her salacious giggle was cut short by a huge yawn. 'There, you see,' she said. 'To put it bluntly, I'm shagged out. So, thank you very much, Alex. It's been a very pleasant evening and I hope we can do it again some time.' She took his hand and gave it a formal shake. Then she got up and climbed out of the cab.

Somewhat bewildered, Alex followed her. After he'd paid the driver he turned to her.

'Are you sure you don't fancy a coffee or something?' he asked. The suggestion behind his offer was obvious. To his dismay she shook her head firmly.

'No,' she said, 'I told you I'm tired. But thank you for asking and I want you to know that I'm looking forward to our next adventure. Call me. Anytime.'

To Alex, there didn't seem to be anywhere left to go. Meredith had made it clear where she stood. She had drawn the demarcation lines and if he wanted to continue the game it would be up to him.

'OK, I will,' he responded with more confidence than he actually felt. 'I've got something in the pipeline as a matter of fact. Something that will do your career some good as well as—'

'That's great,' she interrupted him. 'Just let me know when and where and I'll be there.' So saying, she smiled sweetly at him, gave him the merest glance of a kiss on the cheek and sauntered off down the tow path.

Meredith thought she'd done pretty damn well with Alex – all things considered. Her act, and that's the only way she could look at it, had been convincing enough for Steven Spielberg let alone someone like Alex. In truth she wished she could have been more honest with him. But, she reasoned, if she'd gone with her feelings then she might have risked losing her chance with him altogether.

I won't be just another quick fuck to him, she said to herself determinedly as she got ready for bed. He'll want me so badly... And, when he does finally get me, he'll damn well want to keep having me. I'll make sure of that. And anyway, she mused as she slipped under the duvet, I'm enjoying the game too much to stop now.

It was her last thought before sleep claimed her sore and aching body.

* * *

For a while Meredith thought she had blown it with Alex. After three days, when he still hadn't made any attempt to contact her, she began to seriously panic. What made matters worse was that she could see him moving about in his flat, though he rarely came to the window. And when he did, it seemed he studiously avoided looking across to her flat.

To compensate, Meredith threw herself wholeheartedly into her work. She enjoyed a brief meeting with Camilla. It was only for an hour or so and much of that time was spent discussing Camilla's forthcoming wedding. Even so, the short bout of sex they enjoyed was enough to quell Meredith's frustration for a little while. Also, it was some consolation that Camilla was thrilled with the lingerie Meredith presented her with and she promised to recommend Meredith to all her friends.

Back at her flat, Meredith still had various orders to fill. Reluctantly she picked up her sewing and it was just as she was engrossed in a particularly tricky bit of stitching – and for once not thinking about Alex at all – that the phone rang. With a sigh of annoyance she put her work down carefully and picked up the cordless phone.

'Yes, can I help you?' she said tersely.

'Meredith, it's me, Alex.'

For a moment Meredith was speechless. Then she recovered and said, 'Alex. How are you?'

'I'm fine, how about you?'

She sensed him smiling that warm, intimate smile as he spoke, which made her toes curl.

'Busy,' she said lightly.

'Too busy to go somewhere tomorrow evening?' Alex asked.

Meredith felt her heart begin to pound. 'When? Where?'

'Do you remember I told you about someone who might possibly be a good contact for you?' he said.

Meredith found herself nodding. Then she realised Alex wouldn't be able to see her. He was not calling from his flat. She'd already seen him go out first thing this morning.

'I remember,' she said. 'Have you managed to set something up then?'

'Oh, yes.' Alex's voice was full of promise. 'I think you'll be delighted with the outcome of this meeting.'

'Well,' Meredith urged, tingles of anticipation stealing over her, 'who's the meeting with – will I have heard of him?' She assumed Alex would be talking about a man.

'I don't know,' Alex responded. 'His name is Cosimo Guiardini. He's the editor of a male fashion magazine.'

Meredith felt her excitement quadruple as he mentioned the name of the magazine. It was one of the market leaders.

'He wants to see some samples of your work,' Alex went on. 'I persuaded him that a photographic spread, giving men sexy gift ideas for their wives and girlfriends, might be a good concept. Fortunately, he agrees with me. He knows as well as I do that the average male hasn't a clue when it comes to women's underwear.'

'Lingerie,' Meredith corrected him automatically. 'No, you're right of course. The imagination of most men seems incapable of extending beyond red and black nylon, crotchless panties, suspenders and peephole bras.'

'Absolutely,' Alex agreed. 'So, can I take it you're quite keen on this idea?'

'Oh, yes,' Meredith said. She hesitated for a moment. 'So – this is just a business meeting – nothing else?'

Alex's throaty chuckle ticked her eardrums.

'Don't be silly,' he said. 'I think you'll be pleasantly surprised by what Cosimo and I have in store for you.'

The intervening hours seemed like torture to Meredith. Try as she might she couldn't concentrate on her work, though the prospect of having to present a good selection of her designs spurred her on to a certain extent. She also had some shopping to do. Alex had made it quite clear that he wouldn't accept anything less than his precise terms of dress.

The smart suit he asked her to wear was easy, Meredith already had a couple of those. But she needed to buy new shoes – higher and spikier than the ones she had worn before – and black stockings. She groaned inwardly at this, noting that even a man as imaginative as Alex could still harbour certain stereotypical notions about dressing sexily.

It was only when Meredith found herself delighting to the sensuality and texture of the sheer nylons, as she rolled them up her legs, that she began to appreciate their aesthetic value. And when she stood up and regarded the reflection of herself, clad only in stockings and suspender belt, that she experienced the singular pleasure of desiring herself.

In her mind she pictured Camilla clad in much the same way and was shocked by the sharp frisson of desire that spiked the thought. There and then she resolved to take Camilla a pair when, or if, she ever saw her again. They hadn't made any definite arrangements.

The suit she chose was also black and tailored to outline every curve of her body. Her choice of lingerie was, naturally, one of her own designs – a black satin pushup bra and matching g-string with a tiny bow positioned to grace the uppermost point of the cleft between her buttocks.

This is it then, she thought, pushing her feet into black leather stilettos and wincing as she stood up. The heels were extremely high, much higher than she was used to, and the toe was quite sharply pointed.

These shoes are a real foot fetishist's dream, she mused as she glanced in the mirror and saw the reflection of her feet. Her naturally high arches were even more defined by the shape of the shoe. And the high heels forced her into adopting an unnaturally provocative stance – shoulders thrown back and spine arched, thereby thrusting her breasts and buttocks into tantalising prominence.

Pausing to take a deep breath for courage, Meredith stooped to pick up her black samples case and gave her reflection one last quick appraisal before picking up her shoulder bag and keys and heading for the door.

'This is the place,' Alex said as the taxi drew to a halt outside a tall, glass-walled building.

He glanced sideways at Meredith, noting with pleasure the soft curve of her cheek, the long feathery lashes, straight nose with a slight uptilt at the tip and full, pouting lips. Without meaning to his gaze drifted down to the slightly gaping neckline of her jacket. Nestling between the edges of her jacket he could see the tantalising, golden mounds of her breasts, revealing that she was wearing very little underneath.

Drawing in his breath sharply he recalled his first sighting of her that evening. It had had the effect of stopping him completely in his tracks. Not used to seeing her in a business suit, he was instantly struck by the contrast between her severe clothing and the soft, womanly body underneath. As always, she wore her hair down and unadorned. Obviously freshly washed, it hung around her shoulders in a sleek, shining curtain.

Alex couldn't help wondering what Cosimo would make of her. Rather a lot if I know Cosimo, he mused wryly, remembering the Italian's penchant for blondes. Straight away Alex realised how unfair he was being to Cosimo. The truth was his friend had a genuine appreciation for women of all types and ages – from children to grandmothers and everyone in between. And they loved him in return.

Bloody hell, some men have all the luck, Alex thought grimly. Then he admonished himself. He wasn't doing too badly really, compared with a lot of guys. And if he didn't have Meredith, well, whose fault was that?

They paused on the pavement before entering the building. With a proprietary air Alex brushed a few stray hairs from Meredith's shoulder. Then he tugged down the hem of her jacket and righted the neckline. As he did so he couldn't help the backs of his fingers brushing the smooth mounds of her breasts. He felt her tremble and wondered if it was with annoyance, or something else. Maybe he was kidding himself but perhaps she did desire him after all.

'Will I do now?' Meredith asked, shrugging him off.

In truth, she didn't think she could bear to let Alex touch her the way he had. The unintentional caress had an electrifying effect on her and she was scared of betraying her true feelings for him. There was a hotel situated on the opposite corner and she had an overpowering urge to suggest they forget all about the meeting and go to the hotel instead.

'You look beautiful,' Alex said truthfully. 'I almost wish–' He broke off hastily. Shit! He'd almost given himself away then.

'Yes?' Meredith gazed innocently at him. Inside, her pulse was racing. Her legs trembled so much she could almost hear her knees knocking together and there was a moistness between her thighs that hadn't been there a few minutes earlier. To her disappointment Alex shook his head.

'Nothing,' he said tersely. 'I think we should go inside now, don't you? We don't want to keep Cosimo waiting.'

Her disappointment was so acute Meredith felt a lump form in her throat. She swallowed deeply, trying to dislodge it.

'No of course not.' She forced a bright smile. 'Lead on McDuff.'

Chapter Eleven

The multi-storey building housed a number of different companies, each having a floor of their own, Meredith discovered. The floor they wanted was the penthouse and so Alex led her over to the lift.

The door of the lift closed behind them, sealing them together in the confined space. And though Alex stood slightly apart from her, Meredith felt his closeness and their aloneness so keenly she could have wept. Desire made her feel that way. The fact that she wanted him and needed him to want her in return had fast become irrefutable.

She sighed inwardly, wondering how could she possibly communicate her feelings to him. It should have been simple – she managed it effortlessly enough with other men. In a similar situation – if she had been alone in a lift with anyone but Alex – she could easily make the most of this opportunity for erotic adventure. She reminded herself that with other men she didn't dread the possibility of her advances being rebuffed. If they were, so what? But with Alex it was different. He mattered to her. And what they did share, though obscure, wasn't worth risking on a capricious whim.

Despite her reasoning half of her felt as though it was worth taking the chance with Alex anyway. She banished the thought immediately. Though she trusted Alex implicitly when it came to the game they had chosen to play, in all other respects he was a complete stranger to her. Not only had she no knowledge of his everyday existence – his goals, or what motivated him – neither did she have any insider knowledge about Alex the person. For goodness sake, I don't even know his last name! she realised all of a sudden. What am I doing here with him?

She realised it was already too late for her to start

backtracking. The digital display on the lift panel showed they only had one more floor to go. Feeling daring she shot Alex's profile a desperate, questioning look. When he glanced round at her she felt all her fears evaporate in an instant. His eyes locked into hers, his penetrating gaze warm and intimate.

'You don't have anything to worry about,' he assured her, misunderstanding her pensive expression. 'Cosimo is a great guy. One of the best.'

'I'm not worried about Cosimo, or the meeting,' she said.

He raised his eyebrows just a fraction. 'What then?' he asked. He reached out, his arm spanning the short divide between them. Then he took her hand and squeezed it reassuringly, his expression now one of concern.

'It's you who worries me,' she admitted, avoiding his searching gaze. 'Or rather me. Oh, God, I don't know. Don't ask me. Forget I said anything.'

To Meredith's surprise Alex touched a button on the lift control panel. The lift stopped immediately.

'What are you doing?' she exclaimed. 'We're trapped in here now. Oh, God. This is my worst nightmare.' Dropping Alex's hand she began to pace nervously back and forth.

With a heavy sigh, Alex grabbed her by her shoulders, halting her in her tracks.

'Stop it, Meredith!' he said sternly. 'What's all this about? Look at me for God's sake.' After a moment, when she still refused to look at him, Alex adopted a gentler tone and lifted her chin so that her eyes were forced to meet his. 'Please, look at me. I don't like seeing you like this.'

She felt lulled by the warmth of his tone and the gentle way his fingers supported her chin. His gaze was deep and searching, sending liquid fire down to her toes.

'I'm sorry,' she mumbled, feeling stupid now, 'I think I must have been having a panic attack or something. I'm all right now,' she added. She felt desperate to reassure him. If he continued to probe too deeply she was scared she might reveal everything to him.

Alex continued to gaze deeply into her eyes. It was as though he was trying to see right into her soul. 'Honestly?' he asked.

'Yes.' Meredith nodded. 'Honestly. Please, forget everything. Let's just go and see your friend.'

Alex still didn't look entirely convinced, she noticed, but he pressed the button again and the lift continued on its upward journey. In seconds it stopped, this time at the penthouse suite.

The lift door slid smoothly open, admitting them straight into a square lobby. The carpeting was dark blue and the lobby was unfurnished save for a tall, blue and white Chinese patterned vase which stood in one corner. The plain cream walls were enlivened by framed covers of various issues of the magazine. Meredith recognised some of them straight away and others she wandered over to look at. Meanwhile, Alex announced their arrival on an internal phone which was attached to the wall.

'Cosimo's secretary will come out for us in a moment,' he told her. 'Are you sure you're feeling OK?'

Meredith turned her head and smiled at him. 'Yes, I told you,' she said. 'Please don't go having second thoughts, I'm not.'

He shook his head disbelievingly. 'If you say so. Believe me, Meredith, whatever else you may think of me I am far from a misogynist. I wouldn't be going to these lengths if I didn't think you wanted me to.'

'Oh, but I do,' she assured him. She spoke the truth. Since they stepped out of the lift she had felt a faint tingle of anticipation which was growing stronger by the second.

At that moment they were interrupted by a door opening. A young woman in a red suit – which should have clashed with the auburn hair piled on top of her head – came up to them.

'Mr Guiardini will see you now,' she said. 'Please, follow me.'

'With pleasure,' Alex murmured.

He was charm itself until the young woman turned back to the door. Then he pretended to wipe his brow before throwing Meredith an ironic look, followed by a broad wink.

Despite the nervous fluttering in her stomach Meredith was forced to stifle a giggle. However little she knew about Alex there was one thing she was certain of – he really was incorrigible.

The young woman sashayed through an outer office which Meredith assumed was hers – judging by the filing cabinets, desk and computer terminal. She stopped outside a black hardwood door and rapped her knuckles smartly on it.

'Come,' a deep voice commanded from within.

Again, Meredith felt like giggling. For God's sake get a grip girl, she warned herself. This is business as well as pleasure remember. As she watched the black door swing slowly open she couldn't help wondering which prospect made her feel more eager – the business or the pleasure.

Her first impression of Cosimo was of a handsome, sophisticated man of indeterminate age. He was seated behind an obscenely large desk, his fingers playing idly with a gold pen as he watched Meredith and Alex approach him.

As she drew closer, Meredith noticed that the man's jet black hair was feathered with silver at the temples and the deep laughter lines around his sloe eyes and full-lipped mouth revealed him to be past the first flush of youth. However, it couldn't be denied that he was exceptionally attractive for an older man. His dark suit was superbly tailored and his fingernails well manicured. Beneath the desk she could see his feet. Crossed at the ankles they were clad in black leather loafers that looked expensive and hand made.

She reminded herself that Cosimo was Italian, and a fashion editor, so of course he would be dressed to perfection. However, there was something about the way he held himself, with a relaxed elegance which, when added to his general air of wealth and confidence, told her his sartorial elegance was inherent.

He didn't bother to get up when Alex and Meredith reached his desk but nodded to two chairs positioned at the side of it. He gave Alex a broad smile and held out his hand to Meredith.

'Hello, Alex,' he said, 'it's good to see you again.' He turned his attention to Meredith. 'And this must be the young woman you told me about.' As he shook her hand he gave her the benefit of a thorough appraisal. The expression in his eyes was genial, with more than a hint of interest.

Straight away Meredith felt herself responding to him. Her cheeks flushed warmly and it took every ounce of willpower not to avert her gaze. Get a grip, she admonished herself for the second time. He's only a man for goodness sake and you're hardly a blushing virgin. Stop being so coy.

'Pleased to meet you, Mr Guiardini,' she said. She was pleased to note her voice hardly shook at all. 'Alex says you may be interested in some of my designs for a magazine layout.'

Cosimo nodded and let go of her hand. 'This is true,' he said, allowing his fingertips to linger caressingly on her palm for a moment before withdrawing them. 'We, that is Alex and I, are of the opinion that men do not know how to treat their women properly. And that includes the gifts they buy for them.'

Forgetting her nervousness, Meredith laughed. 'Yes, all that red see-through nylon and fishnet. I—'

Cosimo held up his hand to silence her. 'Yes, thank you. I have the general idea.'

Meredith forced herself not to hang her head in shame. What is the matter with you, she asked herself, babbling on like some silly teenager?

'I am so sorry,' Cosimo said. His voice was deep and resonant, reminding Meredith of large waves rolling into the shore. 'I didn't mean to be rude. That was unforgivable. It is just that I'm so overwhelmed by your beauty I am finding it hard to concentrate on what you have to say.'

Meredith's lips twitched. 'Very charmingly put, Mr Guiardini,' she countered lightly.

To her surprise he leaned forward, this time taking both her hands in his. 'I am not trying to charm you, Miss Baxter. I am merely stating facts. And please, call me Cosimo.'

She inclined her head. 'Very well, Cosimo,' she said. 'But why don't we drop all the–' She hesitated, the word 'bullshit' hovering on her lips. 'All pretences,' she amended hastily. Reaching down she picked up her samples case and placed it on the desktop. Then she snapped open the catches and raised the lid. 'Here are some samples of my designs. I think you'll agree they cater for every taste.'

Cosimo shared a glance with Alex, then he pulled the case closer to him and began to examine the articles inside.

'This is very attractive,' he said after he had deliberated over the contents of the case for some time. He held up a cream satin bra which was dotted with tiny pink silk rosebuds. Then he turned to Alex. 'This sort of thing is just what I'm looking for. It's very indicative of the Italian and French designs, most of them unfortunately unavailable in England.' Glancing at Meredith, he nodded, 'I suppose there are panties to go with this?'

'Yes,' she replied, rummaging about in the case. 'Three different styles.' She took out a pair of briefs, some bikini pants and a pair that were thong style. She arranged them on his blotter, which she noticed was edged with leather and bore the distinctive Gucci logo. 'Not all women favour the same type of pantie.'

Cosimo nodded approvingly. 'Very astute,' he said, smiling at her as she sat back down. 'And what type do you favour, Miss – er – Meredith?'

Meredith felt her cheeks turning as pink as the rosebuds. 'Well, that very much depends,' she said hesitantly, unused to being asked such a direct and personal question by a client. She was further unnerved by the way Cosimo leaned forward and stared hard at her.

'On what?' he asked.

Clearing her throat, Meredith pondered his question. She supposed the straight answer would be, 'On whoever is likely to see them.'

'It depends on what I'm planning to wear, I suppose,' she said lamely. 'If it was something clingy I would either choose the briefs or the thong, neither present the problem of visible panty line.' She realised her answer sounded stiff and formal . . . and not at all what he wanted to hear.

'And if you were meeting a lover?' Cosimo probed relentlessly, 'What style would you choose then.'

'The thong, definitely,' Meredith countered.

She felt all her muscles tense as she forced herself to gaze levelly at him. If this was going to turn out to be a battle of wills, she was damned if she was going to let him think he had the upper hand. All at once she was unnerved to find he was leaning closer still. So close she could smell his minty breath and the crisp tang of his aftershave. Worse still, she could feel his body warmth enveloping her and her body responding to his animal magnetism. Shifting slightly on her chair, she forced herself to keep her gaze steady. Even when he ran his fingertip lightly up her leg she didn't waver.

The fingertip stopped just beneath the hem of her skirt which reached mid-thigh.

'What type are you wearing now?' he asked in a low voice.

She hesitated, wondering whether to lie. 'I'm wearing a thong style as it happens,' she said truthfully.

His finger began to climb again. Ah, stockings,' he murmured as he encountered a suspender. His finger moved higher still and began to describe small circles on the bare portion of thigh above her stocking top. His caress was mesmerising and seductive.

Meredith inched slightly back in her chair.

A smile played around Cosimo's lips. 'Are you nervous, Meredith?'

She nodded. 'A bit.'

He raised his eyebrows expressively. 'Of me? But there is no need.'

'I've only just met you and already you're investigating my underwear,' she countered in a hoarse voice. 'How should I be expected to feel?'

'Lingerie,' Alex corrected her in an ironic tone.

Feeling as though she was rapidly getting out of her depth, Meredith glanced at him, prepared to offer a counter attack. However, his smile totally disarmed her. Remember why you're here? She reminded herself. Pleasure as well as business. Stop being so standoffish. Chill out.

Instead of glaring at Alex she smiled. She switched her warm gaze to Cosimo.

'I'm sorry,' she said, 'I suppose I've had a bit of rough day.'

At this, Cosimo slapped his palm on his forehead. '*Santo cielo!* Where are my manners? I haven't offered you a drink yet.' He stood up quickly and crossed to a cabinet on the far side of the spacious office. Withdrawing an ice bucket in which nestled a bottle of champagne, he proceeded to pour some of the effervescent liquid into a tall flute glass. He glanced at Meredith, holding the bottle of Dom Perignon aloft. 'Champagne OK?'

She nodded enthusiastically.

'And you, Alex – champagne, or I have a very nice malt?' he said.

'The whisky please,' Alex responded, settling himself more comfortably in his chair.

Cosimo brought their drinks over to them, then resumed his seat in the high-backed leather chair behind his desk. For a while they sipped their drinks in silence. After a few moments Cosimo got up and brought the ice bucket and bottle of malt whisky over and set them down on the desk.

'Indulge yourselves,' he offered, waving his hand expansively. He topped Meredith's glass up and she smiled appreciatively, first at the glass of well chilled, sparkling liquid and then at Cosimo.

'This is lovely,' she said, sighing with pleasure. 'I adore champagne.'

'A woman like you should have only the finest things in life,' Cosimo said. 'I learned a long time ago to settle for nothing less.'

Pausing to sip her drink, Meredith pondered on his flippant remark. How well the other half live, she mused wryly.

'How long have you been an editor?' she asked Cosimo.

He chuckled warmly. 'All my life it seems,' he said. 'But seriously, I have been in this business for quite some time. I started as a humble journalist in Milan and worked my way up to this.' Using his hand he indicated his huge, shades-of-blue office and the panoramic view of London's skyline through the window behind him.

Typically Italian, he used his hands all the time while he was talking, Meredith noticed. And she was having difficulty coming to terms with the notion of him ever being 'humble'.

'It must be fascinating,' she murmured, raising her glass to her lips once again.

Cosimo nodded. 'Ah, yes. It is,' he said, 'but not nearly as fascinating as you.'

Meredith couldn't help marvelling at the way Cosimo managed to grasp every opportunity to flatter her. He had a way of speaking, of turning her words around, so they were directed back at her. This particular characteristic of his made her doubt his sincerity.

She reminded herself that she had no intention of marrying the guy and so it hardly mattered. Her best option would be to simply give in gracefully and enjoy the attention while it lasted. Leaning back she crossed her legs. She dangled the wineglass from her fingertips and regarded him in a thoughtful, if provocative way. Now she was waiting for him to make the next move.

Cosimo refilled all their glasses after a moment or two. Then he gave Meredith a very direct look.

'Would you mind taking off your clothes?' he said.

Meredith nearly choked on her champagne. 'What?'

She felt a tremor start from the tips of her toes and reverberate through her whole body. She realised she could see herself reflected in the dark, shiny marbles of his eyes.

'I said, would you mind taking off your clothes,' he repeated smoothly, his words doing nothing to calm her. 'I would be interested to see your personal choice of lingerie.' Ignoring Meredith's stunned expression he turned to Alex. 'What I always find fascinating,' he continued in a conversational way, 'is the way designers dress themselves. Often their personal taste is totally opposed to the designs they produce for the public.'

Though she found Cosimo's request astounding, Meredith couldn't help privately agreeing with him. As far as she'd noticed, most fashion designers looked a fright. Confident that her underwear would not betray her innate sense of style, and wanting desperately to call his bluff, Meredith stood up and began unbuttoning her jacket.

Ignoring the interested stares of the men, she shrugged off her jacket, hung it neatly on the back of her chair, then proceeded to unzip her skirt. As it hovered on her hips she paused. What the hell was she doing?

'Please,' Cosimo entreated. He turned and tugged repeatedly at a cord behind him until the vertical blinds were almost closed. 'There is that better?' he asked. 'Now no one will be able to see you but Alex and I.'

Meredith shrugged making her conscious of her breasts and the way they jiggled in the black satin cups of her bra. She allowed the skirt to fall to her ankles. When she stooped to pick it up from the floor she heard the men draw in their breath sharply. The skirt joined her jacket. Forcing herself to stay calm she turned around to face them. She wasn't ashamed of her body and was surprised to find herself enjoying their appreciative stares.

'As you can see,' she said in a saleswoman tone, 'this design is both attractive and comfortable. I would have no hesitation in choosing it for everyday wear.'

'If you wore that around me every day, neither of us would ever get any work done,' Alex said. He bit his lip, horrified that he'd managed to let such an admission slip out.

Meredith too was surprised. But pleasantly so. At last, she thought. I have confirmation that Alex sees me as a real woman and not just a playing piece in our 'game'.

'I mean *under* clothes,' she said dryly. Nevertheless, her smile, she felt, gave her away.

For a moment, it seemed, time stood still as she and Alex gazed mutely at each other. Tacit questions, answers and affirmations flew from one to the other, transmitted only by their eyes.

At length, Cosimo interrupted their mutual seduction. 'Turn around please, Meredith,' he said, taking up the reins again.

Conscious that every move she made now would enchant Alex, Meredith turned without argument. Obediently, she posed this way and that according to Cosimo's instructions.

'Come here,' he said eventually, holding out his hands to her.

Moving a chair out of the way, she walked up to him. He pushed his own chair back and motioned to her to stand directly in front of him with her back to his desk.

'Closer,' he breathed seductively. 'Come closer.'

Despite her determination to remain level headed, Meredith felt herself trembling as she moved into the space between Cosimo's open thighs. She felt her knees brush the soft leather of his chair and stopped.

'Is that close enough?' she asked boldly, looking down at him.

Close to, she could see that his hair appeared wiry, as though it was meant to have a curl in it. It was a deep jet black, with only a few silver threads. And thick, so thick there was no hint of pink scalp. Not even on the top of his head where the hair would normally start to thin out.

'You have a good head of hair,' she said, reaching out to run her fingers through it. To her surprise it didn't feel wiry at all but soft and springy.

Cosimo chuckled. 'Thank you,' he said, obviously amused by her observation. 'No woman has ever commented on my hair before. Usually they compliment my eyes, or my mouth, or–' He paused and laughed again. 'This time, Meredith noticed, his laughter was a little self-conscious.

She raised an eyebrow. 'Or?' she persisted wickedly.

'Or my prick,' he said, meeting her challenging stare full on. 'I am told I am rather large.'

Meredith tried but failed to stifle a smile. Oh, wasn't he just typical? she mused wryly. When it came down to it, all men had a sensitive spot and it was usually located just below their navel.

'Haven't you heard, size isn't everything,' she murmured, smiling.

Cosimo's eyes creased beguilingly at the corners as he returned her smile.

'*Touché*,' he said, 'but I wasn't boasting, merely stating a fact.'

Meredith pursed her lips but she knew amusement and a fair amount of erotic interest danced in her eyes.

'If you don't mind, I would like to feel the fabric,' he said, reaching up and running his fingers lightly over the cups of her bra.

Meredith felt herself trembling. There was no question of it, his touch was seductive and the champagne she had drunk had left her feeling light headed and carefree. Damn my precarious inhibitions, she found herself thinking as Cosimo continued to stroke his fingers over her breasts. They loosen all too easily.

After a moment, Cosimo's fingers drifted to her suspender belt and then to the front of her g-string. Ostensibly appreciating the good quality satin she had used on this design, he slipped a couple of fingers under the elastic and rubbed the delicate fabric between his fingers and thumb.

Meredith felt her stomach clench. There was hardly anything to the g-string, just a tiny triangle of satin to the front, which barely covered her pubic mound, and a thin ribbon at the back which snuggled into the cleft between her buttocks. Tingles of excitement ran through her as the backs of his fingers brushed over her pubic hair.

She had trouble focusing properly when he glanced up at her face. His fingers were still examining the satin but now he moved his hand slowly from side to side, the back of it deliberately stroking her pubis. She gasped as he moved his hand a bit lower and his knuckles grazed her outer labia, nudging them apart.

It was as though he had touched her magic button. She could feel her body responding, her moisture increasing and her clitoris and labia swelling and becoming hot and sensitised. To her disappointment he withdrew his hand and stroked it slowly over the curve of her hip. Using both hands he followed the sinuous lines of her body, tracing them with a featherlight touch from armpit to knee. After a few delicious moments of this Meredith felt totally mesmerised.

'Turn around,' he commanded softly, 'and bend forward.'

As if in a dream, Meredith turned. She leaned forward, resting her forearms on the blotter on his desk. Clasping her hands as if in prayer she felt Cosimo's warm breath caress her jutting bottom. She started in surprise as he unexpectedly pulled at the ribbon bisecting her buttocks. It chafed at the delicate flesh there and the satin between her legs was forced between her vaginal lips. She knew her wetness would be obvious to both men and could visualise the contrast between her creamy moisture and the black satin. The dark pink of her sex would provide yet another contrast, she realised and gasped again as she felt Cosimo arrange the satin so that it was pulled tight between her outer lips.

Once again he began to tug gently at the material, working it back and forth so that it rubbed remorselessly against her swollen clitoris and the sensitive puckered flesh of her anus. The caress of the silk upon her most intimate flesh was rhythmic and sensual and she burned with shame as she felt Cosimo bringing her effortlessly to full arousal without actually touching her.

Pain distracted her slightly as she deliberately dug her nails into the palms of her hands. She tried to hold on, to fight him. Presently she heard herself panting and with a sense of inevitability she gave into the wave after wave of hot, aching lust that swamped her.

As her orgasm began to subside she slumped limply upon the desk and rested her burning forehead on the smooth wood. Her whole body felt weak and trembly and she offered no resistance as she felt Cosimo slide her panties down her legs. He raised her feet for her, so that she could step out of the tiny scrap of satin, then positioned them so that her legs were spread.

Resting face down, she was dimly aware of Alex seated somewhere behind her, gazing at her exposed body. It would be the closest view he'd had of her, she realised, the very thought sending fresh tingles of arousal through her. And what of Cosimo? she wondered. Were his plans for her submissive body purely sensual, or more humiliating? Maybe he was a sadist.

She trembled and burned at the thought of him fucking her. Though she was desperate to have her empty body filled by a hard, thrusting cock she was aware that Cosimo didn't seem to share her urgency. If anything his touch, when it came, was light and exploratory. As his fingers gently stroked her quivering sex she marvelled at his self-control, her amazement gradually turning to frustration as he did nothing more than caress her.

Realising it was up to her, she began to move her hips in a tantalising way. Straightening up, with palms flat on the desk top, she gave Cosimo a provocative glance over her shoulder. Her long blonde hair fell over her face and she flicked it away, trying not to let her impatience show.

'Wouldn't you like to take me like this?' she asked, wriggling her bottom.

Glancing up, Cosimo smiled enigmatically. 'Of course,' he said.

Thrilled at her success, Meredith arched her back and deliberately thrust her bottom toward his face. To her dismay he deftly averted his face from her eagerly proffered flesh and broadened his smile. He glanced at Alex.

'*Accidento*, this girl is impatient, Alex!' he said, grinning wolfishly back at her.

Meredith frowned and in retaliation he thrust a couple of fingers deep inside her.

'Bastard!' she gasped, enjoying the game. Provocation always made her hot. She ground herself wantonly against his hand as his probing fingers stroked her inner flesh.

He found her g-spot easily and massaged it until Meredith began to pant again. She could feel her juices trickling out of her and groaned loudly when she felt a tongue lapping at her desperate sex flesh.

'Oh, God. Oh, yes,' she moaned, spreading her legs wider still and cupping her breasts.

She caressed them mindlessly as she gyrated her hips, rubbing her hot flesh eagerly over Cosimo's mouth and lips. Another wave of desire swept over her as she felt his other fingers spreading her labia wide apart. They brushed her clitoris, the piquancy of the caress startling her. After a moment she felt Cosimo's tongue flicker over her swollen bud, pushing her closer and closer to the edge.

Pulling down her bra cups she grasped her aching nipples and pinched them hard. They felt hot and swollen, as if they would burst. Then, as if from nowhere a second pair of hands appeared and took control of her breasts. Half out of her mind with desire, Meredith glanced up. Through the damp strands of hair that streaked her face she saw Cosimo's secretary.

Though their eyes met, the young woman's expression was inscrutable. It was as though she had come into the office and started to take dictation. Averting her gaze, Meredith watched the slim, pale hands cupping her breasts. She moved, taking her weight on her elbows to give the young woman better access to her aching globes.

There was no question of asking her to stop. Meredith felt overwhelmed by a sense of fatality, as though everything that happened to her in this office was entirely beyond her control. Alex had arranged this for their mutual enjoyment and she was wholly prepared to submit to it.

Chapter Twelve

With Cosimo's fingers inside her, his tongue stroking her clitoris and the young redhead's fingers working feverishly at her nipples, Meredith was hardly surprised that she came in moments. More than a simple orgasm, it seemed like an eruption and one that rocked her to her very core.

Afterwards, Cosimo raised her gently and sat her down in his own chair. The leather felt soft and warm against her naked bottom and thighs and Meredith sprawled in it, aware only of the perspiration drying on her skin and the flesh that still pulsated between her spread thighs.

At a nod of instruction from Cosimo, the redhead topped up the flute glass with champagne and handed it to Meredith. She didn't speak to either of the men present, nor to Meredith but her eyes conveyed messages that Meredith felt too exhausted to decipher.

Cosimo squatted down beside Meredith and tenderly cupped her chin, turning her face so that she was looking directly at him.

'Alex is going to leave us now, Meredith,' he said. He spoke slowly, enunciating each word carefully as though speaking to a child. 'He will go into another room where he can observe us on close-circuit TV.' He pointed to a number of small, tube-like cameras positioned high up on the walls.

Meredith followed his moving finger as if in a daze.

'You do understand, don't you, Meredith?' Cosimo prompted.

Slowly, as if she were moving underwater, Meredith nodded. She tried to smile but found her mouth didn't seem to be working properly.

Taking a sip of her champagne to wet her dry throat Meredith said, 'Yes, I understand.'

Though she still felt rapturously languid, Meredith felt her pulse quicken again as Alex stooped over her and planted a kiss on her forehead.

'Don't worry about anything,' he murmured to her. 'You can trust Cosimo. Just enjoy what happens next. Promise me?'

She gave him a faint smile. 'I promise.'

As she watched Alex walk across the office and disappear through a different door to the one they had entered by, Meredith slowly felt herself return to normal. She sipped her champagne and wondered what the next move was going to be.

She didn't have to wait very long. As soon as Alex had gone Cosimo opened the top right hand drawer of his desk. Inside was a small console of buttons. When he pressed one of them a large bookcase slid across the wall to reveal a hidden room.

Craning her neck Meredith saw that the interior of the room was heavily shaded. All she could make out was a huge bed covered in midnight blue satin.

'My home away from home,' Cosimo explained. 'Often I work late – too late according to Nadine here.' He paused and flashed his secretary a sheepish grin. 'When that happens I sleep here.'

I bet that's not all you do on those satin sheets, Meredith found herself thinking. All at once she felt a quickening sensation inside her. Excitement reared its tantalising head as she realised Cosimo had no intention of using the bed for sleeping on now either.

'I suppose you and I–' she began, glancing at the bed and then at Cosimo.

To her frustration he shook his head. An enigmatic smile played about his lips.

'Then me and Nadine?' she glanced at the secretary and found herself wondering what it would be like to caress that pale alabaster flesh. Did the heart of a siren lurk beneath that efficient façade?

Annoyingly, Cosimo shook his head again.

Meredith began to find herself running out of patience. 'Then I may as well get dressed,' she said brusquely, making as if to get up.

'My, you are an impatient one, Meredith,' Cosimo said,

placing a gentle but restraining hand on her shoulder. 'But I appreciate your spirit. It makes the game more interesting.'

Sinking back into the butter soft leather, Meredith regarded him thoughtfully.

'Alex has told you about our game?' she asked.

'Of course,' Cosimo said. He reclined against the edge of his desk and picked up his whisky tumbler.

They both sipped their drinks in silence for a moment. Then, without warning, Cosimo put his glass down and reached into the open drawer again. This time he withdrew a long silk scarf. For a few moments he toyed with the sky blue silk, drawing it through his hands, gradually pulling it into a long, narrow strip.

All at once it occurred to Meredith that he intended to use it to bind her in some way – perhaps her wrists?

'I'm not into bondage,' she said quickly as he moved towards her. To further thwart him, she sat on her hands. To her chagrin, both Cosimo and Nadine laughed.

'I intend to blindfold you, Meredith, not tie you up,' Cosimo said, speaking to her as though she were a child again.

Meredith wanted to argue that she wasn't stupid, that she realised what he wanted to do but realised any counter attack would be pointless. She had misread his intentions. Still, the thought of being blindfolded instead of tied up didn't exactly quell her nerves.

She began to shake her head. 'I'm not sure if I—'

Cosimo silenced her argument by placing a finger upon her lips. 'Please stop fighting me, Meredith,' he said gently. 'Remember how you felt just now. When you finally conceded to my whim.'

Meredith felt herself going hot and cold as she remembered.

Taking her silence as acquiescence, Cosimo placed the strip of silk across her eyes. Nadine lifted Meredith's hair at the back allowing Cosimo to knot the scarf behind her head.

'There now, *cara mia*,' he crooned, stroking her face and shoulders soothingly. 'You will enjoy this, I promise you.'

'I'll take your word for that,' Meredith muttered ungraciously. She had begun to tremble with apprehension again but Cosimo's subtle caresses were having a tranquillising effect on her. All at once, as Cosimo and Nadine helped her to stand up and began to guide her across the room, something else occurred to her. 'If you and Nadine are not going to give me all this pleasure you've promised,' she said. 'Then who do you intend—?'

Cosimo shushed her. 'So many questions, Meredith,' he admonished softly. 'Just relax and trust us. Alex knows what is going to happen to you – and who with. He has vetted them himself. You know he wouldn't allow anyone – how shall we say? – undesirable, to enjoy your gorgeous body.'

Meredith fell silent. She couldn't help fixating on Cosimo's use of the plural when he referred to her unknown lovers – for some reason she had imagined only one other person would be involved. Nor could she begin to grasp the trouble Alex must have taken to set this little scenario up. No wonder it had taken him several days to contact her again.

'OK,' she conceded with a shrug, 'I trust you and Alex.'

It seemed as though she had been lying in the still, dark room for hours. From time to time Nadine came in and helped Meredith to sit up and sip some more champagne. And just once Cosimo sat down beside her and apologised for the delay.

'This wasn't meant to happen,' he said, sounding anxious. 'Apparently the traffic is murder out there.'

Inexplicably, Meredith started to giggle. She had drunk far too much champagne and now all she could think about were faceless men, coming from all directions, anxiously fighting their way through the London traffic to get to her.

'I hope they'll think I am worth all the trouble,' she mused aloud.

To her surprise Cosimo touched his mouth to hers. His tongue forced her lips apart and tantalised her gums. Meredith was still reeling from the shock of his kiss when he took his mouth away.

'Of course they will, who wouldn't?' he said gruffly. 'Ah, *per amore di Dio!* Those superb breasts, that lovely wet pussy, so soft, so fragrant – why they will consider themselves the luckiest men and women on earth.' As he spoke he touched her in the places he mentioned, caressing her breasts and between her parted thighs with agonizingly tantalising strokes of his fingertips.

'Men *and* women?' Meredith repeated in a husky voice. She squirmed under Cosimo's sensual touch, feeling her desire spark and flame all over again.

'There,' Cosimo said, sounding satisfied, 'that is better now, no?' Parting her outer lips gently, he began to stroke her clitoris.

'Oh, yes,' Meredith breathed, feeling herself skyrocket toward the stars again, 'that's much better.'

Her rise toward orgasm was frustrated by the arrival of Cosimo's expected guests. Coming from the outer office Meredith heard the sound of four distinct voices, two male and two female. They all spoke in Italian and when Nadine answered in their native tongue the combination of musical tones sounded like an operetta. A moment later Cosimo left her and soon his voice joined the chorus.

Meredith lay on the bed feeling abandoned and highly aroused. Thanks to Cosimo's expert handling of her body she now awaited the arrival of her unseen 'lovers' with impatience.

She sensed them come into the room. Hushed murmurs told her they were appraising her body, which was clad only in the black bra, stockings and suspender belt; her g-string long since discarded.

Deprived of her sight, Meredith felt all her other senses more acutely tuned. She felt the mattress give on either side of her and the mingled caresses of clothing, long hair and warm breath on her skin told her that all four were grouped around her. The combined scent of the women's perfume and the men's aftershave was heady but not unpleasant and Meredith heard herself whimper with pleasure as deft, unseen fingers tucked the cups of her bra under her breasts.

'*Bella*,' came the unified response to the revelation of her breasts. '*Bellissima!*'

Eager hands caressed her then, the women's fingers decipherable from the men's because of their long nails and lighter touch. The hands were everywhere, stroking her hair, her face, her shoulders, her torso ... They moulded themselves around her breasts and followed the contours of her legs. Frustratingly, none of them touched her sex. Not at first.

Then, when came the first featherlight caress on her vulva, Meredith found herself jerking her hips up in dramatic response.

Her body had been primed by Cosimo, she realised. And she was further aroused by the reality of so many unseen hands and eyes enjoying her body at the same time.

'Yes!' she cried encouragingly. 'Yes, touch me there. Stroke me. Lick me. Oh, God, make me come!'

As fingers slipped inside the wet, waiting channel of her vagina she felt soft feminine lips brush her face. A sweet, musky scent filled her nostrils and when she reached out blindly with her tongue it encountered the delicate petals of woman flesh.

She lapped eagerly, her hips still churning to the tune invoked on her lower body by probing, stroking fingers. A tongue on her clitoris made her cry out and she almost choked. Her mouth was full of fragrant, sensual flesh and her blindly grasping hands encountered softly rounded buttocks and, in contrast, a thick, stiff cock.

The owner of the cock tried to pull away. 'This is not for our pleasure but yours,' a masculine voice said. There was a pause then he added, 'Maria you are a naughty girl, offering your pussy in such a way.'

'No, no that's all right,' Meredith managed to gasp out. 'I want to. With both of you. It is giving me pleasure.' She grasped the cock more tightly and was pleased to hear the man groan.

'If you are sure,' he said huskily.

Meredith hoped the way she caressed his thick stem was proof enough. Above her, she felt the girl, Maria, in the throes of orgasm. Her body shuddered and her clitoris nudged Meredith's tongue repeatedly as if she were simply using Meredith's mouth as a way to bring herself off. A moment later Meredith was rewarded by the sensation of warm, sticky fluid coating her hand and more flooding her mouth. A double whammy, she thought deliriously as she licked the honeyed juices from her lips.

Now she had succeeded in pleasuring two people simultaneously, Meredith felt able to allow herself to sink into the luxury of her own orgasm. She gave herself up to the sensuous caresses which left no part of her body untouched and let out an enormous cry of joy as her orgasm was ripped from her writhing body.

That night was like no other. Lost in her own dark world of

sensuality and bliss, Meredith experienced the hitherto unknown pleasure of having four lovers at once. Gentle, feminine fingers and hands stroked where strong masculine ones had a moment ago, though she couldn't say whether the tongues that entered her were male or female. There seemed no end to it and nor did she want it to end.

Finally, she heard herself calling out to be fucked. It was the only thing that hadn't happened to her all evening and by this time she felt a need bordering on desperation.

'My pleasure, if you don't mind, Meredith,' she heard a familiar voice whisper in her ear at long last.

'Oh, yes, Cosimo, I'd love it to be you,' Meredith gasped.

Gradually all other hands receded from her body and she felt herself being turned over. Strong hands smoothed over her shoulders and a tongue flickered tantalisingly down the length of her spine. It stopped at the crest of her buttocks and Meredith found herself raising her hips, offering herself wantonly to him.

'Now, now!' she urged, arching her spine so that her bottom jutted into the air.

She circled her hips and was pleased to feel those same strong hands covering her buttocks. The splayed fingers massaged her flesh and in a moment she felt the delicious sensation of Cosimo's glans nudging her vaginal lips apart. He grasped her hips, drawing her to her knees and thrusting deeply, right to the hilt.

With her face buried in the satin sheets Meredith smothered her gasps of pleasure. After a moment, when Cosimo remained motionless inside her, she was able to raise the top half of her body and allow her forearms to take her upper body weight.

Then he began to move inside her with slow, measured strokes, eliciting every possible ounce of pleasure. Gradually she picked up his rhythm and worked her pelvis against his. She could feel his balls slapping against her thighs and his cock stretching and tantalising her woman flesh. As his pace increased so his fingertips dug harder into her hips. Meredith felt her breath coming in short, sharp gasps. Perspiration trickled between her breasts and she lowered her upper body so that the hard buds of her nipples brushed sensuously against the fine satin.

She felt suffused by sensation and though she sensed that he was holding back for her benefit Meredith couldn't stop herself from coming and coming . . .

Eventually, as her strong vaginal muscles tightened around Cosimo's hard shaft for the umpteenth time she heard him groan loudly. His body jerked against hers and after delivering a few more slow, deep strokes, he withdrew from her. A few moments later she felt his hand stroking her shoulders and his lips brush her cheek.

'Enough?' he murmured.

Slumping face down on the bed, Meredith smiled contentedly.

'Enough,' she said.

Having lost all sense of time and space, Meredith was surprised to see the first purplish light of dawn tinting the dark sky outside. She clung to Alex's arm like a limpet feeling as though she needed all the support he could offer her. Her body felt heavy, her legs leaden and it seemed as though her feet literally dragged across the pavement as Alex helped her into the waiting minicab.

It was not until the taxi drew away from the kerb that Alex finally spoke to her.

'Are you feeling all right?'

Meredith nodded, feeling absurdly grateful for his concern. She hadn't been able to help wondering if she had finally overstepped the mark with him. Surely he couldn't respect her now, after all that had happened in Cosimo's office.

Her emotions were in turmoil. At once she felt both elated and abused. Only Alex's opinion of her exploits would give her the salvation she craved. No matter how often she reminded herself that all that had happened had been Alex's idea, she still couldn't help feeling as if she had betrayed him somehow – and possibly herself.

Mustering all her courage she glanced sideways at him. Though in profile, she could see his face was expressionless.

'Alex?' she began.

He turned his head and to her relief his eyes were warm as they glanced across her face.

'Don't even say it,' he murmured, touching his fingers to her face at the same time.

His fingers traced the contour of her cheek and when he rested his palm flat against the side of her face Meredith allowed herself to relax against it. Like a cat she rubbed her face against his palm. The gesture was so comforting she almost purred.

He leaned forward, his lips brushing the hair away from her forehead. They felt dry and warm and against her feverish skin. Then he drew back from her again, leaving his hand in place. His fingertips entwined in the roots of her hair and he began to massage her scalp gently.

They travelled like that all the way to their respective homes. Neither speaking. The one simply content to caress, and the other content to be caressed. Through eyes heavy-lidded with fatigue they gazed through the windows of the cab and watched the dawn breaking over city streets that were already filling up as the new day began.

Once again, Meredith felt slightly let down when she and Alex parted company. It was true they were both dog tired but was that any reason to break the spell that bound them? Or was their closeness merely a figment of her imagination? Meredith wondered. Did she want him so badly that she would deliberately misinterpret his words and his gestures toward her?

'Well, Meredith, once again a parting of the ways,' Alex said lightly. He chucked her under the chin and assumed an American twang as he added, 'You were really something kiddo.'

'Yes, I was, wasn't I,' Meredith concurred. She hoped her deliberate immodesty would cover up her true feelings, which she felt sure were written all over her face. Take me to bed, was what she really wanted to say. Let me spend all day making love to you.

She was disappointed when Alex glanced at his watch. 'I just have time for a shower and a coffee before I have to be on set,' he groaned.

'Oh, dear,' Meredith sympathised, realising how selfish her thoughts were. She must remember that Alex had a life that didn't include her. 'Is it far away?'

He mentioned a location south of the river that she had never heard of.

'It's on a disused garage lot of all places,' he said with a wry chuckle. Briefly he explained what he was working on.

Meredith hugged this new information to her. It was the first time he had opened up and told her anything about himself. One small step, she mused, but a giant leap for womankind.

She smiled. 'Well, I mustn't keep you.'

For a few moments they both lingered awkwardly, as though neither wanted to be the first to break away. But, finally, Alex leaned forward and kissed her cheek lightly.

'See you then, Meredith,' he said.

'Yeah,' she replied, unable to disguise the longing in her voice, 'see you, Alex.'

Up in his flat, Alex closed the door on the outside world and sagged against it, feeling as though he had no energy left in him whatsoever. It had taken every last ounce of strength to behave in such an offhand manner with Meredith. And leaving her on the tow path had been like wrenching one of his own legs off and leaving it behind – and that was no mean feat for a dancer.

Despite his weariness, Alex smiled at the analogy. You're going soft in your old age, he told himself as he straightened up and headed for the bathroom. Do you seriously think a girl as wonderful as Meredith is going to be interested in you? His immediate response was, why not? But he already knew why not. Because Meredith was not like any other woman he had ever met. She was a beautiful, sexually sophisticated enigma. She allowed him to dictate the pace of the game solely because it suited her. Her needs. If they had met under any other circumstances, she wouldn't have given him a second glance.

Alex truly believed this. In the shower he allowed himself the luxury of mentally replaying the scenes from the night before. The whole thing had worked out superbly. Far better than he could have hoped. And that was in no small way due to Meredith herself. How many women could embrace their sexuality as totally as she did – to take such pride and delight in her own body?

It came as no surprise to Alex to find his cock stiffening as he recalled the way her body had blossomed under Cosimo's skilful touch. It had truly been a sight to behold and it had taken every ounce of willpower he possessed to keep himself from touching her. Time and again he'd had to remind himself that his role in the game was as a voyeur, not a participant. Still, it didn't stop him from mentally putting himself in Cosimo's place and imagining that it had been his fingers and cock that had entered her inviting portal.

As the warm water cascaded over him he took pleasure in the fantasy. The sensation of water droplets rebounding off his stiff shaft merely added to his arousal. In his mind the warm wetness engulfing him came from deep inside Meredith's body. Switching the spray from a steady flow to a massaging jet, he positioned himself deliberately so that the pulsating jet was concentrated on his cock. Holding it under the relentless beat of the water, he began to stimulate himself with swift, sure strokes . . .

'For Chrissakes, Alex, you look as though you've been run over by a steamroller!' Regina greeted him as he strolled on to the lot an hour later. 'I don't need to ask what sort of night you've had.'

'Well, you'd be wrong,' Alex countered.

Clearly disbelieving, Regina gave him an arch look. 'When are we going to get together again, Alex?'

'Not now, Regina,' Alex muttered. 'We've got work to do.'

'Fine,' she said, turning her back on him huffily. 'You take that attitude, Alex. See if I care.'

As he watched the young black woman stride away from him, her full hips twitching angrily under lime green lycra, Alex groaned. This was the last thing he needed. And he didn't like the way she managed to make him feel so guilty. It wasn't as though he'd promised to marry her or anything. It had just been a fuck.

A moment later Lisa Blair arrived, making Alex groan again. He hadn't been expecting her on the set today and he could tell, just by her general brisk air, that she was fighting fit and wouldn't be taking any prisoners. Just what I need, he mused, feeling his spirits slump even further. Two women on my case.

Only the intense, stifling heat of the midday sun managed to wake Meredith. Even though her head had been full of the previous night's events and her confusion over Alex, she had managed to fall straight into a deep and surprisingly restorative sleep. Now, some seven hours later, she awoke to the sensation of the sheet clinging damply to her perspiring body.

'Bloody hell,' she gasped, as she came awake, 'What temperature is it today?' Pausing only to open her bedroom window to let some fresh air in, she tumbled into the bathroom and straight under the shower.

It was only as she walked into the kitchen, stark naked, did she remember that at some point while she was asleep she had dreamed of seducing Alex. Resting her bare behind against the counter top as she waited for the kettle to boil she brought the dream fully to mind. Although some of the points were hazy the key factor in her dream had been her assertiveness.

You've been too submissive up to now, she told herself. Perhaps Alex doesn't like that in a woman. She reminded herself that what had started out as a two-way street had quickly developed into something entirely different. Stop being a pawn, Meredith, she warned herself firmly. Take control now or you're going to lose your chance with him for ever.

When Alex finally arrived home the first thing he did was walk to the window and stare across the canal to Meredith's flat. He couldn't tell if she was home or not, she wasn't seated at her cutting table. Feeling disappointed he decided to take a nap. It had been a gruelling day and to cap it all, he hadn't been able to argue when Regina insisted on inviting herself over to his flat that evening.

One quick drink and she's out of here, Alex promised himself as he stretched out on the bed, still fully dressed. No funny business. And definitely no fucking. Just one drink and that's all . . .

Meredith was feeling like Mata Hari. When Alex had walked straight up to his window she had had to flatten herself against the wall so he wouldn't see her. Convinced that he might be feeling too exhausted to carry on working and knock off early, she had been looking out for him since about three o'clock onwards. Naturally, his actual return had caught her while she was temporarily off her guard and she had rushed to the window only to dive for cover the moment she realised he was going to look into her flat.

Her plan, such as it was, was still a bit fuzzy around the edges and she felt thwarted when he turned away from the window almost immediately. For twenty minutes she waited, still in hiding and just peeking around the corner occasionally, until she finally accepted he had found something else to occupy him and wouldn't be coming back to the window just yet.

Skirting around the edges of the room, lest he should catch a glimpse of her, Meredith made her way to her bedroom. She sat down on the bed and picked up the piece of paper by the telephone. This was it – her secret weapon. The question was, did she dare use it?

It hadn't needed much ingenuity to find out Alex's telephone number. A bit of sweet-talk to their joint caretaker was all it took. As she turned the scrap of paper with the number scribbled on it over in her hands, she recalled something one of her old school teachers had been fond of saying: knowledge is power.

Well, she thought, picking up the phone decisively. I have the knowledge and therefore the power, now I'm going to use it.

Alex was deeply asleep when the phone rang. Gradually, the sound of the ringing filtered through his unconscious state and took the form of a dream.

'Alex, is that you?'

'Meredith?' Even fast asleep, Alex recognised her voice instantly. He was surprised to find his heart was beating fast inside his inert body.

'I'm coming across to see you tonight, Alex,' Meredith said. 'You will be in, won't you?'

'For you, anything.'

'Good, that's what I like to hear.' There was a pause during which Alex dreamed he rolled over and held the receiver more firmly to his ear.

'Are you still there?' he whispered.

'Yes,' came the reply. 'I'm still here. Hearing your voice I just had to touch myself. I'm doing it now. Stroking all those places you saw so clearly last night. Do you remember, Alex?'

'Remember?' He cleared his throat hastily, feeling his cock start to rise. 'How could I forget?'

'Good,' Meredith murmured back. 'Well, hold on to that memory, Alex. Tonight we're going to take the game on to the next stage.'

Alex hung on, waiting for her to say something else. His only reward was the soft 'click' as she disconnected the call.

When he finally awoke it was to find he had had a wet dream. The sheet was moulded around his groin and when it peeled it away from his sticky body he groaned. Christ! He thought, feeling ashamed. This hasn't happened to me since I was a teenager.

Immediately he recalled his dream about Meredith calling him. No wonder I shot my load, he thought wryly as he got up stiffly and began to strip the bed. Shame it *was* only a dream.

A glance at the clock beside his bed showed he still had time for a shower and a bite to eat before Regina turned up. He amended his thoughts about her proposed visit to his flat. Despite the physical proof that he had orgasmed, his dream had left him feeling oddly frustrated and unfulfilled. Perhaps he would let Regina stay a bit longer than he'd originally intended, he mused, recalling the young black girl's enthusiastic approach to sex. If he couldn't have the real object of his desire – well, any port in a storm . . .

Chapter Thirteen

Meredith dressed with care that evening. She wanted to look casual yet seductive. Which was no mean feat, she mused, for a woman who felt something akin to a bitch on heat. She chuckled, imagining herself walking into Alex's flat and then wandering around him, sniffing, like a dog would do. I wonder if he's ever been sniffed before, she thought as she picked up her eyeliner pencil and prepared to do battle with her too-small eyes. It could certainly add something to the usual ritual of foreplay.

She finally decided upon a short dress in aquamarine silk. It contrasted beautifully with her golden tan and the long, silky strands of her hair which fell in a pale blonde curtain around her shoulders. Feeling daring, she dispensed with any thoughts of lingerie and instead let the cool silk slide down over her naked body. It fitted her like a sheath, moulding itself around the curves of her breasts, hips and buttocks and lightly caressing the tops of her bare thighs.

When she looked at herself in the mirror she saw that her nipples were clearly visible. The sight of those round, hard buds peaking insolently at the fine fabric made her stomach clench. She couldn't help wondering what Alex would think when he saw her. Would his eyes be immediately drawn to those distended nubs of flesh, or would his gaze be solely concentrated on hers in that disturbing, mesmerising way of his?

As she slipped her feet into a pair of leather wedge-heeled sandals and tied the thongs around her ankles, she glanced up. Through her bedroom window she could see Alex's shadow moving behind the blind that obscured his own bedroom. How long will it take for my shadow to join his, she asked herself – how long will either of us be able to hold out?

* * *

When Alex answered the door on the third ring of the bell he was totally taken aback to find a vision of loveliness standing on his doorstep. He had been expecting Regina, who although lovely in her own way, was nothing like Meredith.

'You look like a sea nymph,' he said before he could stop himself. He took a step back and was surprised when Meredith pushed her way confidently past him and entered his flat. The soft brush of silk against his bare arm as she passed him almost took his breath away. 'Come in,' he murmured, his mind racing.

He watched in stunned silence as she sashayed across the room, her hips swinging under the fine sheath of silk. Was it his imagination, he asked himself, or did she look more naked than naked in that dress?

Stopping in front of the window she glanced down at his favourite chair, then back at him.

'So this is where it all began,' she said with a smile.

Alex nodded dumbly as he stared back at her. He was sure his mouth was hanging open in surprise and tried desperately to collect himself before she noticed. He couldn't help admiring the way she looked: like a beautiful watercolour of a mermaid in the guise of a human, her sinuous form framed by the huge window. The sea green shade of her dress suited her colouring to perfection and its simple cut served as an adornment to a body that he already knew to be perfect in every way.

It occurred to him now that what he had assumed to be a dream had been real. His telephone conversation with Meredith had taken place. She had invited herself to his flat and he had accepted. Now she was here.

'If I look stunned it's because you look so lovely in that dress,' he said, surprising himself at the smooth way he managed to offer a plausible – and charming – explanation for his odd behaviour.

She smiled. 'Thank you,' she said. Without waiting to be invited, she sat down in the chair and crossed one slender leg over the other. Her skirt rode up to the tops of her thighs as she did so and Alex licked his lips at the sight of so much golden tanned flesh. Tossing her hair over her shoulder she glanced around. 'Do you have something I could drink?'

Alex leaped into action at once. 'Oh, yes. Of course. I'm sorry, I should have offered . . .'

She put up her hand to silence him. 'You seem flustered, Alex,' she observed. 'Why is that?'

He felt he could hardly claim that he hadn't been expecting her and so instead he said, 'I was just napping. I feel a bit disoriented to tell the truth, what with the lack of sleep and all that.'

Their eyes met, each sharing the memory of the previous evening. In response, Meredith blushed pinkly which made Alex feel a little more in control at last.

'Would you like a glass of wine?' he offered. 'Or maybe a soft drink?'

'Wine would be lovely,' Meredith answered. 'White if you have it.'

Just as Alex returned from the kitchen with a bottle of chilled Chardonnay and a couple of glasses the doorbell rang again. Swiftly, he remembered Regina. Oh, shit!

'Are you expecting someone else?' Meredith asked, raising her eyebrows in surprise.

'A prior arrangement,' Alex explained, putting down the wine and glasses. He made for the door as Regina's ringing became more insistent. 'She's just one of the dancers I'm working with.' Confusion gave him temporary amnesia, making him forget that Meredith had viewed he and Regina fucking like crazy on his studio floor.

The moment he opened the door he realised his *faux pas*. Meredith stared at Regina as though she was looking at a ghost. In contrast, when Regina noticed Meredith sitting by the window she stared at Alex. The expression in both women's eyes seemed to scream: what's *she* doing here?

'Just one of the dancers, eh?' Meredith muttered archly when Alex was in earshot.

Alex assumed a forced smile to go with his air of false levity. 'Regina, this is Meredith. Meredith, Regina. She—'

'I know, she's a fellow dancer,' Meredith interrupted him smoothly. 'A colleague.' The scornful tone of her voice made Alex's spirits plummet to the soles of his feet.

'So who're you then?' Regina asked, resting her ample

bottom on the window ledge and staring suspiciously at Meredith.

Meredith debated her options for a moment. 'A friend,' she said. 'Well, more of a neighbour really. I live in the flat opposite.' She inclined her head toward the window.

'How cosy,' Regina murmured. She shot Alex a 'Get rid of her look,' which he chose to ignore.

'I'll get another glass,' he said.

He was grateful for the excuse to escape for a moment and leaned against the kitchen cabinets feeling like a fugitive around whom the web of imminent capture was tightening. He had never felt so awkward, or less in control of a situation. The tense atmosphere between Meredith and Regina was palpable. Both women it seemed were spoiling for a fight and though it was flattering to imagine a 'pistols at dawn' scenario on his account, he didn't feel he could cope with the reality.

Both women turned their heads to look at him as he walked back through the door. He glanced furtively from one to the other. Whereas Regina's expression was accusative, Meredith's was completely inscrutable. He didn't know which was worse.

'Here we go,' he said with a false bonhomie that shattered the tense silence. He busied himself pouring out the wine and handing out glasses.

The only other seats in the room were well away from the window so Alex had no option but to join Regina. From such a distance he felt as though they were on trial, with Meredith as presiding judge – and jury.

Though he felt guilty for doing so, he allowed Regina to divert his attention away from Meredith by talking about the video. Presently, to his relief, Meredith got up and came over to join them. As she sat down on the sofa next to Regina – the only vacant seat – Alex couldn't help making mental comparisons between the two women. They were as different from each other as it was possible to get.

'Is Alex a good choreographer?' Meredith found herself asking Regina.

Regina paused and smirked at Alex. 'The best,' she said. 'At everything.'

'So I recall,' Meredith said drily.

Alex wanted to put his head in his hands and groan. Meredith must think I'm such a shit, he thought despairingly. It looks as though I deliberately lied to her about Regina. Seizing all his courage he met Meredith's steady gaze head on.

'I forgot,' he said simply, 'about a lot of things.'

Regina interrupted. 'Forgot about what – what are you going on about, Alex?'

'I think Meredith knows,' Alex said, risking Regina's wrath.

The nod Meredith gave him was barely discernible. Now, he was relieved to notice, a twinkle had replaced the hardness in her gaze. Though he failed to see how diabolical it was.

For her part, Meredith came to an instant decision. If she had the courage to carry out her plan the evening wouldn't go the way she had originally intended. But the temptation was irresistible.

'I think Alex is playing games with both of us,' she said, turning to Regina.

Regina eyed her warily. 'What do you mean?'

'I mean,' Meredith continued, forcing herself to keep a straight face, 'he is a two-timing bastard. I think he deliberately invited us both here to play one off against the other.' She risked a sideways glance to see how Alex was taking things. By the look on his face, she could see he appeared as perplexed as anyone could be.

It was fortunate for Meredith that Regina conveniently forgot that it was she who had invited herself to Alex's flat and not the other way round. She turned to face Alex, her expression livid.

'Of all the–' she spluttered, hardly able to contain herself. Jumping to her feet she stunned Alex by throwing the remainder of her wine in his face. 'You bastard! So that's your little game, is it? Well, you can stuff it, Alex.'

Before Alex could do or say anything, Regina was halfway across the room. Just as he made a move to go after her Meredith rounded on him.

'I'm going too,' she announced. 'This time the game's gone too far. Regina's right, you are a bastard!' With that she got to her feet and dashed out of the door after Regina before she lost her nerve.

'Wait, Regina, stop!' Meredith called after the girl as they both raced down the concrete staircase.

Regina didn't even look back and soon Alex's voice joined Meredith's as he hung over the stair rail on the third floor and called down to them both.

'Please, there's been a misunderstanding—'

Meredith and Regina resolutely ignored him and it was only once both were out on the tow path that Regina stopped and turned to face Meredith. Her bitter chocolate eyes blazed with undisguised contempt.

'Fuck off — I don't want to talk to you, you bitch!'

'Regina, please, just listen to me for a moment,' Meredith pleaded. She put her hand on the other woman's arm but Regina shook her off. 'Please,' Meredith repeated. 'I'm playing a trick on Alex. Come up to my flat for a drink and I'll explain.'

Regina eyed her warily. 'A trick?'

'Yes,' Meredith said, still panting from running down the stairs. 'Please, just one drink. I promise when I've finished explaining you'll see the funny side. You can go back over there and tell him everything afterwards if you want to.'

Regina gave a disbelieving snort but she allowed Meredith to lead the way across the tiny bridge that spanned the canal and up to her flat.

'This had better be good,' Regina said, once Meredith had got her sitting down and sharing a bottle of wine.

'Oh, it is,' Meredith assured her as she picked up her glass. 'But I'd better start at the beginning—'

Tears of laughter coursed down Regina's face. 'I was right, Meredith,' she gasped out between sobs of laughter, 'you are a bitch.'

Meredith smiled. 'I know. I can't help myself sometimes. Did you see Alex's face?'

Both girls went off into renewed peals of laughter.

'Oh, God,' Regina gasped. She clutched at her sides. 'I've got a stitch. Oh, Christ!' She stood up and bent over double.

Meredith found her eyes wandering over the delicious sight of the black girl's rump which was clad in purple denim. To complement the jeans she wore a white halternecked body-hugging tee-shirt that clung to her ample breasts. Meredith blushed when Regina glanced over her shoulder at her.

'You looking at my arse, girl?' the young woman demanded.

Dumbly, Meredith nodded. 'I'm sorry—' she began.

'Ah, shit, don't be,' Regina said, straightening up. She slapped her palms against her bottom. 'Everyone loves my backside. Men and women alike. No need to be shy about it. It's my best feature.'

'I wouldn't say that exactly,' Meredith mused aloud as her eyes were immediately drawn to the jutting mounds of Regina's bra-less breasts. Her gaze roved freely, visually devouring her.

Though the young black woman was not overweight, Meredith couldn't help marvelling at how much of her there seemed to be. All that lovely ebony flesh simply oozing out of her clothes and straining at the seams . . .

'You're bi aren't you?' Regina said, interrupting Meredith's visual assessment of her. When Meredith didn't answer straight away she added. 'Don't worry, I don't mind you looking at me like that.' She paused and glanced around Meredith's flat as though seeing it for the first time. 'Hey, we could have some real fun, you and me.'

Meredith felt excitement quicken inside her. She had taken a gamble suggesting to Regina that they play up to each other for Alex's benefit. Far from appearing shocked, the young woman had embraced Meredith's idea wholeheartedly. Now, it seemed, she was planning to take things a lot further than Meredith had intended.

'Real fun?' Meredith asked.

Regina nodded enthusiastically. 'Yeah, fun? You know, like proper sex, not just mucking about? Good job I brought my bag of tricks with me. I thought Alex might like – Oh, shit, I forgot about him for a minute.' She looked shamefaced.

At the mention of Alex's name Meredith glanced to the window automatically. It didn't surprise her to see him sitting in his usual chair.

'Don't worry about Alex,' Meredith said confidently. 'I think he'll end up enjoying this evening almost as much as we will.'

With the dark cloud of depression enveloping him, Alex hardly noticed Meredith and Regina moving the cutting table out of the way. His first inkling that something interesting was about to occur was when Meredith flung open the French windows that led out to her tiny balcony. An orange light – strong and blinding – flashed into his eyes, temporarily blinding him. It was the reflection of the setting sun on the metal frames of the French window.

His first thought when he saw Meredith and Regina settle into deckchairs opposite each other on the balcony was, thank God, at least they haven't killed each other. In a way he wasn't surprised to see them talking and sipping wine, neither woman had struck him as the sort to be deliberately hostile.

'Here's to sisterhood, honey pie,' Regina drawled in a Southern gal accent as she touched the rim of her wine glass to Meredith's.

'And to fun,' Meredith added.

As their glasses touched Meredith felt a sharp ripple of desire run through her. Their camaraderie was light and unforced, yet there was an underlying tension between herself and Regina that was distinctly sexual. She found herself envying Regina her experience with Alex. She had yet to achieve that level of intimacy with him. And yet, she reminded herself, haven't you and Alex already shared something much deeper and more intimate? A curious erotic, sensual knowledge that bound them more securely than a one off fuck.

'Have you and Alex been lovers for long?' Meredith found herself asking.

Regina laughed, the ensuing ripples of her laughter making her unfettered breasts jiggle under the stretched cotton. 'No, I haven't known him long. Only since we started working on this video. And as for being lovers, to tell the truth we've only screwed each other once.'

'You really enjoyed it.' It was a statement rather than a question.

Regina flashed Meredith a look of surprise. 'I'll say. But you talk as if you were there.'

For a moment Meredith considered telling Regina the truth. Then she stopped herself. It would serve no good purpose. Pretending to concentrate on the glowing sunset, Meredith surreptitiously glanced across to Alex's window. Just for the briefest moment she experienced a flicker of guilt. She hated to think how awful Alex must have felt when she and Regina turned on him like that. She only hoped that, when he looked on this evening in retrospect, he would think the end justified Meredith's rather cruel and devious means.

Meredith put down her glass. The wine made her feel pleasantly loose and uninhibited. Leaning forward she began to trace an idle path along one of Regina's denim-clad thighs. Crossing over to the other thigh just before she reached the sharp 'v' at the top, she traced another path down to the knee. Beneath the denim she could feel the firm texture of Regina's tautly muscled legs and the overpowering heat of her body.

'You must be feeling ever so warm in those,' Meredith murmured, nodding at the jeans. She looked up at Regina's face, fixing her with a gaze that was at once innocent and meaningful. 'I couldn't bear to wear something as constricting as jeans on a night like this.'

It was true, the air temperature was incredibly sultry.

'You're right, they are making me feel a bit sticky,' Regina said, standing up. 'I'll take them off if you don't mind.'

The expression in her eyes was hazy with anticipation as she undid the button on the waistband and pulled down the zipper. The purple denim parted to reveal a slightly curved brown belly. A faint line of dark hairs arrowed down from a deep navel to the elasticated top of white lace panties.

Meredith watched her ease the jeans over her ample hips. Her mouth felt dry, she realised and she picked up her glass and took a large, unladylike slug of her wine. This time when she put her glass down her hand was shaking.

'Here, let me help,' Meredith offered as Regina struggled with the skin-tight jeans.

Indicating that the girl should sit down again, Meredith first pulled off her brown leather ankle boots, then began to ease the denim down her legs and over her feet. When she had freed one leg of the jeans Regina placed her foot on Meredith's shoulder. She smirked at Meredith and when Meredith glanced up, she realised why the girl was looking at her in such a provocative way. With her leg raised Regina offered her a blatant view of her crotch.

Feeling emboldened by Regina's free and easy manner, Meredith allowed her gaze to travel deliberately up the length of the young black girl's legs. The skin on her inner thighs had a satiny sheen and at their apex the dark, mysterious pouch of Regina's sex was encased by sheer white lace. Meredith felt transfixed by the sight. The soft vulva bulged seductively at the lace but the flimsy panties failed to contain all its lusciousness. From around the edges of the lace Meredith could see a few dusky curls.

Those curls of pubic hair seemed to beckon to her flirtatiously and when she reached up and stroked them with tentative fingertips, Meredith delighted to their soft, springy texture. Her knuckles brushed Regina's sex and encountered wetness. Regina moaned softly and kicked off the remaining leg of her jeans so that she could spread her thighs wide, encouraging Meredith to explore further.

For a while Meredith deliberately teased the black girl. Purposefully avoiding the hot, wet place between her thighs, she concentrated on following the outline of the panties with her fingertip, disturbing the escaping curls and tantalising the sensitive flesh of Regina's groin.

With a desperate groan Regina arched her back and thrust her pelvis toward Meredith. 'For fuck's sake touch me,' she urged.

Never having met someone quite so earthy and uninhibited before, Meredith felt temporarily stunned. Her lesbian experience wasn't all that great and, certainly, Regina was nothing like the refined Camilla. Nothing at all.

Knowing she was prolonging the agony – but needing to all the same – she turned and picked up her wine glass, downing the rest of the contents in one go. When she turned back it was to see Regina's fingers unselfconsciously stroking her sex through her panties. She had untied the halterneck on her tee-shirt and now her breasts thrust forward from her ribcage like two huge mounds of chocolate blancmange.

Blancmange tipped by morello cherries, Meredith thought wickedly as she eyed the dark buds of Regina's nipples.

Entranced by the sight of those breasts, Meredith moved onto her knees and cupped them both, drawing the pliant mounds together. Eagerly, she began to tongue each burgeoning nipple, flicking her tongue back and forth between them rapidly. The black girl moaned and began to writhe in the deckchair, her fingers still working feverishly between her legs.

Taking pity on her, Meredith reluctantly released her breasts and moved her face down to the stretch of smooth brown stomach beneath the white band of her top. She lapped delicately at the silky skin, enjoying its texture and its peculiar taste. A light sheen of perspiration mingled with some sort of fruit scented body lotion, lending Regina's skin a slightly sweet and sour flavour. Meredith lapped it up, working her way gradually down, over the slight curve of the girl's belly to the white lace panties.

When she reached the panties she paused. Then she slid her fingers under the thin bands that encircled Regina's hips and tugged gently. Regina aided her by lifting her bottom off the seat making it easy for Meredith to pull the scrap of lace down her legs. When they were off she gently pressed her palms against Regina's inner thighs, opening her legs wider and wider.

Of course, she can probably do the splits, Meredith found herself thinking as the girl opened her legs so wide apart Meredith feared she would do herself some damage. And, as Regina parted her legs, so the outer lips of her plump sex blossomed outward, revealing the dusky petals of her inner flesh.

Unconsciously, Meredith licked her lips. The girl's sex was like a ripe fruit – a split plum, the dark outer flesh parted and the succulent inner flesh simply oozing with lusciousness and dripping with juice. She could see Regina's clitoris quite clearly. Budding from its surrounding leaves of flesh it was dark red and heavily engorged, reminding Meredith of one of the girl's nipples.

Without even thinking twice about it Meredith stroked the flat part of her tongue over its pearly tip and watched with delight as the muscles in the young woman's belly rippled with pleasure. As she continued to tantalise Regina's clitoris her eager fingers explored the rest of her sex. The flesh her questing fingertips encountered was so succulent Meredith couldn't resist raising one hand to her lips and licking her fingers clean.

As she did so her other hand kept up a steady rhythm, gently stimulating the flesh around the large, hard clitoris.

She glanced up and noticed that Regina was watching her through heavy-lidded eyes. Her expression was one of acute sensual longing.

'Please,' she gasped hoarsely, 'please make me come.'

With a knowing smile, Meredith slid both hands down between Regina's thighs, her fingers skilfully parting her sex lips even further. Pausing only to circle the moist rim of the girl's vagina and slick some of the juices over her most intimate flesh, she slid a couple of fingers inside her gaping channel. She began to move them rhythmically, deliberately hooking them to rub the sensitive spot just above the girl's pubic bone.

Regina began to weave her hips in perfect accord and without further hesitation Meredith dipped her head and, using the tip of her tongue, began to beat out a sensual tune on the girl's pulsating clitoris. Barely a minute later she felt the first rhythmic spasms of Regina's internal muscles. They cramped around her fingers, becoming tighter and faster as the tune Meredith played on her body reached its crescendo.

When the girl's body began to judder uncontrollably Meredith realised she had taken her far enough for the time being. Raising her head, her mouth and chin smeared with Regina's glistening juices, Meredith caught her languid gaze and smiled.

'Will that do?' she asked softly.

It seemed to take a great effort for Regina to nod. 'For now,' she managed to gasp out, after a moment. A confident, if wobbly, grin spread across her face. 'But just you wait, you bitch. I'm going to have you screaming for mercy.'

Chapter Fourteen

The sun seemed to take its time about setting. The sky was still ablaze with streaks of fiery red and shades of pink, the sun itself a glowing orange orb. It slipped slowly lower and lower, neither diminishing in its colourful intensity nor its command of the sky. Alex sensed its surreal power and let out a deep sigh.

As if she could hear him Meredith turned her head. Across the great divide of the canal he could feel the poignancy of her gaze. He noticed that Meredith was leaning against the balcony. She had her back to him, her silk covered buttocks striped by the railings. In the next instant, Regina stood up and stripped off the white top she'd been wearing. It was her only remaining bit of clothing and now she stood proud and naked. Like one of those wood carvings of fertility goddesses he'd seen in ethnic shops. Graced by the reflection of the setting sun, her ebony skin glowed a deep ochre on the rounded parts of her body: her shoulders, her hips . . .

Alex found himself licking his lips, an aesthetic appreciation of grace and beauty banishing the hurt and disappointment which had prowled like an angry leopard inside his psyche a moment before. And yet there was more to it than that. He knew, expected, anticipated, that in a few moments Meredith's body would be revealed to him again. He wasn't wrong.

Regina walked up to Meredith and placed her hands either side of her on the railing. She pressed her body up close to Meredith's, so close Alex could hardly see any of her. Just the merest shadow of her hips and shoulders. They were kissing. Meredith was bent back over the railing by the force of Regina's kiss.

He watched with growing anticipation as Regina stooped and caught the hem of Meredith's flimsy dress in her hands. He imagined the delicate fabric creasing and bunching in the grip of those strong, dark fingers. She lifted the hem, higher and higher, gradually revealing the perfect peach of Meredith's bottom.

Meredith helped her by raising her arms aloft and shimmying out of the silken sheath. Then she too was naked. Stark. Glorious. The total embodiment of all things womanly.

Alex's gaze swept appreciatively from the tip of her golden head, down the smooth sweep of her back, to the roundness of her buttocks. Envious of Regina, he coveted her. Her nakedness. Her submissiveness. It surprised him that he hadn't felt that way before. Not in the beer garden of the pub, nor in Cosimo's office. On those two occasions he had simply been content to be a part of the proceedings and yet apart from Meredith.

Now, he wanted her. Now he yearned for her with every fibre of his being. Now, more than any time during the past weeks, he felt he could never have her. Before he could stop himself he stumbled to his feet, flung open the windows that led to his balcony and cried out, 'Meredith! Why are you torturing me like this?'

The shout came from across the water, carried on the sultry evening air like the plaintive call of a seagull. Despite the anguish evident in the sound, Meredith resolutely refused to turn. To look at Alex. To acknowledge him in any way.

'Don't,' she muttered to Regina when she glanced up. 'This is all part of the game. For me at any rate.'

'Fine, have it your way,' Regina responded with a shrug. 'Do you still want to carry on, or would you rather I went home now?'

Meredith smiled down at her and placed a hand on the top of her head. She could have been an empress conferring a great honour. Or she could simply be a girl who placed physical pleasure above all else. Regina preferred to think of Meredith as the latter.

'Stay,' Meredith said simply.

A lascivious smile gave Regina a predatory look. 'OK. But if I do I'm going to fuck you.'

Meredith shrugged. 'So, fuck me.' She grinned inwardly,

enjoying the verbal sparring and not believing for one moment that Regina was serious.

To her surprise, Regina got up. 'Just give me a moment, I've got to get something from inside,' she muttered.

With a nod of her head, Meredith watched the black girl retreat into the shadowy recesses of her flat. Then she turned and looked across the water. Alex was still there. Standing on the threshold of his balcony.

'Enjoying the view?' she called across to him.

He raised his hand in a half salute. Meredith smiled back at him, though she wasn't sure if he could read the pertness in her body language. She felt wicked. But there was a new pleasure to be had in her wickedness. A perversion of desire.

She heard Regina's footsteps softly padding across the floorboards and back on to the tiny balcony. She felt the brush of her hard nipples between her shoulder blades. She didn't turn around.

'Bend forward,' Regina ordered in a low, confident voice. 'You'll have to come back a bit. That's it. Bend a bit more. Right, stay like that.'

A knot of excitement began to gather inside Meredith again. She rested her forearms on the balcony railing and felt her breasts swing freely. Her bottom was thrust outwards, her legs spread. She could feel Regina's hands sweeping over her body, caressing her sides, her back, her hips and buttocks, down the length of her thighs. Then a hand snaked between her open legs, cupping her sex. Another stroked her bottom, a couple of fingers sliding effortlessly down the cleft between. The fingers sank into wetness. Her own wetness.

'You're juicy, babe,' Regina murmured behind her. 'I think you're ready for this.'

The fingers withdrew and a moment later a surprising hardness nudged at Meredith's vaginal lips. It felt familiar yet unfamiliar.

'What is that?' Meredith asked, turning her head.

Swiftly, Regina cupped the back of her head and made Meredith face the front again.

'I told you I'm going to fuck you. What do you think it is?' she said.

Meredith decided to hazard a guess. 'A bottle?' She glanced down to her feet. It wasn't the bottle they'd been drinking from.

A deep chuckle, rich as a fudge brownie, touched her ears. 'Nope. Guess again.'

She didn't feel in the mood for guessing games. Risking Regina's wrath she turned her head quickly, then gaped at the sight that met her eyes. Strapped around Regina's waist was a black leather contraption of some kind.

'It's a dildo,' Regina explained, a wicked excitement lighting her eyes. 'Ever tried one of these before?'

'Not when it's strapped to someone else I haven't,' Meredith murmured.

She felt appalled. Then a thrill of anticipation ran through her. And, hot on its heels, a huge surge of lust.

'Christ!' Regina exclaimed. 'What just happened then?' She ran her fingertips around the puffy flesh of Meredith's vaginal lips and added, 'You just soaked my cock.'

Meredith felt herself blushing. She was mortified and aroused. Incredibly aroused.

'If you're going to use that thing,' she said hoarsely, 'please, hurry up.'

A gasp of surprise was all she could managed when she felt the dildo suddenly thrust into her body. It felt so real, so lifelike, that for a moment she forgot it wasn't a real cock. And it was huge. It felt gigantic as it stretched her sex flesh beyond all reason.

'I'm going to tear,' she gasped, panicking.

Regina's voice was soothing. 'No you're not. You can take it. Just relax.'

The young woman began to slide the dildo in and out of her, her clever fingers seeking and caressing the hard bud of Meredith's clitoris at the same time.

'That's it, baby,' Regina crooned, 'just go with the flow.'

In moments Meredith felt her entire body turn liquid. A forest fire of sensual passion ran through her, melting down her resistance. She whimpered, feeling the deep thrusting of the dildo and its corresponding pull on her intimate flesh. All her nerve endings were alive and tingling. Her clitoris swelled under the softly stroking pads of Regina's fingers. Instinctively, she began to buck her hips, meeting the black girl thrust for thrust.

'I told you!' Regina cried out triumphantly as Meredith tensed, became still, then began to writhe through a crashing orgasm. 'Now you've got the taste for it, I'm going to fuck you into oblivion.'

Without her noticing it, sunset gave way to sunrise. In between, Meredith rode the dark hours on a sea of ecstasy. Now, finally, she was left alone. She lay on her bed. Aching. Satiated. Sore.

She smiled, thinking of Regina. Then her thoughts immediately turned to Alex and she frowned. Perhaps she had gone too far this time. By turning the tables on him, she may have ruined her chances. The ominous shape of the telephone beckoned to her. With a deep sigh of resignation she picked it up. It was now or never. She had to know where she stood.

'Alex?'

'Meredith?'

'You're still speaking to me then?'

'Do I have a choice? You rang me.'

Meredith gulped. She wasn't to know that a fiesta – complete with music, brilliant costumes and fireworks – had started up in Alex's head.

'I want to apologise.'

'What for?'

'You know what for. What I did tonight – last night – was unforgivable.'

'Was it?'

'You know it was.'

'Why?'

Meredith paused. It was a good question.

'Because–' she began hesitantly.

'Because you thought you'd give me a taste of my own medicine?'

'You're not angry then?' Meredith held her breath waiting for his answer.

When it came, it was riding the create of a rolling chuckle. 'No. Oh, I was a bit at first. Though angry is not really the right word. Suicidal might be more apt.'

'Oh, God!' Meredith felt overcome by remorse.

'Only teasing,' he said warmly. He'd forgive her anything now. It was just such a relief to hear her voice again. 'So you and Regina enjoyed yourselves then, eh?'

'You could tell?' Meredith's tone was light and teasing. She felt as though a weight equivalent to the Statue of Liberty had been taken off her shoulder.

Alex's tone was as dry as the finest champagne and every bit as exhilarating. 'I may be stupid but I'm not blind.'

'Oh, Alex, don't call yourself stupid.' Meredith's response came out in a rush. 'You're not. Far from it. If anything I'm the idiotic one.'

'How come?' His voice was gentle again, probing.

Meredith felt about three years old. 'Because I risked everything between us. Just for the sake of devilment.'

'Don't you know I like you when you're at your devilish best. Especially the horns.'

Meredith giggled. 'You haven't seen my horns yet.'

'Ah, no, that's right, I haven't.' Alex made a low murmuring sound as though he were considering something. 'We'll have to rectify that, won't we.'

Excitement galloped through Meredith. 'Will we – when?'

'When do you suggest?'

She thought quickly. 'Tomorrow. Six o'clock. On the tow path.'

Alex chuckled. 'OK. But tell me, how will I recognise you? What will you be wearing.' He hoped she was as spontaneous and creative as he'd surmised.

'School uniform,' she said, saying the first thing that came into her head. 'I shall need some help with my homework,' she continued, warming to the theme. 'Biology. Do you think you could oblige?'

'Biology is my best subject,' Alex replied, laughing. 'I take it there'll be a lot of practical?'

'Oh, absolutely.'

'Good,' Alex murmured, relaxing his grip on the receiver, 'You'd better make sure you get some sleep then. You'll need to be particularly alert tomorrow evening.'

It seemed to Alex as if he spent the whole day moving about in a fog. He was on set first thing and for once everything seemed to flow smoothly. The only hitch was the unexpected arrival of Lisa Blair half way through the afternoon.

'Don't mind me,' she called out airily to the assembled troupe, 'I'll just sit over here and watch.'

One of the set assistants produced a director-style chair for her to sit in and a freestanding parasol to provide some much needed shade. The temperature was well up in the eighties and everyone was wearing as little as possible, including Lisa who wore the tiniest dress Alex had ever seen on a full grown woman, the short hem and shoestring straps revealing the full extent of her lithe, tanned limbs.

As far as Alex was concerned, she could have been wearing an old flour sack. And the same went for all the scantily-clad female dancers, including Regina, who had steadfastly – though pleasantly – shrugged off when she tried to draw him out about his opinion of her and Meredith's escapade.

'It was entertaining,' was all he would say. 'Now, let's concentrate on getting that jump and twist movement just right.'

He deliberately forced himself not to think about the previous night, nor the coming evening. Just the idea of Meredith in school uniform was enough to turn his entire body to jelly. Which was not a good idea when he was supposed to be demonstrating his superior skills as a dancer.

'Was that a *grande jeté*, Alex, or did you just trip over your own feet?' one of the dancers ribbed him when he cocked up a perfectly simple move for the umpteenth time.

'It's the heat,' he said lamely. 'Or perhaps I'm coming down with something.'

To his annoyance, Lisa called him over. 'I can't help noticing you're not on form, Alex,' she commented with a superior smile.

Fighting back a scathing retort, Alex merely shrugged. 'It's the heat,' he repeated. He paused and glanced around the garage lot. The concrete surface shimmered in a haze of heat and he couldn't help noticing how shabby everything looked under the unforgiving rays of the sun. 'I don't think we're going to get much more out of that lot today,' he added, wanting desperately to go home, shower and have a nap before meeting Meredith. If Lisa hadn't turned up he'd planned to send everyone home early.

'They've put in some good work today but I think we've all had it.'

Lisa gave him a narrow-eyed stare. 'We start shooting the damned video in less than a week,' she pointed out tersely. 'From what I've seen, I don't think any of you can afford to slacken off now.'

Feeling like a schoolboy being reprimanded by the headmistress, Alex clasped his hands behind his back and stared down at the ground, which he scuffed idly with his toe.

Lisa sighed. 'OK,' she conceded, glancing at her watch, 'perhaps I am being a bit hard on you all. What do you say you put in another hour and then we'll call it a day?'

Her change of heart caused Alex to look up and give her a grateful smile. 'Thanks, Lisa,' he said. 'I think the others will appreciate it.'

She nodded, smiling back. 'Don't think I'm doing this out of the goodness of my heart,' she warned him, her smile broadening, 'I have an ulterior motive.'

'Oh, yes?' Alex's spirits, which had just begun to rise, began to descend again just as quickly.

Lisa reached out and grasped him by the wrist. She tugged at his arm, pressing his hand flat against her breast. 'Yes,' she murmured huskily,' I haven't forgotten that you and I have a bit of unfinished business, Alex. I thought this evening would be the perfect time to continue things.' Her eyelashes fluttered as she gazed up at him. Beneath his palm, Alex could feel her nipple stiffening. 'We'll go for a drink first,' she continued, releasing his hand. 'Then we'll take it from there.'

Feeling as though she had backed him against a wall, blindfolded him and called a firing squad to take aim, Alex gave her a weak approximation of a smile.

'We'll have that drink,' Alex promised. 'Just as soon as we finish up here.'

As for the rest of her plans, he thought as he turned and walked back across the lot, I'll have to find a way out. He prayed his powers of ingenuity wouldn't let him down. If the worst happened and it came to a choice between his work and Meredith, he didn't know what he would do.

* * *

Unaware that she was in danger of being stood up, Meredith hummed happily to herself as she glanced down at the items she had laid out on the bed. It had taken her most of the day to find exactly what she was looking for in her size. It had meant braving the intrigued stares of shop assistants as she explained that she was buying the clothes for her niece, who just happened to be the same size as her.

I wonder if they get a lot of people like me? she mused as she stroked her hand down the pleats of the short, black skirt she had chosen. As fantasy dressing went, she didn't think school uniforms were all that unusual, which made her wonder if there were special shops that catered specifically to adult sizes. She supposed she was lucky that a lot of genuine schoolgirls were about the same size as her – some, she had noticed, were even a lot larger.

With less than an hour to go before her tryst with Alex, she decided to start dressing. Hold-up stockings went on first – black, with a deep lacy welt – then a white cotton bra and pants. She wanted to look as authentic as possible, with the sexy garnish of the stockings, which Alex wouldn't know were stockings until she revealed them to him. A proper white cotton, short sleeved school blouse went on next. Then the skirt.

Meredith smoothed the skirt down and eyed herself critically in the mirror, bending this way and that to make sure her stocking tops didn't show. The skirt was short, ending at midthigh, but not too short. Later on, she supposed, she could always roll the waistband over to make it shorter and sexier.

Next came a tie, with yellow, black and cream stripes. This she kept deliberately loose, with the top couple of buttons of her blouse undone. The effect appeared genuine, given the heat and the fact that school was over for the day, yet undeniably sluttish. Last but not least was a black felt boater banded by yellow ribbon which she crammed on her head. Glancing in the mirror again, she tilted the hat rakishly to one side then stuck her tongue out at her reflection.

'Good one, Meredith,' she congratulated herself. 'Alex won't be able to keep his hands off you in that get up.'

Seated outside an Italian restaurant just around the corner from the garage, Alex glanced covertly at his watch for the umpteenth time. He groaned inwardly. It was ten to six and he still hadn't managed to come up with a plausible enough excuse to get away from Lisa. Reaching a decision he stood up abruptly.

'Just give me a minute, Lisa,' he said, interrupting her mid-sentence. 'I have to make an urgent call and my mobile's not picking up a good signal here.'

She smiled up at him. 'Don't be long,' she said, 'I'll order us another bottle of wine while you're gone.'

Alex nodded, grateful to get away from her at long last. He wandered down the street, pretending to check the signal level on his mobile phone When he felt he was far enough away from Lisa's probing gaze and well out of earshot, he dialled Meredith's number. To his frustration, the phone just kept ringing and ringing.

To his dismay, he realised she had probably already gone downstairs to meet him. He pictured her standing on the tow path, glancing in the direction of the High Street, waiting to catch her first glimpse of him. Or perhaps she thought he was already at home, he mused. Now he pictured her leaning against the wall of the converted warehouse where she lived, gazing up at his flat. He liked that image better, he decided, feeling his arousal grow. He could picture the casual insolence of her stance. One leg bent, foot placed flat against the wall, hands on hips. Perhaps she would be chewing gum in a kind of lazy, sluttish way. That definitely would complete the image.

Though the phone still rang on interminably, Alex pretended to be talking to someone in case Lisa was watching him. He desperately needed a moment to think. To come up with some reason to make his escape that sounded so plausible Lisa would let him go quite happily. The last thing he wanted to do was jeopardise the future of this video. It wasn't just his career, or his credibility at stake, he owed it to the rest of the dancers too.

In the end he disconnected the abortive call by flipping the mouthpiece shut. Inside his head he could still hear the ringing sound. It changed to a dull thudding. Christ! His mind had gone completely blank. For once, he was lost for ideas. Feeling thoroughly defeated, he dragged his feet back down the pavement to the table where Lisa sat waiting for him and slunk into his seat.

'Everything OK?' she asked him brightly.

All Alex could do was nod dumbly and reach for the bottle of wine. If he couldn't have Meredith, he may as well get pissed.

Meredith had gone past the point of feeling frantic. First of all she'd felt slightly anxious. Then increasingly panicky. Then frantic. Now she was steaming. How dare he stand her up, the bastard! Was this his idea of a joke, a way of getting his own back on her? Her anger made her want to do serious harm to him. She wished him under the wheels of a bus. Then she retracted the idea just as quickly. It made her feel too guilty. And sad. She didn't really want anything bad to happen to him. All she wanted was for him to walk around the corner.

No matter how much she willed him to put in an appearance he didn't come. She had no idea what the time was. She knew she had left her flat about a quarter to six. Then it must have taken her all of two minutes to walk downstairs. Whichever way she looked at it, Alex must be getting on for an hour late.

OK then, mister, she thought angrily. If Mohammed won't come to the mountain, then the mountain will bloody well go to Mohammed. And you can bet your life it's going to erupt when it sees him.

Thinking Alex might be in his flat, she marched across the bridge that spanned the canal. But her journey proved fruitless. After five minutes spent hammering on his door she gave up and conceded that he wasn't at home after all.

So, what do I do now? She wondered. All at once it occurred to her that he might have been held up at work. If that was the case she would accept his grovelling apology with good grace. Feeling much better now, she tried to recall the address of the set where he was working. Then she marched up the tow path and on to the High Street. Ignoring the interested stares of passers-by, who gawped quite blatantly at the young schoolgirl with the long, flashing legs, bouncing breasts and wearing a determined expression, Meredith got into the first taxi that came along.

Chapter Fifteen

'Alex, I don't think you're listening to me. Alex!'

'What?' Alex jumped. The sharp tone of Lisa's voice succeeded in startling him out of his reverie. He picked up his glass and downed its contents in one go. With a lopsided grin, he looked across the table at Lisa. 'I'm sorry,' he amended politely, 'I didn't quite catch what you said.'

Lisa glared stonily at him. 'I'm not surprised,' she said. 'How many of those have you had now?'

Alex gazed blankly into his empty glass. Feeling thoroughly despondent and frustrated by the situation, he had swapped wine for scotch. He shrugged.

'I dunno,' he slurred. 'Just a couple.'

Lisa made a tut-tutting sound which grated on Alex's nerves. He hated women who tried to monitor him: what he ate or drank, how many girls he chatted up . . .

'Don't be such a party-pooper, Lisa,' he said daringly. 'It was you who suggested we come here for a drink.'

'*A* drink, Alex,' she corrected him. 'Not two bottles of wine. Oh, shit–' she sat back in her chair an sighed, 'what the hell has got into you? I thought you wanted this. Any other man in his right mind would be chuffed to little mintballs – as my grandmother used to say – to be sitting and drinking with Lisa Blair.' She gazed thoughtfully at him. All at once her face broke into a smile.

Alex gazed back at her. He was relieved to note she didn't look angry any more. And when she smiled like that she looked very attractive. More than attractive. He could really go for her looking like that . . .

'Alex, you've gone blank again,' Lisa chided him gently.

'Sorry.' He grinned ruefully and pushed his fingers through

his hair. If only he could clear his head a bit he could really enjoy himself with Lisa. Provided he could also get rid of the nagging feeling that he was supposed to be doing something else . . .

Just at that moment both Alex and Lisa were distracted by the loud rattle of a black cab pulling up at the kerbside. A young girl emerged backwards from it and Alex could hardly help but gawp when he saw the way her short, pleated skirt rode up over her bum to reveal a flash of thigh above lacy stocking tops.

'Jesus!' he breathed.

Lisa he noticed, when he glanced back at her, didn't look quite as gobsmacked as he felt.

'What can her parents be thinking of, letting her go to school dressed like that?' Lisa said tersely. 'She looks like a right little tart.'

'Yes, she does, doesn't she?' Alex mused aloud. Just the sort of tart he could easily imagine sinking his teeth into.

He turned back to the girl and noticed that she was paying the taxi driver. Her long blonde hair was caught up in a high ponytail. Its pointy end brushed her bra strap, which he could clearly make out through her thin cotton blouse.

'Alex, for Chrissake stop staring!' Lisa hissed at him. 'She's jail bait. Don't even think about it.'

Alex pursed his lips. He pondered the word 'jailbait,' liking the sound of it. Beneath the cover of the table top, he felt his cock growing hard. In the briefest of fleeting fantasies, he imagined the schoolgirl coming over to him, throwing her shapely, stocking-clad legs astride him and impaling herself on his stiff cock. That would wipe the smile of Lisa's face, he thought.

With a feeling of elation he watched as the girl turned and looked straight at him. All at once he felt his leery-smile disintegrate. At the same time his cock shrivelled.

'Meredith?' he gasped, the memory of where he was supposed to be suddenly coming back to him.

She smiled and flicked at her pony tail in a gesture that was at once pert and yet horribly ominous. She advanced towards him.

'Uncle Alex,' she said, still smiling sweetly, 'I hoped I'd bump into you.'

Alex felt himself drowning. Or wished he could drown. How wonderful it would be if, right at that moment, a sea of quicksand would appear beneath him and suck him right down.

'Do you know this girl, Alex?' he heard Lisa asking. Her voice seemed to come from a long way off, drowned out to some extent by the loud booming noise inside his head.

Meredith answered Lisa. She sat down and pulled her chair very close to Alex so he had no option but to feel her thigh brushing against his.

'Of course he knows me,' she said, glancing sideways at him and grinning. 'He's my daddy's youngest brother. But I always think he's too scrummy to be an uncle. Don't you agree?'

'Oh, absolutely,' Lisa mumbled, looking almost as dumbstruck as Alex. 'He certainly is very, er, scrummy.'

They were interrupted by the waiter coming over to their table. 'More drinks, sir, madam?' he asked, pencil poised over his pad.

Meredith leaned across the table, deliberately brushing her breast against Alex's arm. 'You look nice,' she purred lasciviously.

The waiter, a young Italian barely out of his teens, looked unnerved by her overt interest in him.

'Should I bring another bottle of the Chianti?' he asked, deliberately keeping his gaze fixed on Lisa.

Meredith gave an unconcerned shrug and after a moment, sat back and made a great show of tightening the band around her ponytail. When she reached up and arched her back her breasts thrust outwards, commanding every one's attention, including Lisa's.

'Yes, we'll have another bottle of Chianti,' Lisa ordered, turning her attention quickly back to the stunned looking waiter. 'And you'd better bring another glass and a bottle of mineral water for the young lady here.' Her words dripped with sarcasm.

The waiter hurried off gratefully, though he had to be aware that Meredith was deliberately following him with her eyes. Then Meredith turned back to Alex and winked at him.

'Funny,' she said, 'for some reason I feel like eating a nice juicy piece of salami now.'

Alex, who was still in a state of total panic and – desperately in need of alcohol's numbing effect – had reverted to drinking wine, spluttered.

Lisa looked frostily at them both. 'Shouldn't you be doing your homework or something?' she said to Meredith, glancing pointedly at her watch.

Meredith nodded. She took Alex's glass off him and sipped at the wine, much to Lisa's obvious annoyance. 'Uh-huh,' she responded after a minute, 'that's why I came looking for Uncle Alex. He promised to help me with my biology assignment.'

A thousand questions seemed to leap from the glance Lisa threw in Alex's direction. He groaned inwardly. Try as he might, he couldn't quite sink low enough in his chair to become invisible.

The waiter returned and began setting down fresh glasses in front of them all. Still obviously in wanton slut mode, Meredith caught him by the wrist just as he put the wine bottle on the table.

'My, what strong hands you have,' she murmured seductively, glancing up at him through her eyelashes. 'Why don't you come round to my side of the table? I could see if your bum's as tight as Lisa's smile.'

Flashing an apologetic glance at Lisa and Alex, the waiter hastily put down the bottle and fled.

Reclining back in her chair, Meredith chuckled. 'What's eating him?' she said to no one in particular. Then she added on a more thoughtful note, 'Wish it was me.'

Ignoring the stunned atmosphere surrounding their table she reached out and helped herself to the bottle of wine. As she poured, she crossed her legs, surreptitiously hitching up her skirt so that her lacy stocking top showed.

About a dozen men seated at nearby tables craned their necks to look at her.

Grinning pertly, Meredith raised her glass to them. 'Well, bottoms up, everyone,' she said.

To Alex, the next half hour or so seemed interminable. Meredith kept up a steady stream of schoolgirlish chatter which, under other circumstances, he would have applauded. Her act was totally convincing. She was at once innocent and yet whorish. A combination he found incredibly alluring despite his discomfort. If only Lisa would simply disappear, he prayed silently. Even a bomb scare would be a welcome diversion right now.

As luck would have it, a few moments later Lisa's mobile phone rang. She answered it straight away and then glanced apologetically at Alex.

'This is a bit private,' she muttered to him. 'Do you mind if I move to another table for a moment?'

Overwhelmed by relief, Alex nodded. 'Of course. In fact, don't bother to move. I need to make a call of nature and I'm sure Meredith wouldn't mind—'

'No, not at all,' Meredith chirped, jumping to her feet once. 'I could do with a pee myself. You just lead the way, *Uncle* Alex.'

The ladies' and gents' lavatories were at the bottom of a long, narrow staircase. Glancing around to make sure no one was watching them, Alex grabbed Meredith and hauled her into the ladies' loo. Once inside, he checked they were alone, wedged a chair under the door knob, then turned to her, his face dark with fury.

Meredith stared back at him open mouthed. For the first time she felt the rapid rise of anxiety. His eyes glinted dangerously, his expression having the look of a madman.

She unclenched her hands and held one up as if to defend herself against him. 'Now don't be mad with me, Alex—' she began.

Alex interrupted her by grabbing her and slamming her back against the wall. He pressed his body up close against hers and stared down into her wide, frightened eyes.

'Don't be mad,' he growled ominously. 'What the fuck do you think you're playing at?'

Despite her rapidly beating heart, Meredith stood her ground. 'What the fuck am I playing at? What the fuck are you playing at you mean. I waited for you for over an hour, you bastard, wondering if you'd been knocked down by a bus or something and all the time you were here, drinking and flirting with Miss Tightarse!'

Despite his anger, Alex felt his lips twitch at Meredith's description of Lisa.

'Miss Tightarse, as you call her,' he pointed out, still trying to sound seriously angry, 'is Lisa Blair. You know – the singer? She's the one I'm working for at the moment.'

Meredith's eyes widened again. 'She is – you are?' she stammered.

Alex nodded. 'I tried to call you,' he said, 'at about ten to six but there was no answer.'

'I'd already left,' Meredith replied, looking downcast. 'I couldn't wait to see you. I–' She glanced up and noticed that Alex was looking strangely at her. All at once she felt her pulse quicken.

'Why couldn't you wait to see me?' he asked in a low voice.

She shrugged. His hands, which were still gripping her shoulders, slackened.

'Tell me.' he commanded, his tone much softer.

Meredith gazed steadily back at him, her blue eyes shining and alive. 'Because I desire you like crazy, that's why,' she said, horrified at herself for admitting it to him. 'All those times when you were watching me, I kept wishing you would touch me too, just once–' her words trailed off.

'Touch you?' Alex pretended to look confused. 'How – like this?' His tone was gently teasing as he slowly raised his hand and ran the backs of his fingers down the side of her face.

Meredith held herself very still, hardly daring to breath. His caress was like angel's breath.

His fingers continued to stroke her face, then travelled down the side of her neck. They glanced over the collar of her blouse and continued a path to her breast. There the fingers stopped. They spread out and enclosed the mound of flesh beneath.

'Ah!' Meredith cried, pushing her aching breast harder against his hand. 'Yes, like that. Oh, God, yes.'

He rotated his palm, grinding at the malleable flesh. With his other hand he cupped her chin and pressed his lips fiercely against her own.

Caught in the grip of something exhilarating, Meredith felt herself floundering. She was pinned to the wall by the hard pressure of his body, his hand, his lips. Her arms flailed wildly.

Then she clutched at him, grasping his shirt in her hands. She could feel the ridges of his muscles beneath her knuckles as she kneaded his back.

His mouth upon hers was hot and wet. The lips pressed harder, his tongue forcing them open and probing deeply into the wet cavern of her mouth. She felt her heart beating rapidly, her breath trapped in her throat. Help me, she cried silently in her head. I'm drowning.

She was drowning. She knew it from the suffocating tightness in her chest and the moisture trickling between her legs. An ocean of lust had claimed her and she was helpless in the grip of its powerful current. It dragged her along, pulling her deeper and deeper until velvety blackness obscured her sense of reason.

'Fuck me now!' she cried. 'Fuck me, Alex, or God help me I'll kill you.'

To her complete surprise Alex pulled back from her and laughed. It was the laugh of a maniac. 'Fuck you?' he said. 'What happened to the game, Meredith? What about the rules?'

Meredith shook her head wildly from side to side. 'Bugger the rules – and the game! I want you, you bastard, and you know it.'

She began to rip desperately at his shirt, sending buttons flying everywhere. One pinged off the tiling just to the right of her. Just the sound of it made Meredith want to laugh. She wanted to laugh and laugh until she couldn't laugh any more.

Alex regarded her with an enigmatic expression. Inside he felt a surge of conflicting emotions. Then he heard voices outside the door. If he was going to do anything, it was now or never, they couldn't remain undiscovered for long. Lisa would be sure to send out a search party. Or, worse still, come looking for him herself.

He stopped thinking and looked properly at Meredith. Her hair was dishevelled, her eyes wild. Her mouth looked bruised from his kisses and he could see her breasts rising and falling under the blouse with each heaving breath she took.

'If I fuck you, it'll be the end of the game,' he said slowly.

'No, it doesn't have to be.' Meredith shook her head. Her expression was at once earnest and hopeful. Passion blazed in her eyes as her fingers eased the edges of his shirt apart and began to stroke his chest. 'Don't talk about it now, Alex,' she urged him breathlessly. 'Don't talk at all. Just fuck me.'

Almost against his will, Alex felt his cock rise inside his trousers and somehow his fingers found their way to the buttons on her blouse. He undid them quickly, feeling his breath grow shorter as the heaving mounds of her breasts came into view. Encased in a simple white bra, they looked innocent and delectable.

As he lowered his head and began to nibble at her bared flesh his hands travelled up her thighs. They brushed over the lacy welt of her stockings and continued up over silky flesh. At the edge of her knickers they stopped for a moment until Meredith began to writhe urgently against him. Then he pulled really hard, ripping the scrap of white cotton off her with one swift tug.

'Oh,' she gasped feeling cool air snake between her legs and caress her naked buttocks. 'God, Alex!'

As his fingers sank deeply into her aching wetness she ground herself upon them, hooking one leg over his hip.

Lifting her up, he manoeuvred her over to the basin, setting her down so that her bare bottom was perched on the edge of the white porcelain. Meredith gasped when she felt its coldness beneath her buttocks and watched as though in a trance while Alex positioned a chair under one of her feet and a laundry bin under the other. She glanced down, noticing with a lustful thrill how wide apart he had positioned them.

Her sex pouted enticingly at him beneath the pelmet of her skirt, which was rucked up around her waist. Desperate to release her breasts, Meredith unhooked her bra and pulled it up over the aching globes of flesh. She felt wild. Abandoned. Like a woman possessed. She cupped her breasts in her hands and stroked her thumbs over the swollen buds of her nipples.

Another frisson of desire ran through her as she caught the way Alex was looking at her, devouring her with his eyes as he unzipped his trousers. Unhampered by pants of any kind, his stiff cock sprang free.

Meredith gazed at it through glazed eyes. It looked eager and rampant. Keen to enter her desperate body.

'Yes, oh, yes,' she found herself gasping as Alex advanced toward her and grasped a buttock with one hand, a breast with the other. Her head lolled back, her eye lids closing under the weight of her desire as she felt the smooth roundness of his glans nudge determinedly at her moist opening. Slowly it slid inside her. *God, yes*, she thought, almost mindless with arousal. *At last . . .*

He plunged in deeply, taking her breath away. Wrapping her legs around him she pulled him closer to her. Her vagina seemed to yearn for him, her muscles gripping him hard as though trying to draw all of him inside her. She wobbled precariously on the cool porcelain, the edge of the basin dug into the soft flesh of her buttocks and, as if he sensed her discomfort, Alex slid his hands under her, taking some of her weight.

Sliding her hands under his shirt she gripped his shoulders, her fingernails pressing into his flesh. Alex groaned, whether with pain or pleasure Meredith couldn't be sure. Perhaps it was a combination of both. Clinging to him like a limpet she ground herself harder against him, smothering her breasts against the hard wall of his chest, forcing her greedy vulva to rub against his groin.

Alex took her fiercely. This wasn't how he had imagined their first encounter would be. He had fantasised about taking her slowly and sensuously in an intimate setting. There was nothing intimate about a public lavatory, with voices and footsteps and an occasional metallic clang coming from the other side of the door.

However, he couldn't help relishing the moment for what it was. Its heat and intensity were overwhelming. Meredith was passionate in her response to him. He thrilled to the sensation of her lovely breasts and hard nipples crushed against his bare skin and the feel of her delicious buttocks in his hands. Most of all he felt overcome by the sensation of actually being inside her. His cock, so hard and eager plundering her wet, open little body.

Despite his overwhelming desire, he succeeded in delaying his own orgasm until he felt her body tense. He looked into her face, noticing with pleasure the glazed, otherworldly expression on her face, as if she were transported to some far off realm of ecstasy. Then her internal muscles began to spasm around him, squeezing him, milking him.

He groaned loudly, his groan turning to a cry of horror as the door to the lavatory was suddenly flung open. He stared wide-eyed at the woman standing on the threshold, her mouth hanging wide open in disbelief.

'Lisa!' he gasped as the power of his orgasm began to recede. 'It's not what you think.'

Though he knew the wisest thing would be to withdraw, Alex kept his cock firmly embedded in Meredith's body. Her expression, he noticed was similar to the one he could see reflected on his own face in the mirror behind her. He felt Meredith's legs slacken around him and he slowly eased his hands out from under her bottom.

Then he turned back to Lisa. She was still standing there, he noticed, hands on hips, looking totally aghast and, for once, apparently lost for words.

Flashing him a look of pure scathing, Lisa turned and closed the door behind her.

When they were sure she had gone, Meredith stared at Alex. 'Bloody hell,' she muttered, feeling herself come crashing back down to earth with a vengeance. 'I've really dropped you in it now, haven't I?'

Alex withdrew slowly from her and attempted a smile that didn't quite come off. He helped her down from the basin.

'I think I had something to do with it as well,' he said. He cleared his throat, wishing he could clear his head as easily.

Meredith smoothed down the pleats of her skirt and began buttoning up her blouse. She felt really shitty now. What had seemed like a good idea at the time – and had produced a wonderful result – now seemed destined to have horrendous consequences for Alex.

He zipped up his trousers and tucked his shirt back into the waistband, trying without much success to make it look as though his shirt still had buttons on it. Then he wet his hands under the tap and used them to smooth his hair back. Feeling more human again, he turned to look at Meredith.

'Whatever happens from now on,' he said looking serious, 'I will never regret what just happened between us. It was wonderful. And you are too. Wonderful and beautiful.' Cupping Meredith's face between his still damp hands he kissed her.

Meredith clung to him as though she were drowning all over again. Her passion temporarily sated, she still desired more of him and yet felt an aching tenderness and remorse that she had never felt before. Her concern was not with herself but with Alex. What would happen to him now? Would Lisa fire him – tell him she didn't want him to have any more to do with her blasted video?

'Bloody bitch,' Meredith muttered.

At long last, Alex felt able to conjure a smile. 'No she's not,' he said softly. 'How could she possibly know what's been going on between us? As far as she's concerned I'm your Uncle Alex, remember? Wicked Uncle Alex who just fucked his schoolgirl niece.' With that he threw back his head and began to laugh.

After a moment Meredith joined in his laughter. She was glad he could see the funny side. And there was one. She couldn't deny that. Perhaps, she thought hopefully, when we're about ninety we'll look back on this incident and have another good chuckle about it.

'I'd better go,' she muttered.

Turning, she glanced at her reflection in the mirror over the basin. Her ponytail was wrecked and so she pulled at the fabric covered band that had secured it and let her long hair tumble free over her shoulders.

Alex delved into his pocket. He brought out a set of keys. From his other pocket he produced his wallet and extracted a ten pound note.

'It might be better if you did,' he agreed. He handed her the keys and the money. 'Here, take there. The money's for a cab. Go back to my flat and wait for me there. Please,' he added when he noticed Meredith's doubtful expression. 'I'll be as quick as I can,' he said, pressing them into her hand and closing her fingers over the note and keys. 'I just need some time alone with Lisa to explain things. Make yourself at home, have a bath or whatever you want. I'll bring some food back with me.' He paused, his smile becoming wolfish. 'And afterwards,' he went on, 'I'll make love to you properly. The way I intended in the first place.'

Feeling herself go weak with longing, Meredith smiled back at him. 'Now that,' she murmured softly, 'is an offer I can't refuse.' She pushed him gently on the shoulder. 'Now go on. Go after Lisa and explain. I'll try and slip out unobtrusively.'

Alex gave her another quick appraising glance. She still looked achingly gorgeous and eminently fuckable in her school uniform. So much so that, somehow, he doubted she could ever appear unobtrusive. Nevertheless, he was grateful for her understanding and for giving him the space he needed. Now, he thought, brushing his lips lightly against Meredith's own before turning to leave, all he had to do was convince Lisa that he wasn't the lecherous, incestuous bastard she probably assumed him to be.

When he reached the top of the stairs, Alex was relieved to see that Lisa was still sitting at their table. He had wondered if she would simply leave. And now, noting her drumming fingertips and black expression, he almost wished she had. This was not going to be easy.

He slunk into the vacant chair opposite her, wondering where to begin.

She glanced up, preempting the words he had begun to form ever so carefully in his head. 'I think you and I need to sort some things out between us, Alex,' she said.

He nodded. His hands fluttered uselessly on the table top until his fingers encountered a wine glass. He didn't know whether it was his own or Meredith's, but it had wine in it so he raised it to his lips and swallowed the lot.

'Do you really think that is going to help, Alex?' Lisa enquired. She looked stern. 'Obviously, you can't handle your drink. I've been giving it some thought. A talent like yours shouldn't be wasted through alcohol abuse. Perhaps you should think about counselling—'

'I don't need a counsellor,' he interrupted. 'I just need to explain to you what happened back there.' Out of the corner of his eye he couldn't help noticing Meredith. The flash of her blonde hair and black stockinged legs distracted him for a moment. He forced himself to concentrate on Lisa.

To his discomfort, Lisa gave a thin little laugh. 'Explain,' she said. She sat back in her chair and crossed her arms. 'How exactly does one explain how one happened to be fucking one's own niece in a restaurant loo?'

'She's not my niece,' Alex mumbled. 'That's part of what I need to tell you.'

Lisa, he noticed, still kept her arms firmly crossed but her expression softened just a little. 'Go on then,' she said, 'tell me. I'm all ears.'

Chapter Sixteen

Meredith couldn't understand what was taking Alex so long. The strangeness of being in his flat was starting to wear off and now she was becoming bored waiting for him to arrive. One thing that hadn't dissipated however, was the exhilaration she felt every time she thought about the two of them together. Though it had been brief and had ended on a tragic note, their fucking had been wonderful.

'I'll bet she's giving him a really hard time, the bitch,' Meredith muttered to herself as she wandered around his flat.

Idly, she peered at the books and photographs on his shelves and his collection of CD's – mostly classical and Latin American. The rough wooden shelving, which looked as though it had been reclaimed from a building site, even bore several dance awards.

He must be really good, she mused with a surge of pride as she gazed at the small statuettes. For the first time she wondered if Alex was actually famous. Dance wasn't really an area she knew much about but, she reasoned, to win awards and to be working on a video for someone like Lisa Blair, he must be quite renowned in his field.

Meredith sighed at the unwelcome recollection of Alex's nemesis. She found herself wondering if he had fucked her. She wouldn't put it past a woman like Lisa to make a play for him. Perhaps that was what she was doing right now. Using Alex's guilt to extract her pound of flesh. The bitch! Meredith pounded her first on the arm of the sofa. It was the only way she could think of Lisa Blair – as a tight-arsed, superficious she-devil.

Realising she needed to do something to calm herself down, Meredith wandered into Alex's bathroom. The white pedestal bath looked large and inviting. She stooped to put the plug in, then turned the gold taps, watching as the hot water gushed out and sent up a cloud of steam.

She went into Alex's bedroom and began to undress slowly, savouring the memory of his caresses as she uncovered each new portion of her body. After she had finished undressing she placed her clothes neatly on a low, armless chair. Pausing to check that the bath hadn't filled yet, she walked back into the sparsely furnished studio cum living room. There she helped herself to the bottle of wine she had found in the fridge earlier and her empty glass. She carried them with her into the bathroom, filling the glass and setting it down on top of a low, wicker laundry hamper. After making sure the water temperature was just right she turned off the taps.

Just before she stepped into the bath she glanced around. For the first time she noticed there were a number of candles on the bathroom shelf. They were all different sized and cream in colour. Hunting through the bathroom cabinet she discovered a box of matches. Feeling thoroughly decadent, she distributed the candles about the tiny bathroom, lit them and then turned off the bathroom light. All at once the functional room was transformed into a place of sensuality and intimacy.

As an afterthought and to add to the mood, Meredith walked back into the studio and selected a CD. She put it in the player, turned the volume up high so that she could hear it in the bathroom and allowed the soothing strains of the Baroque melodies she had chosen to sweep over her.

This, she thought, as she sank effortlessly into the steaming water, is bliss. She had gathered her hair on top of her head in a haphazard topknot, securing it with the covered band she had used for her ponytail earlier. Now she tucked a rolled up towel under her neck and allowed her head to loll back.

Occasionally, she sipped a little wine from the glass by her side. It's alcoholic warmth and the heat of the water soothed her inside and out, smoothing out the mental creases that her unfortunate escapade earlier that evening had left behind. Now all she felt was relaxed. Hedonistic. She anticipated the arrival of her lover with an assured sense of erotic expectation. She wasn't anxious. She wasn't tense. She wasn't . . . even . . . awake any more . . .

* * *

Alex thought he would never get away from Lisa but when he did, finally it was with a profound sense of relief. Fortunately for him she had been prepared to listen and gradually she let it be known that she believed him. And, more importantly, still believed *in* him. She wanted him to carry on working on her video, she said, but work he must. There would be no slacking off, no matter how hot it was, or how tired he felt. Alex concurred with her wholeheartedly. He was so relieved he was prepared to agree to almost anything.

During the taxi ride home he thought about Meredith waiting for him back at his flat. It was such a good feeling to know that she would be there when he got home. He thought back over their encounter that evening. Her body. Her passion. The willing, eager way she took him inside her. So intense were his memories that he found himself growing more excited by the second.

The first thing he noticed when he let himself into his flat with a spare set of keys obtained from the caretaker, was the sonorous rhythm of Vivaldi's bassoon concerto in E minor. Walking quickly over to the CD player he turned down the volume a little, then glanced around, wondering where Meredith had got to.

It didn't take him long to discover her. Half submerged in a bathtub full of water she was snoring gently.

His eyes took in the whole scene. The softly flickering candlelight, the open bottle of wine and Meredith – beautiful, sleeping Meredith whose upswept hair made her neck look swanlike and vulnerable and whose pert, round breasts bobbed gently on the surface of the water.

He looked at her nipples, soft, pink and wrinkled in slumber. And then at the smooth sweep of her throat and shoulders. Moving the wicker basket out of the way, he knelt by the side of the bath and gently deposited a kiss on her bare shoulder. She hardly stirred and he gradually worked his way over her shoulder and up the side of her neck. When he reached the sensitive place just below her ear she opened her eyes and smiled sleepily at him.

'Hi,' she murmured softly, 'I thought you'd never get here.'

She started to sit up but Alex pushed her gently back down.

'No rush,' he said. 'Just relax, we've got all night.' He handed her the glass of wine and watched as she took a sip.

'How did things go?' Meredith asked. She felt her insides tighten as she watched the reflection of Alex's memories flicker across his face. To her relief the tension in his face dissolved into a grin.

'All forgiven,' he said. 'It took some explaining though, I can tell you.'

'Did she give you a hard time?' Meredith couldn't bring herself to actually speak Lisa's name.

'Lisa was all right about it actually,' Alex chided her gently. 'All things considered.'

'So you're not joining the ranks of the dole queue just yet then?' Meredith kept her question light but Alex could sense she had been more concerned than she was willing to admit.

'No, thank goodness,' he said. 'Lisa just gave me a bit of a lecture that's all. Warned me to pull my socks up and all that.'

Meredith giggled, her breasts jiggling in the water. With a frisson of anticipation she followed Alex's sweeping gaze.

'There's plenty of room in here for two,' she offered.

Picking up a tube of citrus-scented, liquid soap, Alex shook his head. 'No thanks,' he said, flipping open the cap and squeezing a large, yellow blob into the palm of his hand, 'I discovered ages ago that baths are not the best location for lovemaking. If you don't mind, I'd like to bathe you instead.'

Meredith gazed at him wide-eyed. Mind? She couldn't think of anything more erotic than having his hands soaping every inch of her naked body.

She stretched luxuriously. 'My body is yours,' she murmured, gazing seductively at him. 'I've never been bathed by someone else before. Not since I was a child anyway.'

'There's always a first time for everything,' Alex said, smiling. He rubbed his palms together, working the liquid soap into a lather. 'Just sit up a bit and I'll start with your back,' he added.

Meredith complied dutifully and sighed with pleasure as she felt his soapy hands smooth over her shoulders. He took each arm in turn and soaped it gently. Then he squeezed some more soap from the tube and began to lather her back with seductive, massaging strokes. Every last bit of tension inside her dissolved. She felt her body becoming light. Liquid. Languor tugged at her and when Alex bade her to lie back in the water to rinse the soap off she almost slipped right under the surface.

'I've just died and gone to heaven, I think,' she murmured. 'This is ecstasy.'

Alex took enormous pleasure in her delight but explained regretfully that she would have to stand up if he was going to soap the rest of her.

She pouted a little but got to her feet anyway, turning this way and that as Alex swept the fragrant lather over her legs, hips and buttocks. She realised he was deliberately avoiding her more obvious erogenous zones, though his gently caressing hands seemed to have discovered a hundred others.

'Now for the front,' Alex said after she had dunked herself under the water a second time.

His voice was husky and he felt the catch in it as he anticipated smoothing the rich lather over her breasts and belly. He was so pent up with arousal that he felt himself shaking. To quell his excitement a little he helped himself to a generous gulp of wine.

'Could I have some more of that?' Meredith asked, reaching out her hand. Water dripped from it as she took the glass from him.

Alex tried not to think too hard about what he was about to do as he squeezed some more soap into his palm. His cock already felt at bursting point and he had a long way to go yet before he would allow himself to come again. This time he intended to make sure Meredith was well and truly satisfied before he took his pleasure.

In a way, it was as though what had happened between them in the restaurant had been with someone else. A different Meredith. This one, he thought as he appraised the naked, dripping body which rose out of the steaming water before him like a beautiful nymph, was an entirely different person.

All at once he realised the key to his attraction to Meredith. She was so many different women. Funny. Lustful. Abandoned. Submissive. Assertive. Jealous. Enthusiastic. Intelligent. She was a chimera. A fanciful being who was ever changing and encompassed every possible characteristic a person would possess.

'Oh, that feels so good,' Meredith breathed as Alex put his thoughts on hold and smoothed his soapy palms across her stomach.

He swept his hands upwards, brushing the outer curves of her breasts and then bringing them together in a circular motion. His pulse raced. Her skin felt like the finest satin: soft and glossy. He soaped her again in much the same fashion but concentrating more on her breasts this time, continuing the tantalising circular motion until her nipples swelled and became fully distended.

They nosed through the layer of bubbles like little pink snouts in search of truffles. He smiled, rinsed the lather from her breasts and decided to give her nipples what they so obviously needed. Cupping her breasts in his hands he drew them to his lips, enclosing first one then the other. He suckled them gently, enjoying the way Meredith squirmed and whimpered whenever he flicked the tip of his tongue over those excited little buds.

He glanced up at her face. Her head was tilted back, her eyes closed and she had pressed her palms against the tiled wall behind her to steady herself. He could feel the way her body quivered with desire. Her knees sagged from time to time and when it happened the next time he found he couldn't ignore the temptation of the little pink slit that peeped so beguiling at him through its nest of blonde hair. Her pubic hair was so fine he could see every intimate part of her.

Relinquishing her breasts he moved his head down, nibbling and kissing her torso as he moved closer and closer to his ultimate goal. Meredith was whimpering now, her back arched, her pelvis thrust wantonly toward him. Please, her body language urged him, please put your mouth there.

As delicately as he could, he parted her outer lips, marvelling at their fleshy plumpness and the soft springiness of her pubic hair. Her clitoris stood proud of its little hood of skin, its pearly tip glistening. Tentatively he dabbed at it with his tongue, then he began to lave the swollen bud with more assured strokes.

The trembling in her limbs increased and so he held her steady by gripping her hips. Then he pressed his mouth to her nether lips and began to tongue and lick her entire sex.

'Oh, oh...!' Meredith gripped his head, crushing her desperate flesh against his lips.

She could feel his tongue right inside her, the tip of his nose nuzzling her clitoris. She was seconds away from explosion. And then it happened. He moved his tongue back to her clitoris and began flicking at it, over and over... Waves of hot lust washed over her and all she could do was hold onto him for dear life as she rode the white water rapids of her own sensuality.

Afterwards, he picked her up in her arms and carried her into the sitting room. He set her down on the sofa, left the room and returned a moment later with a heap of towels with which he began to pat her tingling body dry.

'Better than before?' he asked when she opened her eyes and gave him a languid smile.

She nodded. 'Almost,' she said, watching his face crease into confusion, 'but there was one vital bit missing.'

'What was that?' Alex said.

'This.' Meredith reached out and caressed the obvious bulge in his trousers. 'I want to feel you inside me again, Alex,' she murmured softly. 'To feel you moving inside me and being a part of me.'

Relief washed over him, and hot on its heels came a surge of desire. He stood up and began to remove his trousers.

'How remiss of me,' he said teasingly, 'I think I'd better rectify that situation right now.'

He sat on the sofa, his erection pointing straight up and pulled her astride him. A moment later, as he felt her soft wetness encompass him, he immediately recalled his earlier fantasy.

'I imagined you fucking me like this earlier when I saw you get out of the taxi outside the restaurant,' he admitted.

'Oh, yes,' Meredith said as she rose and fell on the hard spear of his cock, 'Was that before or after you realised the sexy schoolgirl was me?'

'Oh, after,' Alex said quickly. He caught the glint in her eye and thrust his pelvis up hard, making her gasp with surprise and pleasure. 'I'll teach you,' he growled, 'I'll teach you to be so fucking pedantic. I'll–'

The rest of his words faded into oblivion as Meredith began to churn her body hard against him, her inner muscles once again milking him of his vitality.

It was much later. They had fallen asleep in each other's arms and awoke to find themselves shivering.

Alex glanced at Meredith. 'I didn't feed you,' he said, sounding disappointed in himself.

Meredith smiled. 'Oh, yes you did,' she said with an impudent grin, 'you gave me *cock au sofa*. I much prefer it to *coq au van* because the gear stick doesn't get in the way.'

He laughed. 'So you've tried it in a van, have you?'

'Well, a car,' she said. 'Hasn't everyone?'

'Not everyone,' Alex countered. 'But, as I said, there's a first time for everything. Perhaps we could hire a car someday and you could show me how it's done.'

Dimples formed at the sides of her mouth as she realised the implication behind his words.

'So this is not the end of the game then?' she said.

Alex put his arm around her and pulled her against him. 'The game,' he mused aloud. 'I'm not sure about the game but I certainly didn't intend us to be a one off – or even a two off.' He laughed lightly.

Meredith looked at him, her expression sincere. 'I don't want the game to stop,' she said. 'Unless you feel really strongly about it.' She paused and glanced down at her hands before looking back at him. 'Our relationship started out in a very odd way but it seems to have worked for us. I'm an adventurer, Alex. I like to experience new things, with different people. What has happened to me over the past few weeks has been a fantasy come true as far as I'm concerned. And it's all thanks to you.'

Alex silenced her by kissing her. He wanted to kiss her and he also desperately needed the space to gather his thoughts. Whether Meredith liked to admit it or not, things had changed drastically between them. And he wasn't at all sure how he felt about continuing the game now.

To put her off talking any more Alex picked up her glass of wine and tilted it, allowing the cold wine to slowly trickle over her naked breasts. Her nipples hardened instantly, her whole body readying itself for yet more pleasure.

It was as though the lovemaking they had enjoyed already that evening had been nothing more than foreplay – a prelude to the final opus.

'You'll never make it through tomorrow,' Meredith protested as Alex cupped her breasts and began to lick the wine from them. She moaned with pleasure as his tongue laved her bare flesh with long, assured strokes. 'Don't forget what Lisa said,' she managed to gasp out. 'No excuses.'

Alex glanced up, his expression wolfish. 'Tomorrow is tomorrow,' he murmured. 'Let me worry about that. Your job is to lie back and enjoy what I'm about to do to you.'

Meredith smiled lazily. 'Are you for real?' she said. 'I keep expecting to wake up at any moment and find myself back in Nottingham, still struggling to make my mark.'

'Is that where you come from then?' Alex asked.

As he spoke his hands caressed her torso, his fingertips lightly skimming her sides, her breasts, the slight curve of her belly. He felt he couldn't get enough of her. She was the most sensual, sexually exciting woman he had ever met. Bold and wanton one minute. Soft and acquiescent the next.

'No,' she said, her silken tresses fanning out across the duvet as she shook her head. 'I come from down here but I trained up there. The trouble is, London is where everything seems to happen in fashion, despite what a lot of the provincial designers say.'

Alex understood. 'It's the same in dance and choreography,' he said.

'I suppose we're both artists in our own ways,' Meredith continued. 'And we both deal with the aesthetics of the human body.'

'True,' Alex concurred, liking the idea that there was more than simply sexual attraction between himself and Meredith. 'Most people think choreography is about devising a sequence of steps but it's not. It's more about the organisation of the body within a given area. A good choreographer can't just stand on the sidelines and shout orders at a dancer, he has to put himself inside her, or him.'

Meredith flashed him a provocative smile. 'Sounds good to me,' she murmured lasciviously. 'I know I'm not a dancer but how about putting yourself inside me?'

'Wicked woman,' Alex responded, already easing his body over hers. He lay between her open thighs, the tip of his cock nudging her succulent flesh. 'What do I have to do to wear you out?'

Her lips curved seductively. 'Fuck me,' she said. 'All you have to do is fuck me and fuck me and – ooh . . . !'

Alex felt it would be very bad of him not to oblige her. A long gasp broke from her lips as he slid his hardness right inside her. The velvety texture of her inner walls delighted and stimulated him. Her moisture oozed around him, lubricating the slow in-out thrusting and grinding motion that he used to take her to the pinnacle of pleasure.

Supporting himself on his hands, he dipped his head and nuzzled at the enticing mounds of her breasts. He could feel his desire growing beyond control. Everything about her was so luscious, so totally delectable, he could go on fucking her for ever. If only his body would allow him to . . .

They moved into his bedroom after that where they eventually dozed off and it seemed to Alex only minutes after his eyes closed that the alarm on his wristwatch began buzzing. He rolled over and silenced the insistent noise before rolling back to Meredith. As he deposited a light kiss on her bare shoulder she stirred.

'Wha – what time is it?' she mumbled sleepily.

'Don't you bother about that,' Alex reassured her, 'Go back to sleep. I'll call you later, if you're not still here I'll try your flat.'

Ignoring him, Meredith struggled to sit up, the duvet slipped down to her waist and Alex couldn't help his gaze straying to her breasts.

'So tempting,' he murmured as he reached out to them.

Laughing, Meredith slapped his hand away. 'Remember, you'll be in trouble with Lisa if you don't get a move on,' she teased.

Alex was tempted to say, 'Sod Lisa,' but knew there was no way he could. Not if he wanted to keep his career intact. He gave Meredith a rueful smile.

'That woman is really beginning to bug me,' he said.

'It's not her fault,' Meredith pointed out. 'Perhaps this was the wrong time for you and I to happen.'

'No way.' Alex's denial was firm. Just in case she was still harbouring any misconceptions, he grabbed her by the shoulders and kissed her deeply. When they broke apart he said, 'Don't you ever go thinking that way again. My problems with Lisa are my problems.' He paused, remembering something. 'I only hope she doesn't still want me to repay the sexual favour she gave me.'

Meredith looked quizzically at him. 'Why?' she asked. 'You may not like her very much at the moment but you find her attractive, don't you?'

Alex nodded, wondering where this was leading.

'Then what's the problem?' Meredith continued.

Alex was certain he must look as baffled as he felt. 'I wasn't sure if – well, since you and I – what I mean is–'

Meredith's burst of laughter served to add to his confusion. 'Stop torturing yourself, Alex, for goodness sake,' she said. 'We might have something special starting here but we're hardly engaged or anything. Lighten up.'

A huge wave of relief washed over Alex. Although he felt far more for Meredith than he'd ever had for another woman, it was early days. Once again he realised how futile it was simply to assume things about her.

'In that case, I'll stop worrying about it,' he said. 'If she comes on to me again I'll deal with it as and when.'

To his surprise, Meredith knelt up and put her arms around him. He could feel her naked body pressed up against him. Her skin felt soft and still warm from being under the duvet.

'Just promise me one thing,' Meredith murmured as she began to rub her palm suggestively over his groin.

Alex felt his body start to come alive under her seductive caresses. 'Mm?' he mumbled.

'If she does want you to repay the compliment, try and call me first.'

Alex felt confused. 'Why's that?' he asked.

'Because,' Meredith said, her eyes twinkling lasciviously, 'if it's at all possible, I'd like to watch.'